No word was spoken. No word was necessary. Khosatral spread his great arms, and Conan, crouching beneath them, slashed at the giant's belly. Then he bounded back, eyes blazing with surprise. The keen edge had rung on the mighty body as on an anvil, rebounding without cutting. Then Khosatral came upon him in an irresistible surge.

There was a fleeting concussion, a fierce writhing and intertwining of limbs and bodies, and then Conan sprang clear, every thew quivering from the violence of his efforts; blood started where the grazing fingers had torn the skin. In that instant of contact he had experienced the ultimate madness of blasphemed nature; no human flesh had bruised his, but metal animated and sentient; it was a body of living iron which opposed his.

Khosatral loomed above the warrior in the gloom . . .

Cover painting by Frank Frazetta . . . with grateful acknowledgement to Roy Krenkel, adviser.

Conan the Wanderer

ROBERT E. HOWARD,
L. SPRAGUE de CAMP and LIN CARTER

SPHERE BOOKS LIMITED
30/32 Gray's Inn Road, London WC1X 8JL

First published in Great Britain by Sphere Books Ltd 1974
Copyright © L. Sprague de Camp 1968

'Black Tears' by L. Sprague de Camp and Lin Carter was first
published in the original Lancer Inc edition; copyright © 1968
by L. Sprague de Camp.

'Shadows in Zamboula' was first published in *Weird Tales* for Nov-
ember, 1935; copyright 1935 by Popular Fiction Publishing Co. It
was reprinted in *Skull-Face and Others*, Sauk City: Arkham House,
1946; in *Conan the Barbarian*, N.Y.: Gnome Press, 1954; and in
The Spell of Seven, N.Y.: Pyramid Publications, 1965.

'The Devil in Iron' was first published in *Weird Tales* for August,
1934; copyright 1934 by Popular Fiction Publishing Co. It was reprinted in *Conan the Barbarian*.

'The Flame Knife' was first published in *Tales of Conan*, N.Y.:
Gnome Press, 1955; copyright 1955 by Gnome Press.

TRADE
MARK

Set in Intertype Times

Printed in Great Britain by
Hazell Watson & Viney Ltd
Aylesbury, Bucks

ISBN 0 7221 4698 1

CONTENTS

Pages 6 & 7: A map of the world of Conan in the Hyborian Age, based upon notes and sketches by Robert E. Howard and upon previous maps by P. Schuyler Miller, John D. Clark, David Kyle, and L. Sprague de Camp, with a map of Europe and adjacent regions superimposed for reference.

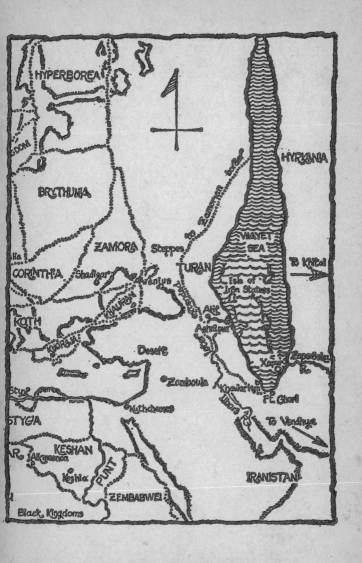

INTRODUCTION

Robert E. Howard (1906-36), the creator of Conan, was born in Peaster, Texas, and spent most of his life in Cross Plains, in the center of Texas. During his short life (which ended in suicide at the age of thirty) Howard turned out a large volume of popular fiction: sport, detective, Western, historical, adventure, science fiction, weird, and ghost stories, besides his verse and his many fantasies. Of his several series of heroic fantasies, the most popular have been the Conan stories. Eighteen of these were published in Howard's lifetime; eight others, from mere fragments and outlines to complete manuscripts, have been found among his papers since 1950. The incomplete stories have been completed by my colleague Lin Carter and myself.

In addition, in the early 1950s, I rewrote four unpublished Howard manuscripts of Oriental adventure, with medieval and modern settings, to convert them into Conan stories by changing names, deleting anachronisms, and introducing a supernatural element. This did not prove hard, since Howard's heroes are pretty much cut from the same cloth, and the resulting stories are still about three-quarters or four-fifths Howard.

Of these, the story *The Flame Knife* is the longest. Howard originally wrote it in 1934 as a 42,000-word novella of adventure in modern Afghanistan, called *Three-Bladed Doom*. The hero was Francis X. Gordon, one of Howard's large fictional family of brawny, brawling Irish adventurers and the hero of several published stories of Oriental adventure. In *Three-Bladed Doom*, the cult exposed by the hero is a modern revival of the medieval Assassins. When the original version failed to sell, Howard in 1935 rewrote it to a length of 24,000 words; but that version likewise failed to find a market. The story showed the influence of Harold Lamb and Talbot Mundy. The present collaborative version, with 31,000 words, is intermediate in length between Howard's two original versions.

Carter and I have also written several pastiches, based upon hints in Howard's notes and letters, to fill up gaps in the saga. *Black Tears*, in the present volume, is one of these.

All these stories belong to a sub-genre of imaginative fiction that connoisseurs call 'heroic fantasy', or, sometimes, 'swordplay-and-sorcery fiction'. Such a story is laid in an imaginary ancient or medieval setting – perhaps this world as it is supposed to have been long ago, or as it will be in the remote future, or on another planet, or in another dimension – where magic works and modern technology has not yet been discovered. Examples of the genre – outside the Conan stories – are E. R. Eddison's *The Worm Ouroboros*, J. R. R. Tolkien's trilogy *The Lord of the Rings*, Fletcher Pratt's *The Well of the Unicorn*, and Fritz Leiber's stories of Fafhrd and the Gray Mouser. When well done, stories of this kind provide the purest *fun* fiction of any kind.

Of the several larger-than-life characters who stride through Howard's pages, Conan the Cimmerian is his hero of heroes. Conan lived, loved, and moved in Howard's imaginary Hyborian Age, about twelve thousand years ago, between the sinking of Atlantis and the beginnings of recorded history. A gigantic barbarian adventurer from the bleak, backward northern land of Cimmeria, Conan brawled and battled his way across half the world of his time, wading through rivers of gore and overcoming foes both natural and supernatural to become, at last, king of the mighty Hyborian kingdom of Aquilonia.

Arriving as a raw, hulking, lawless youth in the kingdom of Zamora (see the map), Conan for a few years made a precarious living there and in the neighbouring lands as a thief. Tiring of this starveling existence, he enlisted as a mercenary in the armies of Turan. For the next two years he traveled widely and refined his knowledge of archery and horsemanship.

As a result of a quarrel over a woman with a superior officer, Conan fled from Turan. After an unsuccessful try at treasure-hunting in Zamora and a brief visit to his Cimmerian homeland, he embarked upon the career of mercenary soldier in the Hyborian kingdoms. Circumstances – violent as usual – made him a pirate along the coasts of Kush, with a Shemitish she-pirate, Bêlit, as his partner and a crew of bloodthirsty black corsairs. After Bêlit was slain, he became the chief of a black tribe, then served as a mercenary in Shem and among the most southerly Hyborian nations.

Later still, Conan appeared as a leader among the *kozaki*, a horde of outlaws who roamed the steppes between the Hyborian lands and Turan. He captained a pirate craft on the great inland Sea of Vilayet.

While serving as captain of the royal guard of Queen Taramis of Khauran, Conan was captured by the queen's enemies, who crucified him. When a vulture flew down to try to peck his eyes out, Conan bit the bird's head off. (You can't have a tougher hero than that.) Olgerd Vladislav, Zaporoskan leader of a band of Zuagirs, the nomadic, desert-dwelling eastern Shemites, happened upon Conan at this juncture and rescued him – for his own purposes – from the cross. When friction arose between Conan and Olgerd, the hard-bitten Cimmerian ruthlessly ousted Olgerd from the leadership of the band, which – after overthrowing the enemies of Queen Taramis and restoring her to her throne – he led off eastward to plunder the Turanians. At that point, the present story begins.

Because of legal complications, it was not possible to publish the books of Lancer Books' present Conan series in chronological order. A total of eleven or twelve books are planned, of which more than half have already been published. When the series is complete, this will be the fourth volume, following *Conan the Freebooter* and preceding *Conan the Adventurer*.

Readers who wish to know more about Conan, Howard, or heroic fantasy in general are referred to two periodicals and one book. One periodical is *Amra*, published by George H. Scithers, Box 9120, Chicago, Ill., 60690; this is the organ of the Hyborian Legion, a loose group of admirers of heroic fantasy and of the Conan stories in particular. The other periodical is *The Howard Collector*, published by Glenn Lord, literary agent for the Howard estate, Box 775, Pasadena, Texas, 77501; this is devoted to articles, stories, and poems by and about Howard. The book is *The Conan Reader*, by the present writer, published by Jack L. Chalker, 5111 Liberty Heights Ave., Baltimore, Md., 21207; this consists of articles on Howard, Conan, and heroic fantasy previously published in *Amra*. I also listed many works by Howard and sword-and-sorcery stories by other writers in my introduction to the volume *Conan* of the present series.

L. Sprague de Camp

BLACK TEARS

After the events narrated in 'A Witch Shall be Born' (in Conan the Freebooter), *Conan heads his band of Zuagirs eastward to raid the cities and caravans of the Turanians. He is about thirty-one years old at this time and at the height of his physical powers. He spends, altogether, nearly two years with the desert Shemites, first as Olgerd's lieutenant and then as their sole chieftain. But the fierce and energetic King Yezdigerd reacts swiftly to Conan's pinpricks; he sends out a strong force to entrap him.*

1. *The Jaws of the Trap*

The noonday sun blazed down from the fiery dome of the sky. The harsh, dry sands of Shan-e-Sorkh, the Red Waste, baked in the pitiless blaze as in a giant oven. Naught moved in the still air; the few thorny shrubs that crowned the low, gravel-strewn hills, which rose in a wall at the edge of the Waste, stirred not.

Neither did the soldiers who crouched behind them, watching the trail.

Here some primeval conflict of natural forces had riven a cleft through the escarpment. Ages of erosion had widened this cleft, but it still formed a narrow pass between steep slopes – a perfect site for an ambush.

The troop of Turanian soldiery had lain hidden atop the hills all through the hot morning hours. Sweltering in their tunics of chain and scale mail, they crouched on sore hams and aching knees. Cursing under his breath, their captain, the Amir Boghra Khan, endured the long, uncomfortable vigil with them. His throat was as dry as sun-baked leather; within his mail, his body stewed. In this accursed land of death and blazing sun, a man could not even sweat comfortably; the desiccated desert air greedily drank up every drop of moisture, leaving one as dry as the withered tongue of a Stygian mummy.

Now the amir blinked and rubbed his eyes, squinting against the glare to see again that tiny flash of light. A forward scout, concealed behind a dune of red sand, caught the sun in his mirror and flashed a signal toward his chief, hidden atop the hills.

Now a cloud of dust could be seen. The portly, black-bearded Turanian nobleman grinned and forgot his discomfort. Surely his traitorous informant had truly earned the bribe it took to buy him!

Soon, Boghra Khan could discern the long line of Zuagir warriors, robed in flowing white khalats and mounted on slender desert steeds. As the band of desert marauders emerged from the cloud of dust raised by the hoofs of their horses, the Turanian lord could even make out the dark, lean, hawk-faced visages of his quarry, framed by their flowing headdresses – so clear was the desert air and so bright the sun. Satisfaction seethed through his veins like red wine of Aghrapur from young King Yezdigerd's private cellars.

For years, now, this outlaw band had harried and looted towns and trading posts and caravan stations along the borders of Turan – first under that black-hearted Zaporoskan rogue, Olgerd Vladislav; then, a little more than a year ago, by his successor, Conan. At last, Turanian spies in villages friendly to the outlaw band had found a corruptible member of that band – one Vardanes, not a Zuagir but a Zamorian. Vardanes had been a blood brother to Olgerd, whom Conan had overthrown, and was hungry for vengeance against the stranger who had usurped the chieftainship.

Boghra thoughtfully tugged his beard. The Zamorian traitor was a smiling, laughing villain, dear to a Turanian heart. Small, lean, lithe, and swaggering, handsome and reckless as a young god, Vardanes was an amusing drinking companion and a devilish fighter but as cold-hearted and untrustworthy as an adder.

14

Now the Zuagirs were passing through the defile. And there, at the head of the outriders, rode Vardanes on a prancing black mare. Boghra Khan raised a hand to warn his men to be ready. He wanted to let as many as possible of the Zuagirs enter the pass before closing the trap upon them. Only Vardanes was to be allowed through. The moment he was beyond the walls of sandstone, Boghra brought his hand down with a chopping motion.

'Slay the dogs!' he thundered, rising.

A hail of hissing arrows fell slanting through the sunlight like a deadly rain. In a second, the Zuagirs were a turmoil of shouting men and bucking horses. Flight after flight of arrows raked them. Men fell, clutching at feathered shafts, which sprouted as by magic from their bodies. Horses screamed as keen barbs gashed their dusty flanks.

Dust rose in a choking cloud, veiling the pass below. So thick it became that Boghra Khan halted his archers for a moment, lest they waste their shafts in the murk. And that momentary twinge of thrift was his undoing. For out of the clamor rose one deep, bellowing voice, dominating the chaos.

'Up the slopes and at them!'

It was the voice of Conan. An instant later, the giant form of the Cimmerian himself came charging up the steep slope on a huge, fiery stallion. One might think that only a fool or a madman would charge straight up a steep slope of drifting sand and crumbling rock into the teeth of his foe, but Conan was neither. True, he was wild with ferocious lust for revenge, but behind his grim, dark face and smouldering eyes, like blue flames under scowling black brows, the sharp wit of a seasoned warrior was at work. He knew that often the only road through an ambush is the unexpected.

Astonished, the Turanian warriors let bows slacken as they stared. Clawing and scrambling up the steep slopes of the sides of the pass, out of the dust-clouded floor of the defile, came a howling mob of frenzied Zuagirs, afoot and mounted, straight at them. In an instant the desert warriors – more numerous than the amir had expected – came roaring over the crest, scimitars flashing, cursing and shrieking bloodthirsty war cries.

Before them all came the giant form of Conan. Arrows

15

had ripped his white khalat, exposing the glittering black mail that clad his lion-thewed torso. His wild, unshorn mane streamed out from under his steel cap like a tattered banner; a chance shaft had torn away his flowing kaffia. On a wild-eyed stallion, he was upon them like some demon of myth. He was armed not with the tulwar of the desert folk but with a great, cross-hilted western broadsword – his favourite among the many weapons of which he was master. In his scarred fist, this length of whirling, mirror-bright steel cut a scarlet path through the Turanians. It rose and fell, spraying scarlet droplets into the desert air. At every stroke it clove armor and flesh and bone, smashing in a skull here, lopping a limb there, hurling a third victim mangled and prone with ribs crushed in.

By the end of a short, swift half-hour it was all over. No Turanians survived the onslaught save a few who had fled early – and their leader. With his robe torn away and his face bloody, the limping and disheveled amir was led before Conan, who sat on his panting steed, wiping the gore from his steel with a dead man's khalat.

Conan fixed the wilting lordling with a scornful glance, not unmixed with sardonic humor.

'So, Boghra, we meet again!' he growled.

The amir blinked with disbelief. 'You!' he gasped.

Conan chuckled. A decade before, as a wandering young vagabond, the Cimmerian had served in the mercenaries of Turan. He had left King Yildiz's standards rather hurriedly over a little matter of an officer's mistress – so hurriedly, in fact, that he had failed to settle a gambling wager with the same amir who stood astonished before him now. Then, as the merry young scion of a noble house, Boghra Khan and Conan had been comrades in many an escapade from gaming table to drinking shop and bawdy house. Now, years older, the same Boghra gaped up, crushed in battle by an old comrade whose name he had somehow never connected with that of the terrible leader of the desert tribesmen.

Conan raked him with narrowing eyes. 'You were awaiting us here, weren't you?' he growled.

The amir sagged. He did not wish to give information to the outlaw leader, even if they were old drinking companions. But he had heard too many grim tales of the

16

Zuagirs' bloody methods of wringing information from captives. Fat and soft from years of princely living, the Turanian officer feared he could not long keep silent under such pressure.

Surprisingly, his coöperation was not needed. Conan had seen Vardanes, who had curiously requested the post of advance scout that morning, spur ahead through the further end of the pass just before the trap had been sprung.

'How much did you pay Vardanes?' Conan demanded suddenly.

'Two hundred silver shekels . . .' the Turanian mumbled. Then he broke off, astonished at his own indiscretion. Conan laughed.

'A princely bribe, eh? That smiling rogue – like every Zamorian, treacherous to the bottom of his rotten black heart! He's never forgiven me for unseating Olgerd.' Conan broke off, leveling a quizzical glance at the bowed head of the amir. He grinned, not unkindly. 'Nay, berate yourself not, Boghra. You did not betray your military secrets; I tricked you out of them. You can ride back to Aghrapur with your soldierly honor intact.'

Boghra lifted his head with astonishment. 'You will let me live?' he croaked.

Conan nodded. 'Why not? I still owe you a bag of gold from that old wager, so let me settle the debt this way. But next time, Boghra, have a care how you set traps for wolves. Sometimes you catch a tiger!'

2. *The Land of Ghosts*

Two days of hard riding through the red sands of Shan-e-Sorkh, and still the desert marauders had not caught up with the traitor. Thirsty for the sight of Vardanes' blood, Conan pressed his men hard. The cruel code of the desert demanded the Death of Five Stakes for the man who betrayed his comrades, and Conan was determined to see the Zamorian pay that price.

On the evening of the second day, they made camp in the shelter of a hillock of parched sandstone, which thrust

17

up from the rust-colored sands like the stump of some ruined ancient tower. Conan's hard face, burnt almost black by the desert sun, was lined with fatigue. His stallion panted at the edge of exhaustion, slobbering through frothy lips as he set the water bag to the animal's muzzle. Behind him, men stretched weary legs and aching arms. They watered the horses and lit a campfire to keep the wild desert dogs away. He heard the creak of ropes as saddle-bags disgorged tents and cooking equipment.

Sand crunched under a sandaled heel behind him. He turned to see the lined, bewhiskered face of one of his lieutenants. This was Gomer, a sloe-eyed, hook-nosed Shemite with greasy, blue-black ringlets escaping from the folds of his headdress.

'Well?' growled Conan as he rubbed down the tired stallion with long, slow strokes of a stiff brush.

The Shemite shrugged. 'He's still making a straight path to the southwest,' he said. 'The black-hearted devil must be made of iron.'

Conan laughed harshly. 'His mare may be iron, but not Vardanes. He's flesh and blood, as you shall see when we spread him out to the stakes and slit his guts for the vultures!'

Gomer's sad eyes were haunted by a vague fear. 'Conan, will you not give over this quest? Each day takes us deeper into this land of sun and sand, where only vipers and scorpions can live. By Dagon's tail, unless we turn back, we shall leave our bones here to bleach forever!'

'Not so,' grunted the Cimmerian. 'If any bones are left to bleach here, they'll be Zamorian. Don't fret, Gomer; we'll catch up to the traitor yet. Tomorrow, perhaps. He can't keep up this pace forever.'

'Nor can we!' Gomer protested. He paused, feeling Conan's smoldering blue gaze searching his face.

'But that's not all that's eating at your heart, is it?' demanded Conan. 'Speak up, man. Out with it!'

The burly Shemite shrugged eloquently. 'Well, no. I— the men feel—' His voice trailed away.

'Speak, man or I'll kick it out of you!'

'This – this is the Makan-e-Mordan!' Gomer burst out.

'I know. I've heard of this 'Place of Ghosts' before. So what? Are you afraid of old crones' fables?'

18

Gomer looked unhappy. 'They are not just fables, Conan. You are no Zuagir; you do not know this land and its terrors, as do we who have long dwelt in the wilderness. For thousands of years, this land has been a cursed and haunted place, and with every hour that we ride, we go deeper into this evil land. The men fear to tell you, but they are half mad with terror.'

'With childish superstition, you mean,' snarled Conan. 'I know they've been quaking in their boots over legends of ghosts and goblins. I've heard stories of this country, too, Gomer. But they are only tales to frighten babes, not warriors! Tell your comrades to beware. My wrath is stronger than all the ghosts that ever died!'

'But, Conan!'

Conan cut him off with a coarse word. 'Enough of your childish night fears, Shemite! I have sworn by Crom and Mitra that I will have the blood of that Zamorian traitor or die trying! And if I have to scatter a little Zuagir blood along the way, I'll not scruple to do so. Now cease yammering and come share a bottle with me. My throat's as dry as this blasted desert, and all this talk dries it out the more.'

Clapping Gomer on the shoulder, Conan strode away toward the campfire, where the men were unpacking stores of smoked meat, dried figs and dates, goat cheese, and leathern bottles of wine.

But the Shemite did not rejoin the Cimmerian at once. He stood long, gazing after the swaggering chieftain he had followed for nearly two years, ever since they had found Conan crucified near the walls of Khauran. Conan had been a guard captain in the service of Queen Taramis of Khauran until her throne was usurped by the witch Salome, leagued with Constantius the Falcon, the Kothic *voivode* of the Free Companies.

When Conan, realizing the substitution, took his stand with Taramis and was defeated, Constantius had him crucified outside the city. By chance, Olgerd Vladislav, chief of the local band of Zuagir outlaws, had come riding by and had cut Conan down from his cross, saying that if he survived his wounds he might join their band. Conan not only survived but also proved so able a leader that in

19

time he ousted Olgerd from the band, which he had led from that day to this.

But this was the end of his leadership. Gomer of Akkharia sighed deeply. Conan had ridden before them for the last two days, sunk in his own grim lust for revenge. He did not realize the depth of the passion in the hearts of the Zuagirs. Gomer knew that, although they loved Conan, their superstitious terrors had driven them to the brink of mutiny and murder. To the scarlet gates of Hell they might follow the Cimmerian – but no further into the Land of Ghosts.

The Shemite idolized his chieftain. But, knowing that no threat would swerve the Cimmerian from the path of vengeance, he could think of but one way to save Conan from the knives of his own men. From a pocket in his white khalat he withdrew a small, stoppered phial of green powder. Secreting it in his palm, he rejoined Conan by the campfire, to share a bottle of wine with him.

3. Invisible Death

When Conan awoke, the sun was high. Heat waves shimmered across the barren sands. The air was hot and still and dry, as if the heavens were an inverted brazen bowl heated to incandescence.

Conan staggered to his knees and clutched his throbbing brow. His aching skull felt as if he had been clubbed.

He lurched to his feet and stood swaying. Through bleary eyes, squinted against the glare, he looked slowly about him. He was alone in this cursed, waterless land.

He croaked a curse on the superstitious Zuagirs. The entire troop had decamped, taking with them all the gear, the horses, and the provisions. Two goatskin water bags lay beside him. These, his mail shirt and khalat, and his broadsword were all that his erstwhile comrades had left him.

He fell to his knees again and pulled the stopper from one of the water bags. Swirling the lukewarm fluid about, he rinsed the vile taste from his mouth and drank sparingly, reluctantly replacing the stopper before his fiery thirst was half assuaged. Although he longed to up-end the bag over his aching head, reason asserted its dominance. If he were lost in this sandy waste, every drop would be needed for survival.

Through the blinding headache and the groggy state of his wits, he could see what must have occurred. His Zuagirs were more fearful of this dubious realm than he had supposed, despite Gomer's warnings. He had made a serious – perhaps a fatal – error. He had underestimated the power of superstition over his desert warriors and overestimated his power to control and dominate them. With a dull groan, Conan cursed his own arrogant, bull-headed pride. Unless he learned better, it might some day be the death of him.

And perhaps this was the day. He took a long, stony look at his chances. They seemed slim. He had water for two days on short rations – three, if he would risk madness by limiting his intake further. No food and no horse, which meant he must wend afoot.

Well then, on he would go. But whither? The obvious answer was: back the way he had come. But there were arguments against that course. Of these, the most eloquent was that of distance. They had ridden for two days after leaving the last water hole. A man on foot could travel at best at only half the speed of a horse. For him, then, to return by the route they had come would mean he must travel for at least two full days without any water at all . . .

Conan rubbed his jaw reflectively, trying to forget the throbbing in his skull and to cudgel some sense out of his groggy wits. Retracing his steps would not be the best idea, for he knew there was no water closer than four days' march away.

He looked ahead, where the trail of the fleeing Vardanes stretched straight from this place to the horizon.

Perhaps he should continue to follow the Zamorian. While the path led into unknown country, the mere fact that the land was unknown was in its favor. An oasis might lie just beyond the nearest dunes. It was hard to reach a sensible decision under such circumstances, but Conan resolved upon what seemed the wiser course.

21

Girding his khalat about his mailed form and slinging his sword across his shoulders, he strode off along Vardanes' track, the water bags slapping against his back.

The sun hung forever in a sky of burning brass. It blazed down like a fiery eye in the brow of some colossal cyclops, gazing upon the tiny, slow-moving figure that trudged across the baking surface of the crimson sands. It took forever for the afternoon sun to glide down the vast, empty curve of the sky, to die on the flaming funeral pyre of the west. Then purple evening stole on shadowy wings across the vault of the heavens, and a trace of blessed coolness crept across the dunes, with soft shadows and a light breeze.

By then, Conan's leg muscles were beyond pain. Fatigue had numbed the ache in them, and he stumbled forward on limbs like stone columns animated by sorcery. His great head was bowed on his massive chest. He plodded on numbly, needing rest but driven by the knowledge that now, in the coolness of evening, he could make the most distance with the least discomfort.

His throat was caked with dust; his swarthy visage was dusted brick-red with a mask of desert sand. He had drunk a mouthful an hour ago and would drink no more until it became so dark that he could no longer see to follow Vardanes' trail.

His dreams that night were turgid and confused, filled with shaggy nightmare figures with one glaring eye in their bestial brows, who beat his naked body with whips of red-hot chain.

When he blinked awake, he found the sun already high and another hot day before him. It was agony to rise. Every muscle throbbed as if tiny needles had been thrust deep into his tissues. But rise he did, to drink lightly and go forward.

Soon he lost track of time, but still the tireless engine of his will drove him on, step after staggering step. His mind wandered away into shadowy bypaths of delusion. But still he held three thoughts before him: to follow the trail of hoofprints, to save water stringently, and to stay on his feet. If once he fell, he knew he would be unable to rise again. And if he fell during the scorching day, his bones would desiccate and whiten amidst these scarlet wastes for ages to come.

4. *The Deathless Queen*

Vardanes of Zamora halted at the crest of the hills and stared down at a sight so strange that it struck him dumb. For five days, since the botched ambush against the Zuagirs had rebounded upon the Turanians, he had ridden like a madman, scarcely daring to snatch an hour or two of rest for himself and his mare. A terror so great that it robbed the very manhood from within him goaded him on.

Well did he know the vengeance of the desert outlaws. His imagination was filled with sickening scenes of the price the grim avengers would exact from his body if ever he fell into their hands. Thus, when he saw that the ambush had failed, he had galloped straight out into the desert. He knew that devil, Conan, would flay the traitor's name from Boghra Khan and then would come howling on his heels with a bloodthirsty mob of Zuagirs. Nor would they easily give up the quest of their treacherous former comrade.

His one slim chance had been to head out into the trackless reaches of Shan-e-Sorkh. Although Vardanes was a city-bred Zamorian of culture and sophistication, the fortunes of his age had flung him in with the desert outlaws, and he knew them well. He knew they dreaded the very name of the Red Waste and that their savage imaginations peopled it with every monster and devil ever dreamed of. Why the desert tribesmen feared the Red Waste so terribly he neither knew nor cared, so long as their fear would keep them from following him very far into that deadly desert.

But they had not turned back. His lead on them was so slight that, day after day, he could see the clouds of dust raised by the Zuagir horsemen behind him. He pressed ahead with every moment, eating and drinking in the saddle and pushing his mount to the verge of exhaustion in order to widen that narrow gap.

After five days, he knew not whether they were still on his track; but soon it mattered little. He had exhausted the food and water for himself and his mare and pressed on in the faint hope of finding a water hole in this endless waste.

His horse, caked with dry mud where desert dust had stuck to lathered sides, staggered forward like a dead thing driven by a sorcerer's will. Now it was near to death. Seven times this day it had fallen, and only the lash of the whip had driven it to its feet again. Since it could no longer support his weight, Vardanes walked, leading it by its rein.

The Red Waste had taken a fearful toll of Vardanes himself. Once handsome as a laughing young god, he was now a gaunt, sunblackened skeleton. Bloodshot eyes glared through matted, stringy locks. Through cracked, swollen lips he mumbled mindless prayers to Ishtar, Set, Mitra, and a score of other deities. As he and his trembling steed lurched to the crest of yet another row of dunes, he looked down and saw a lush green valley, dotted with clumps of emerald-green date palms.

Amid this fertile vale lay a small, walled city of stone. Bulging domes and squat guard towers rose above a stuccoed wall, wherein was set a great gate whose polished bronzen hinges redly reflected the sun.

A city in this scorching waste? A lush valley of cool, green trees and soft lawns and limpid lotus pools, in the heart of this bleak wilderness? Impossible!

Vardanes shuddered, shut his eyes, and licked his cracked lips. It must be a mirage, or a phantom of his disordered wits! Yet a shard of half-forgotten lore, gleaned from his youthful studies long ago, came back to him. It was a fragment of legend called Akhlat the Accursed.

He strove to recover that thread of memory. It had been in an old Stygian book, which his Shemite tutor kept locked in a sandalwood chest. Even as a bright-eyed lad, Vardanes had been blessed or cursed with greed, curiosity, and nimble fingers. One dark night, he had picked that lock and pored with mingled awe and loathing through the portentous pages of that dark grimoire of elder necromancy. Penned in a spidery hand on pages of dragon parchment, the text described strange rites and cere-

24

monies. The pages crawled with cryptic hieroglyphs from elder kingdoms of sorcerous evil, like Acheron and Lemuria, which had flourished and fallen in time's dawn.

Among the pentacle-crowded pages had been fragments of some dark liturgy designed to draw down undying demon-things from dark realms beyond the stars, from the chaos that ancient mages said reigned beyond the borders of the cosmos. One of these liturgies contained cryptic references to '*devil-cursed and demon-haunted Akhlat in the Red Waste, where power-mad sorcerers of yore called down to this earthly sphere a Demon from Beyond, to their unending sorrow . . . Akhlat, where the Undying One rules with a hand of horror to this very day . . . doomed, accursed Akhlat, which the very gods spurned, transforming all the realm round about into a burning waste . . .*'

Vardanes was still sitting in the sand by the head of his panting mare when grim-faced warriors seized him and bore him down from the ring of stony hills that encircled the city – down into the garden valley of date palms and lotus pools – down to the gates of Akhlat the Accursed.

5. *The Hand of Zillah*

Conan roused slowly, but this time it was different. Before, his awakening had been painful, prying gummed lids open to squint at the fiery sun, hoisting himself slowly erect to stagger forward across broiling sands.

This time he awoke easily, with a blissful sensation of repletion and comfort. Silken pillows lay beneath his head. Thick awnings with tasseled fringes kept the sun from his body, which was clean and naked save for a fresh loincloth of white linen.

He sprang instantly to full alertness, like an animal whose survival in the wild depends upon this ability. He stared about with unbelieving eyes. His first thought was that death had claimed him at last and that his spirit had been borne beyond the clouds to the primitive paradise where Crom, the god of his people, sat enthroned amid a thousand heroes.

Beside his silken couch lay a silver ewer, filled with fresh, clear water.

Moments later, Conan lifted his dripping face from the ewer and knew that whatever paradise he was in, it was real and physical. He drank deep, although the state of his throat and mouth told him that he was no longer racked with the burning thirst of his desert trek. Some caravan must have found him and borne him to these tents for healing and succor. Looking down, Conan saw that his limbs and torso had been washed clean of desert dust and smeared with soothing salve. Whoever his rescuers might be, they had fed and cherished him while he raved and slumbered his way toward recovery.

He peered around the tent. His great broadsword lay across an ebony chest. He padded toward it on silent feet, like some wary jungle cat – then froze as he heard the tinkle of a warrior's harness behind him.

The musical sound, however, came from no warrior but from a slim, fawn-eyed girl who had just entered the tent and stood staring. Dark, shining hair fell unbound to her waist, and tiny silver bells were threaded through these tresses. Thence had come the faint tinkle.

Conan took in the girl in one swift glance: young, scarcely more than a child, slim and lovely, with a pale body that gleamed enticingly through gauzy veils. Jewels glistened on her slim, white hands. From the golden bangles on her brow and the look of her large, dark eyes. Conan guessed her to be of some folk akin to the Shemites.

'Oh!' she cried. 'You are too weak to stand! You must rest some more to regain your strength.' Her language was a dialect of Shemitish, full of archaic forms but close enough to the Shemitish that Conan knew for him to understand.

'Nonsense, girl, I'm fit enough,' he replied in the same tongue. 'Was it you who tended me here? How long since you found me?'

'Nay, strange lord, 'twas my father. I am Zillah the daughter of Enosh, a lord of Akhlat the Accursed. We found your body amid the everlasting sands of the Waste three days past,' she replied, veiling her eyes with silken lashes.

Gods! he thought, but this was a fair wench. Conan

had seen no woman in weeks, and he frankly studied the swelling contours of her lithe body, scarcely hidden by the gauzy veils. A trace of scarlet rose to her cheeks.

'So your pretty hand tended me, eh, Zillah?' he said. 'My thanks to you and your sire for this mercy. I was close enough to death, I'll warrant. How did you chance upon me?' He strove without success to recall any city by the name of Akhlat the Accursed, although he thought he knew every city of the southern deserts, by repute if not by an actual visit.

'It was not by chance; indeed, we came in search of you,' said Zillah.

Conan's eyes narrowed as his nerves tingled to the sense of danger. Something in the sudden hardening of his grim, impassive face told the girl that he was a man of swift animal passions, a dangerous man unlike the soft, mild townsmen she had known.

'We meant you no harm!' she protested, lifting one slim hand defensively. 'But follow me, sir, and my sire will explain all things to you.'

For a moment, Conan stood tense, wondering if Vardanes had set these people on his trail. The silver he had carried off from the Turanians should be enough to buy the souls of half a hundred Shemites.

Then he relaxed, deliberately calming the blood lust that rose within him. He took up his sword and slung the baldric over his shoulder.

'Then take me to this Enosh, lass,' he said calmly. 'I would hear his tale.'

She led him from the chamber. Conan squared his naked shoulders and padded after her.

6. *The Thing from Beyond*

Enosh was poring over a wrinkled, time-faded scroll in a high-backed chair of black wood, as Zillah conducted Conan into his presence. This part of the tent was hung with dark purple cloth; thick carpets muffled the tread of their feet. On a coiling stand composed of intertwined serpents of glinting brass, a black mirror of curious design reposed. Eery lights flickered in its ebon depths.

Enosh rose and greeted Conan with courtly phrases. He was a tall, elderly man, lean but straight. His pate was covered with a headdress of snowy linen, his face was lined with age and creased with thought, and his dark eyes were weary with ancient sorrow.

He bade his guest be seated and commanded Zillah to bring wine. When the formalities were over, Conan asked abruptly: 'How did you come to find me, O shaykh?'

Enosh glanced at the black mirror. 'Whilst I am no fell sorcerer, my son, I can make use of some means not altogether natural.'

'How is it that you were looking for me?'

Enosh lifted a thin, blue-veined hand to quiet the warrior's suspicions. 'Be patient, my friend, and I will explain all,' he said in his quiet, deep-toned voice. Reaching to a low tabouret, he set aside his scroll and accepted a silver cup of wine.

When they had drunk, the old man began his tale: 'Ages ago, a wily sorcerer of this land of Akhlat conceived of a plot against the ancient dynasty that had ruled in this place since the fall of Atlantis,' he said slowly. 'With cunning words, he made the people think their monarch – a weak, self-indulgent man – was their foe, and the people rose and trampled the foolish king into the mire. Setting himself up as a priest and prophet of the Unknown Gods, the sorcerer pretended to divine inspiration. He averred that one of the gods would soon descend to earth to rule over Akhlat the Holy – as it was called – in person.'

Conan snorted. 'You Akhlatim, it seems, are no less gullible than the other nations I have seen.'

The old man smiled wearily. 'It is always easy to believe what one wishes to be true. But the plan of this black sorcerer was more terrible than any could dream. With vile and nameless rites, he conjured into this plane of existence a demoness from Outside, to serve as goddess to the people. Retaining his sorcerous control over this being, he presented himself as the interpreter of her divine will. Struck with awe, the people of Akhlat soon groaned beneath a tyranny far worse than that which they had suffered from the old dynasty.'

28

Conan smiled wolfishly. 'I have seen that revolutions often throw up worse governments than those they replace.'

'Perhaps. At any rate, this one did. And in time matters became even grimmer; for the sorcerer lost control over the demoniac Thing he had summoned down from Beyond, and it destroyed him and ruled in his place. And it rules to this very day,' he concluded softly.

Conan started. 'The creature is immortal, then? How long ago was this?'

'More years have passed than these wastes have grains of sand,' said Enosh. 'And still the goddess rules supreme in sad Akhlat. The secret of her power is such that she leaches the life force from living creatures. All this land about us was once green and fair, lush with date palms along the streams and grassy hills whereon the fat herds pastured. Her vampiric thirst for life has drained the land dry, save for the valley wherein the city of Akhlat stands. That she has spared, for without living things to drain to dry, lifeless husks, she cannot sustain herself on this plane of being.'

'Crom!' whispered Conan, draining his wine cup.

'For centuries, now,' Enosh continued, 'this land has been transformed into a dead and sterile waste. Our young go to slake the dark thirst of the goddess, as do the beasts of our flocks. She feeds daily. Each day she chooses a victim, and each day they dwindle and lessen. When she attacks one victim incessantly, day after day, he may last but a few days or he may linger half a moon. The strongest and bravest endure for as many as thirty days before she exhausts their store of life force and must begin on the next.'

Conan fondled the hilt of his sword. 'Crom and Mitra, man, why have you not slain this thing?'

The old man wearily shook his head. 'She is invulnerable, unkillable,' he said softly. 'Her flesh is composed of matter drawn to her and held together by the goddess's unconquerable will. An arrow or a sword could but wound that flesh: it is a trifling matter for her to repair the injury. And the life force she drinks from others, leaving them dry husks, gives her a terrible store of inner strength from which to remold her flesh anew.'

'Burn the thing,' Conan growled. 'Burn the palace down about her head, or cut her into little pieces for the flames of a bonfire to devour!'

'No. She shields herself with dark powers of hellish magic. Her weapon transfixes into paralysis all she looks upon. As many as a hundred warriors have crept into the Black Temple, determined to end this grim tyranny. Naught was left of them but a living forest of motionless men, who served in turn as human banquets for the insatiable monster.'

Canon stirred restlessly. ' 'Tis a wonder that any of you still dwell in this accursed land!' he rumbled. 'How has this damnable leech not drained every last human being in this valley dry long since? And why have you not bundled your belongings and fled from this demon-haunted place?'

'In truth, very few of us are left; she consumes us and our beasts faster than their natural increase can make up the loss. For ages, the demoness sated her lust with the minute life force of growing green things, sparing the people. When the land became a waste, she fed first upon our flocks and then from our slaves and finally from the Akhlatim themselves. Soon we shall be gone, and Akhlat will be one vast city of death. Nor can we leave the land, for the power of the goddess holds us within narrow bounds, beyond which we cannot stray.'

Conan shook his head, his unshorn mane brushing his bare, bronzed shoulders. 'It is a tragic tale you tell, old man. But why do you repeat it to me?'

'Because of an ancient prophecy,' said Enosh gently, picking up the worn and wrinkled scroll from the tabouret.

'What prophecy?'

Enosh partly unrolled the scroll and pointed to lines of writing of a form so old that Conan could not read it, although he could manage the written Shemitish of his own time. 'That in the fullness of time,' said Enosh, 'when our end was near, the Unknown Gods, whom our ancestors turned away from to worship the demoness, would relent of their wrath and send a liberator, who should overthrow the goddess and destroy her evil power. You, Conan of Cimmeria, are that savior . . .'

7. Hall of the Living Dead

For days and nights, Vardanes lay in a dank dungeon cell beneath the Black Temple of Akhlat. He yelled and pleaded and wept and cursed and prayed, but the dull-eyed, cold-faced, bronze-helmed guardsmen paid him no heed, save to tend to his bodily needs. They would not answer his questions. Neither would they submit to bribery, which much astonished him. A typical Zamorian, Vardanes could hardly conceive of men who did not lust for wealth, yet these strange men with their antique speech and old-fashioned armor were so little covetous of the silver he had wrung from the Turanians in payment for his betrayal that they even let his coin-filled saddle bags lie undisturbed in a corner of his cell.

They tended him well, however, bathing his haggard body and soothing his blisters with salves. And they fed him sumptuously with fine roast fowl, rich fruits, and sweetmeats. They even gave him wine. Having known other gaols in his time, Vardanes realized how extraordinary this was. Could they, he wondered uneasily, be fattening him for slaughter?

Then, one day, guards came to his cell and brought him forth. He assumed he was at last to appear before some magistrate to answer whatever absurd charges his accusers might make. Confidence welled up within him. Never had he known a magistrate whose mercy could not be purchased with the silver in those fat saddle bags!

But, instead of to a judge or suffete, he was led by dark and winding ways before a mighty door of greened bronze, which loomed in front of him like the gate of Hell itself. Triply locked and barred was this portal, and strong enough to withstand an army. With nervous hands and taut faces, the warriors unfastened the great door and thrust Vardanes within.

As the door clanged shut behind him, the Zamorian found himself in a magnificent hall of polished marble. It was drowned in deep, purple gloom and thick with dust. On every hand lay tokens of unrepaired decay, of untended neglect. He went forward curiously.

Was this a great throne room, or the transept of some colossal temple? It was hard to say. The most peculiar thing about the vast, shadowy hall, other than the neglect from which it had evidently long suffered, was the statuary that stood about its floor in clusters. A host of puzzling questions rose within Vardanes' troubled brain.

The first mystery was the substance of the statues. Whereas the hall itself was builded of sleek marble, the statues were made of some dull, lifeless, porous gray stone that he could not identify. Whatever the stuff was, it was singularly unattractive. It looked like dead wood ash, though hard as dry stone to the touch.

The second mystery was the amazing artistry of the unknown sculptor, whose gifted hands had wrought these marvels of art. They were lifelike and detailed to an incredible degree: every fold of garment or drapery hung like real cloth; every tiny strand of hair was visible. This astonishing fidelity was carried even to the postures. No heroic groupings, no monumental majesty was visible in these graven images of dull-gray, plaster-like material. They stood in lifelike poses, by the score and the hundred. They were scattered here and there with no regard for order. They were carved in the likeness of warriors and nobles, youths and maidens, doddering grandsires and senile hags, blooming children and babes in arms.

The one disquieting feature held in common by all was that each figure bore on its stony features an expression of unendurable terror.

Before long, Vardanes heard a faint sound from the depths of this dark place. Like the sound of many voices it was, yet so faint that he could make out no words. A weird diapason whispered through this forest of statues. As Vardanes drew nearer, he could distinguish the strains of sound that made up the whole: slow, heart-rending sobs, faint, agonized moans; the blurred babble of prayers; croaking laughter; monotonous curses. These sounds seemed to come from half a hundred throats, but the Zamorian could see no source for them. Although he peered about, he could see naught in all this place but himself and the thousands of statues.

Sweat trickled down his forehead and his lean cheeks. A nameless fear arose within him. He wished from the depths of his faithless heart that he were a thousand leagues from this accursed temple, where voices of invisible beings moaned, sobbed, babbled, and laughed hideously.

Then he saw the golden throne. It stood in the midst of the hall, towering above the heads of the statues. Vardanes' eyes fed hungrily on the luster of gold. He edged through the stony forest toward it.

Something was propped up on that rich throne – the shriveled mummy of some long-dead king? Withered hands were clasped over a sunken breast. From throat to heel, the thin body was wrapped in dusty cerements. A thin mask of beaten gold, worked in the likeness of a woman of unearthly beauty, lay over the features.

A twinge of greed quickened Vardanes' panting breath. He forgot his fears, for, between the brows of that golden mask, a tremendous black sapphire glowed like a third eye. It was an astounding gem, worth a prince's ransom.

At the foot of the throne, Vardanes stared covetously at the golden mask. The eyes were carved as if closed in slumber. Sweet and beautiful slept the drowsy, full-lipped mouth in that lovely golden face. The huge, dark sapphire flashed with sultry fires as he reached for it.

With trembling fingers, the Zamorian snatched the mask away. Beneath it lay a brown, withered face. The cheeks had fallen in; the flesh was hard, dry, and leathery. He shuddered at the malevolent expression on the features of that death's head.

Then it opened its eyes and looked at him.

He staggered back with a scream, the mask falling from nerveless fingers to clatter against the marble pave. The dead eyes in the skull-face leered into his own. Then the Thing opened its third eye . . .

8. *The Face of the Gorgon*

Conan padded through the hall of gray statues on naked feet, prowling the dusty, shadow-haunted aisles like some great jungle cat. Dim light showed along the keen edge of the mighty broadsword in his huge, capable fist. His eyes glared from side to side and the hackles bristled upon his nape. This place stank of death; the reek of fear lay heavy in the still air.

How had he ever let old Enosh talk him into this foolish venture? He was no redeemer, no destined liberator, no holy man come from the gods to free Akhlat from the deathless curse of the demoness. His only purpose was one of red revenge.

But the wise old shaykh had spoken many words, and his eloquence had persuaded Conan to undertake this perilous mission. Enosh had pointed out two facts that convinced even the hard-bitten barbarian. One was that, once within this land, Conan was bound there by black magic and could not leave until the goddess was slain. The other was that the Zamorian traitor was immured beneath the Black Temple of the goddess, soon to face the doom that would, if not averted, destroy them all.

So Conan had come by secret underground ways, which Enosh had shown him. He had emerged from a hidden portal in the wall of this vast, gloomy hall, for Enosh knew when Vardanes was to go before the goddess.

Like the Zamorian, Conan also noted the marvelous realism of the gray statues; but, unlike Vardanes, he knew the answer to this riddle. He averted his eyes from the expressions of horror on the stone faces about him.

He, too, heard the mournful wailing and crying. As he drew nearer to the center of the mighty hypostyle hall, the sobbing voices became clearer. He saw the golden throne and the withered thing upon it, and he crept toward the lustrous chair on silent feet.

As he approached, a statue spoke to him. The shock almost unmanned him. His flesh crawled, and sweat started from his brow.

Then he saw the source of the cries, and his heart pounded with revulsion. For those about the throne were not yet dead. They were stone up to the neck, but the heads still lived. Sad eyes rolled in despairing faces, and dry lips prayed that he would bury his sword in the living brains of these almost – but not completely – petrified beings.

Then he heard a scream, in Vardanes' well-known voice. Had the goddess slain his enemy before he could wreak his vengeance? He sprang forward to the side of the throne.

34

There a terrible sight met his eyes. Vardanes stood before the throne, eyes popping and lips working feverishly. The rasp of stone caught Conan's ear, and he looked at Vardanes' legs. Where the Zamorian's feet touched the floor, a gray pallor crept slowly up them. Before Conan's gaze, the warm flesh whitened. The gray tide had reached Vardanes' knees; but, even as Conan watched, the flesh of the upper legs was transmuted into ashen-gray stone. Vardanes strained to walk but could not. His voice rose in a shriek, while his eyes glared at Conan with the naked fear of a trapped animal.

The thing on the throne laughed a low, dry cackle. As Conan watched, the dead, withered flesh of her skeletal arms and wrinkled throat swelled and became smooth; it flushed from dead, leathery brown to the warm flesh tones of life. With every vampiric draught of vital energy that the Gorgon drained from Vardanes' body, her own body became imbued with life.

'Crom and Mitra!' breathed Conan.

With every atom of her mind focused on the half-petrified Zamorian, the Gorgon paid Conan no heed. Now her body was filling out. She bloomed; a soft rondure of hip and thigh stretched the dull cerements. Her woman's breasts swelled, straining the thin fabric. She stretched firm, youthful arms. Her moist, crimson mouth opened in another peal of laughter – this time, the musical, voluptuous laughter of a full-bodied woman.

The tide of petrification had crept to Vardanes' loins. Conan did not know whether she would spare Vardanes with the semi-petrification of those near the throne or whether she would drain him to the dregs. He was young and vital; his life force must have been a robust vintage to the vampire goddess.

As the stony tide swept up to the Zamorian's panting breast, he uttered another scream – the most awful sound that Conan had ever heard from human lips. Conan's reaction was instinctive. Like a striking panther, he leaped from his place of concealment behind the throne. Light caught the edge of his blade as he swung it. Vardanes' head jumped from its trunk and fell with a meaty smack to the marble floor.

Shaken by the impact, the body toppled and fell. It

crashed to the floor, and Conan saw the petrified legs crack and splinter. Stony fragments scattered, and blood welled from the cracks in the petrified flesh.

So died Vardanes the traitor. Even Conan could not tell whether he struck from lust for revenge, or whether a merciful impulse to end the torment of a helpless creature had prompted the blow.

Conan turned to the goddess. Without meaning to, he instinctively raised his eyes to hers.

9. *The Third Eye*

Her face was a mask of inhuman loveliness; her soft, moist lips were as full and crimson as ripe fruit. Glossy, ebon hair tumbled across shoulders of glowing pearl, to fall in tides of silken night through which thrust the round moons of her breasts. She was beauty incarnate – save for the great dark orb between her brows.

The third eye met Conan's gaze and riveted him fast. This oval orb was larger than any organ of human vision. It was not divided into pupil, iris, and white as are human eyes; it was all black. His gaze seemed to sink into it and become lost in endless seas of darkness. He stared rapt, the sword forgotten in his hand. The eye was as black as the lightless seas of space between the stars.

Now he seemed to stand at the brink of a black, bottomless well, into which he toppled and fell. Down, down through ebon fogs he fell, through a vast, cold abyss of utter darkness. He knew that, if he did not soon turn his eyes away, he would be forever lost to the world.

He made a terrible effort of will. Sweat stood out on his brow; his muscles writhed like serpents beneath his bronzed skin. His deep chest heaved.

The Gorgon laughed – a low, melodious sound with cold, cruel mockery in it. Conan flushed, and rage rose within him.

With a surge of will, he tore his eyes from that black orb and found himself staring at the floor. Weak and dizzy, he swayed on his feet. As he fought for the strength to stand erect, he glanced at those feet. Thank Crom, they were still of warm flesh, not cold, ashen stone! The long moment he had stood ensorcelled by the Gorgon's gaze had been only a brief instant, too short for the stony tide to have crept up his flesh.

The Gorgon laughed again. With his shaggy head bowed, Conan felt the tug of her will. The muscles of his corded neck swelled in his effort to keep his head bent away.

He was still looking down. Before him, on the marble pave, lay the thin golden mask with the huge sapphirine gem set in it to represent the third eye. And suddenly Conan knew.

This time, as his glance rose, his sword swung with it. The flashing blade clove the dusty air and caught the mocking face of the goddess – slashing the third eye in twain.

She did not move. With her two normal eyes of surpassing beauty, she stared silently at the grim warrior, her face blank and white. A change swept over her.

From the ruin of the Gorgon's third eye, dark fluid ran down the face of inhuman perfection. Like black tears, the slow dew fell from the shattered organ.

Then she began to age. As the dark fluid ran from the riven orb, so the stolen life force of aeons drained from her body. Her skin darkened and roughened into a thousand wrinkles. Withered dewlaps formed beneath her chin. Glowing eyes became lusterless and milky.

The superb bosom sagged and shrank. Sleek limbs became scrawny. For a long moment, the dwarfed, withered form of a tiny woman, incredibly senile, tottered on the throne. Then flesh rotted to papery scraps and mouldering bones. The body collapsed, spilling across the pavement in a litter of leathery fragments, which crumbled as Conan watched to a colorless, ashy powder.

A long sigh went through the hall. It darkened briefly as if the passage of half-transparent wings dimmed the obscure light. Then it was gone, and with it the brooding air of age-old menace. The chamber became just a dusty, neglected old room, devoid of supernatural terrors.

The statues slept forever now in graves of eternal stone. As the Gorgon passed from this dimension, so her spells snapped, including those that had held the living dead in

37

a grisly semblance of life. Conan turned away, leaving the empty throne with its litter of dust and the broken, headless statue of what had once been a bold, high-spirited Zamorian fighting man.

'Stay with us, Conan!' Zillah pleaded in her low, soft voice. 'There will be posts of high honour for a man such as you in Akhlat, now that we are freed of the curse.'

He grinned hardly, sensing something more personal in her voice than the desire of a good citizen to enlist a worthy immigrant in the cause of civic reconstruction. At the probing gaze of his hot, male eyes, she flushed in confusion.

Lord Enosh added his gentle voice to the pleadings of his daughter. Conan's victory had lent new youth and vigor to the elderly man. He stood straight and tall, with a new firmness in his step and a new command in his voice. He offered the Cimmerian wealth, honors, position, and a place of power in the newborn city. Enosh had even hinted that he would look with favor upon Conan as a son-in-law.

But Conan, knowing himself ill-suited to the life of placid, humdrum respectability they held out to him, refused all offers. Courtly phrases did not spring readily to the lips of one whose years had been spent on the field of battle and in the wine shops and joy houses of the world's cities. But, with such tact as his blunt, barbaric nature could muster, he turned aside his hosts' pleas.

'Nay, friends,' he said. 'Not for Conan of Cimmeria the tasks of peace. I should too soon become bored, and when boredom strikes, I know of but few cures: to get drunk, to pick a fight, or to steal a girl. A fine sort of citizen I should make for a city that now seeks peace and quiet to recover its strength!'

'Then whither will you go, O Conan, now that the magical barriers are dissolved?' asked Enosh.

Conan shrugged, ran a hand through his black mane, and laughed. 'Crom, my good sir, I know not! Luckily for me, the goddess's servants fed and watered Vardanes' horse. Akhlat, I see, has no horses – only donkeys – and a great lout like me would look like a fool, jogging along on a sleepy ass with my toes dragging in the dust!

'I think I'll bend my path to the southeast. Somewhere

yonder lies the city of Zamboula, to which I have never been. Men say it is a rich city of fleshpots and revelry, where the wine all but flows free in the gutters. I've a mind to taste the joys of Zamboula, to see what excitement it has to offer.'

'But you need not leave us a beggar!' Enosh protested. 'We owe you much. Let us give you what little gold and silver we have for your labors.'

Conan shook his head. 'Keep your treasure, shaykh. Akhlat is no rich metropolis, and you will need your money when the merchants' caravans begin to arrive again from across the Red Waste. And now that my water bags are full and I've provisions aplenty, I must be off. This time, I shall make the journey through the Shan-e-Sorkh in comfort.'

With a last, brisk farewell, he swung into the saddle and cantered up out of the valley. They stood looking after him, Enosh proudly, but Zillah with tears on her cheeks. Soon he was out of sight.

As he reached the top of the dunes, Conan halted the black mare for a last look at Akhlat. Then he rode off into the Waste. Perhaps he had been a fool not to accept their small store of treasure. But there was plenty in Vardanes' saddle bags, which he reached behind him to thump. He grinned. Why squabble over a few shekels like a greasy tradesman? It does a man good, once in a while, to be virtuous. Even a Cimmerian!

SHADOWS IN ZAMBOULA

Canon duly arrives in Zamboula, where he swiftly dissipates the small fortune he brings with him in a colossal debauch. A week of guzzling, gorging, roistering, whoring, and gambling reduce him once more to destitution.

1. *A Drum Begins*

'Peril hides in the house of Aram Baksh!'

The speaker's voice quivered with earnestness and his lean, black-nailed fingers clawed at Conan's mightily-muscled arm as he croaked his warning. He was a wiry, sunburnt man with a straggling black beard, and his ragged garments proclaimed him a nomad. He looked smaller and meaner than ever in contrast to the giant Cimmerian with his black brows, broad chest, and powerful limbs. They stood in a corner of the Sword Makers' Bazaar, and on either side of them flowed past the many-tongued, many-colored stream of the Zamboulan streets, which are exotic, hybrid, flamboyant, and clamorous.

Conan pulled his eyes back from following a bold-eyed, red-lipped Ghanara whose short skirt bared her brown thigh at each insolent step, and frowned down at his importunate companion.

'What do you mean by peril?' he demanded.

The desert man glanced furtively over his shoulder before replying, and lowered his voice.

'Who can say? But desert men and travelers *have* slept in the house of Aram Baksh and never been seen or heard of again. What became of them? He swore they rose and went their way – and it is true that no citizen of the city has ever disappeared from his house. But no one saw the travelers again, and men say that goods and equipment recognised as theirs have been seen in the bazaars. If Aram did not sell them, after doing away with their owners, how came they there?'

'I have no goods,' growled the Cimmerian, touching the shagreen-bound hilt of the broadsword that hung at his hip. 'I have even sold my horse.'

'But it is not always rich strangers who vanish by night from the house of Aram Baksh!' chattered the Zuagir. 'Nay, poor desert men have slept there – because his score is less than that of the other taverns – and have been seen no more. Once a chief of the Zuagirs whose son had thus vanished complained to the satrap, Jungir Khan, who ordered the house searched by soldiers.'

'And they found a cellar full of corpses?' asked Conan in good-humored derision.

'Nay! They found naught! And drove the chief from the city with threats and curses! But' – he drew closer to Conan and shivered – 'something else was found! At the edge of the desert, beyond the houses, there is a clump of palm trees, and within that grove there is a pit. And within that pit have been found human bones, charred and blackened. Not once, but many times!'

'Which proves what?' grunted the Cimmerian.

'Aram Baksh is a demon! Nay, in this accursed city which Stygians built and which Hyrkanians rule – where white, brown, and black folk mingle together to produce hybrids of all unholy hues and breeds – who can tell who is a man, and who is a demon in disguise? Aram Baksh is a demon in the form of a man! At night he assumes his true guise and carries his guests off into the desert, where his fellow demons from the waste meet in conclave.'

'Why does he always carry off strangers?' asked Conan skeptically.

'The people of the city would not suffer him to slay their people, but they care nought for the strangers who fall into his hands. Conan, you are of the West, and know not the secrets of this ancient land. But, since the beginning of happenings, the demons of the desert have worshipped Yog, the Lord of the Empty Abodes, with fire – fire that devours human victims.

'Be warned! You have dwelt for many moons in the tents of the Zuagirs, and you are our brother! Go not to the house of Aram Baksh!'

'Get out of sight!' Conan said suddenly. 'Yonder comes a squad of the city watch. If they see you they may remember a horse that was stolen from the satrap's stable—'

The Zuagir gasped and moved convulsively. He ducked between a booth and a stone horse trough, pausing only long enough to chatter: 'Be warned, my brother! There are demons in the house of Aram Baksh!' Then he darted down a narrow alley and was gone.

Conan shifted his broad sword-belt to his liking and calmly returned the searching stares directed at him by the squad of watchmen as they swung past. They eyed him curiously and suspiciously, for he was a man who stood out even in such a motley throng as crowded the winding streets of Zamboula. His blue eyes and alien features distinguished him from the Eastern swarms, and the straight sword at his hip added point to the racial difference.

The watchmen did not accost him but swung on down the street, while the crowd opened a lane for them. They were Pelishtim, squat, hook-nosed, with blue-black beards sweeping their mailed breasts – mercenaries hired for work the ruling Turanians considered beneath themselves, and no less hated by the mongrel population for that reason.

Conan glanced at the sun, just beginning to dip behind the flat-topped houses on the western side of the bazaar, and hitching once more at his belt, moved off in the direction of Aram Baksh's tavern.

With a hillman's stride he moved through the ever-shifting colors of the streets, where the ragged tunics of whining beggars brushed against the ermine-trimmed khalats of lordly merchants, and the pearl-sewn satin of rich courtesans. Giant black slaves slouched along, jostling blue-bearded wanderers from the Shemitish cities, ragged nomads from the surrounding deserts, traders and adventurers from all the lands of the East.

The native population was no less heterogeneous. Here, centuries ago, the armies of Stygia had come, carving an empire out of the eastern desert. Zamboula was but a small trading town then, lying amidst a ring of oases, and inhabited by descendants of nomads. The Stygians built it into a city and settled it with their own people, and with Shemite and Kushite slaves. The ceaseless caravans, threading the desert from east to west and back again, brought riches and more mingling of races. Then came the conquering Turanians, riding out of the East to thrust back the boundaries of Stygia, and now for a generation Zamboula had been Turan's westernmost outpost, ruled by a Turanian satrap.

The babel of a myriad tongues smote on the Cimmerian's ears as the restless pattern of the Zamboulan streets weaved about him – cleft now and then by a squad of clattering horsemen, the tall, supple warriors of Turan, with dark hawk-faces, clinking metal, and curved swords. The throng scampered from under their horses' hoofs, for they were the lords of Zamboula. But tall, somber Stygians, standing back in the shadows, glowered darkly, remembering their ancient glories. The hybrid population cared little whether the king who controlled their destinies dwelt in dark Khemi or gleaming Aghrapur. Jungir Khan ruled Zamboula, and men whispered that Nafertari, the satrap's mistress, ruled Jungir Khan; but the people went their way, flaunting their myriad colors in the streets, bargaining, disputing, gambling, swilling, loving, as the people of Zamboula have done for all the centuries its towers and minarets have lifted over the sands of the Kharamun.

Bronze lanterns, carved with leering dragons, had been lighted in the streets before Conan reached the house of Aram Baksh. The tavern was the last occupied house on the street, which ran west. A wide garden, enclosed by a wall, where date palms grew thick, separated it from the houses farther east. To the west of the inn stood another grove of palms, through which the street, now become a road, wound out into the desert. Across the road from the tavern stood a row of deserted huts, shaded by straggling palm trees and occupied only by bats and jackals. As Conan came down the road, he wondered why the beggars, so plentiful in Zamboula, had not appropriated these empty houses for sleeping quarters. The lights ceased some distance behind him. Here were no lanterns, except the one hanging before the tavern gate: only the stars, the soft dust of the road underfoot, and the rustle of the palm leaves in the desert breeze.

Aram's gate did not open upon the road but upon the alley which ran between the tavern and the garden of the date palms. Conan jerked lustily at the rope which dangled from the bell beside the lantern, augmenting its clamor by hammering on the iron-bound teakwood gate with the hilt of his sword. A wicket opened in the gate, and a black face peered through.

'Open, blast you,' requested Conan. 'I'm a guest. I've paid Aram for a room, and a room I'll have, by Crom!'

The black craned his neck to stare into the starlit road behind Conan; but he opened the gate without comment and closed it again behind the Cimmerian, locking it and bolting it. The wall was unusually high; but there were many thieves in Zamboula, and a house on the edge of the desert might have to be defended against a nocturnal nomad raid. Conan strode through a garden, where great pale blossoms nodded in the starlight, and entered the taproom, where a Stygian with the shaven head of a student sat at a table brooding over nameless mysteries, and some nondescripts wrangled over a game of dice in a corner.

Aram Baksh came forward, walking softly, a portly man, with a black beard that swept his breast, a jutting hooknose, and small black eyes which were never still.

'You wish food?' he asked. 'Drink?'

'I ate a joint of beef and a loaf of bread in the *suk*,' grunted Conan. 'Bring me a tankard of Ghazan wine – I've got just enough left to pay for it.' He tossed a copper coin on the wine-splashed board.

'You did not win at the gaming tables?'

'How could I, with only a handful of silver to begin with? I paid you for the room this morning, because I knew I'd probably lose. I wanted to be sure I had a roof over my head tonight. I notice nobody sleeps in the streets in Zamboula. The very beggars hunt a niche they can barricade before dark. The city must be full of a particularly bloodthirsty band of thieves.'

He gulped the cheap wine with relish and then followed Aram out of the taproom. Behind him the players halted their game to stare after him with a cryptic speculation in their eyes. They said nothing, but the Stygian laughed, a ghastly laugh of inhuman cynicism and mockery. The others lowered their eyes uneasily, avoiding one another's

44

glance. The arts studied by a Stygian scholar are not calculated to make him share the feelings of a normal being.

Conan followed Aram down a corridor lighted by copper lamps, and it did not please him to note his host's noiseless tread. Aram's feet were clad in soft slippers and the hallway was carpeted with thick Turanian rugs; but there was an unpleasant suggestion of stealthiness about the Zamboulan.

At the end of the winding corridor, Aram halted at a door, across which a heavy iron bar rested in powerful metal brackets. This Aram lifted and showed the Cimmerian into a well-appointed chamber, the windows of which, Conan instantly noted, were small and strongly set with twisted bars of iron, tastefully gilded. There were rugs on the floor, a couch, after the Eastern fashion, and ornately carven stools. It was a much more elaborate chamber than Conan could have procured for the price nearer the center of the city – a fact that had first attracted him, when, that morning, he discovered how slim a purse his roistering for the past few days had left him. He had ridden into Zamboula from the desert a week before.

Aram had lighted a bronze lamp, and he now called Conan's attention to the two doors. Both were provided with heavy bolts.

'You may sleep safely tonight, Cimmerian,' said Aram, blinking over his bushy beard from the inner doorway.

Conan grunted and tossed his naked broadsword on the couch.

'Your bolts and bars are strong; but I always sleep with steel by my side.'

Aram made no reply; he stood fingering his thick beard for a moment as he stared at the grim weapon. Then silently he withdrew, closing the door behind him. Conan shot the bolt into place, crossed the room, opened the opposite door, and looked out. The room was on the side of the house that faced the road running west from the city. The door opened into a small court that was enclosed by a wall of its own. The end walls, which shut it off from the rest of the tavern compound, were high and without entrances; but the wall that flanked the road was low, and there was no lock on the gate.

Conan stood for a moment in the door, the glow of the

bronze lamp behind him, looking down the road to where it vanished among the dense palms. Their leaves rustled together in the faint breeze; beyond them lay the naked desert. Far up the street, in the other direction, lights gleamed and the noises of the city came faintly to him. Here was only starlight, the whispering of the palm leaves, and beyond that low wall, the dust of the road and the deserted huts thrusting their flat roofs against the low stars. Somewhere beyond the palm groves a drum began.

The garbled warnings of the Zuagir returned to him, seeming somehow less fantastic than they had seemed in the crowded, sunlit streets. He wondered again at the riddle of those empty huts. Why did the beggars shun them? He turned back into the chamber, shut the door, and bolted it.

The light began to flicker, and he investigated, swearing when he found the palm oil in the lamp was almost exhausted. He started to shout for Aram, then shrugged his shoulders and blew out the light. In the soft darkness he stretched himself fully clad on the couch, his sinewy hand by instinct searching for and closing on the hilt of his broadsword. Glancing idly at the stars framed in the barred windows, with the murmur of the breeze through the palms in his ears, he sank into slumber with a vague consciousness of the muttering drum, out on the desert – the low rumble and mutter of a leather-covered drum, beaten with soft, rhythmic strokes of an open black hand. . . .

2. *The Night Skulkers*

It was the stealthy opening of a door which awakened the Cimmerian. He did not awake as civilized men do, drowsy and drugged and stupid. He awoke instantly, with a clear mind, recognizing the sound that had interrupted his sleep. Lying there tensely in the dark he saw the outer door slowly open. In a widening crack of starlit sky he saw framed a great black bulk, broad, stooping shoulders, and a misshapen head blocked out against the stars.

Conan felt the skin crawl between his shoulders. He had

bolted that door securely. How could it be opening now, save by supernatural agency? And how could a human being possess a head like that outlined against the stars? All the tales he had heard in the Zuagir tents of devils and goblins came back to bead his flesh with clammy sweat. Now the monster slid noiselessly into the room, with a crouching posture and a shambling gait; and a familiar scent assailed the Cimmerian's nostrils, but did not reassure him, since Zuagir legendry represented demons as smelling like that.

Noiselessly Conan coiled his long legs under him; his naked sword was in his right hand, and when he struck it was as suddenly and murderously as a tiger lunging out of the dark. Not even a demon could have avoided that catapulting charge. His sword met and clove through flesh and bone, and something went heavily to the floor with a strangling cry. Conan crouched in the dark above it, sword dripping in his hand. Devil or beast or man, the thing was dead there on the floor. He sensed death as any wild thing senses it. He glared through the half-open door into the starlit court beyond. The gate stood open, but the court was empty.

Conan shut the door but did not bolt it. Groping in the darkness he found the lamp and lighted it. There was enough oil in it to burn for a minute or so. An instant later he was bending over the figure that sprawled on the floor in a pool of blood.

It was a gigantic black man, naked but for a loin cloth. One hand still grasped a knotty-headed bludgeon. The fellow's kinky wool was built up into hornlike spindles with twigs and dried mud. This barbaric coiffure had given the head its misshapen appearance in the starlight. Provided with a clue to the riddle, Conan pushed back the thick red lips and grunted as he stared down at teeth filed to points.

He understood now the mystery of the strangers who had disappeared from the house of Aram Baksh; the riddle of the black drum thrumming out there beyond the palm groves, and of that pit of charred bones – that pit where strange meat might be roasted under the stars, while black beasts squatted about to glut a hideous hunger. The man on the floor was a cannibal slave from Darfar.

There were many of his kind in the city. Cannibalism was not tolerated openly in Zamboula. But Conan knew now why people locked themselves in so securely at night, and why even beggars shunned the open alley and doorless ruins. He grunted in disgust as he visualized brutish black shadows skulking up and down the nighted streets, seeking human prey – and such men as Aram Baksh to open the doors to them. The innkeeper was not a demon; he was worse. The slaves from Darfar were notorious thieves; there was no doubt that some of their pilfered loot found its way into the hands of Aram Baksh. And in return he sold them human flesh.

Conan blew out the light, stepped to the door and opened it, and ran his hand over the ornaments on the outer side. One of them was movable and worked the bolt inside. The room was a trap to catch human prey like rabbits. But this time, instead of a rabbit, it had caught a saber-toothed tiger.

Conan returned to the other door, lifted the bolt, and pressed against it. It was immovable, and he remembered the bolt on the other side. Aram was taking no chances either with his victims or the men with whom he dealt. Buckling on his sword belt, the Cimmerian strode out into the court, closing the door behind him. He had no intention of delaying the settlement of his reckoning with Aram Baksh. He wondered how many poor devils had been bludgeoned in their sleep and dragged out of that room and down the road that ran through the shadowed palm groves to the roasting pit.

He halted in the court. The drum was still muttering, and he caught the reflection of a leaping red glare through the groves. Cannibalism was more than a perverted appetite with the black men of Darfar; it was an integral element of their ghastly cult. The black vultures were already in conclave. But whatever flesh filled their bellies that night, it would not be his.

To reach Aram Baksh, he must climb one of the walls which separated the small enclosure from the main compound. They were high, meant to keep out the man-eaters; but Conan was no swamp-bred black man; his thews had been steeled in boyhood on the sheer cliffs of his native hills. He was standing at the foot of the nearer wall when a cry echoed under the trees.

In an instant Conan was crouching at the gate, glaring

down the road. The sound had come from the shadows of the huts across the road. He heard a frantic choking and gurgling such as might result from a desperate attempt to shriek, with a black hand fastened over the victim's mouth. A close-knit clump of figures emerged from the shadows beyond the huts and started down the road – three huge black men carrying a slender, struggling figure between them. Conan caught the glimmer of pale limbs writhing in the starlight, even as, with a convulsive wrench, the captive slipped from the grasp of the brutal fingers and came flying up the road, a supple young woman, naked as the day she was born. Conan saw her plainly before she ran out of the road and into the shadows between the huts. The blacks were at her heels, and back in the shadows the figures merged and an intolerable scream of anguish and horror rang out.

Stirred to red rage by the ghoulishness of the episode, Conan raced across the road.

Neither victim nor abductors were aware of his presence until the soft swish of the dust about his feet brought them about; and then he was almost upon them, coming with the gusty fury of a hill wind. Two of the blacks turned to meet him, lifting their bludgeons. But they failed to estimate properly the speed at which he was coming. One of them was down, disemboweled, before he could strike, and wheeling catlike, Conan evaded the stroke of the other's cudgel and lashed in a whistling counter-cut. The black's head flew into the air; the headless body took three staggering steps, spurting blood and clawing horribly at the air with groping hands, and then slumped to the dust.

The remaining cannibal gave back with a strangled yell, hurling his captive from him. She tripped and rolled in the dust, and the black fled in panic toward the city. Conan was at his heels. Fear winged the black feet, but before they reached the easternmost hut, he sensed death at his back, and bellowed like an ox in the slaughter yards.

'Black dog of Hell!' Conan drove his sword between the dusky shoulders with such vengeful fury that the broad blade stood out half its length from the black breast. With a choking cry the black stumbled headlong, and Conan braced his feet and dragged out his sword as his victim fell.

Only the breeze disturbed the leaves. Conan shook his

head as a lion shakes its mane and growled his unsatiated blood lust. But no more shapes slunk from the shadows, and before the huts the starlit road stretched empty. He whirled at the quick patter of feet behind him, but it was only the girl, rushing to throw herself on him and clasp his neck in a desperate grasp, frantic from terror of the abominable fate she had just escaped.

'Easy, girl,' he grunted. 'You're all right. How did they catch you?'

She sobbed something unintelligible. He forgot all about Aram Baksh as he scrutinized her by the light of the stars. She was white, though a very definite brunette, obviously one of Zamboula's many mixed breeds. She was tall, with a slender, supple form, as he was in a good position to observe. Admiration burned in his fierce eyes as he looked down on her splendid bosom and her lithe limbs, which still quivered from fright and exertion. He passed an arm around her flexible waist and said, reassuringly: 'Stop shaking, wench; you're safe enough.'

His touch seemed to restore her shaken sanity. She tossed back her thick, glossy locks and cast a fearful glance over her shoulder, while she pressed closer to the Cimmerian as if seeking security in the contact.

'They caught me in the streets,' she muttered, shuddering. 'Lying in wait, beneath a dark arch – black men, like great, hulking apes! Set have mercy on me! I shall dream of it!'

'What were you doing out on the streets this time of night?' he inquired, fascinated by the satiny feel of her sleek skin under his questing fingers.

She raked back her hair and stared blankly up into his face. She did not seem aware of his caresses.

'My lover,' she said. 'My lover drove me into the streets. He went mad and tried to kill me. As I fled from him I was seized by those beasts.'

'Beauty like yours might drive a man mad,' quoth Conan, running his fingers experimentally through her glossy tresses.

She shook her head, like one emerging from a daze. She no longer trembled, and her voice was steady.

'It was the spite of a priest – of Totrasmek, the high priest of Hanuman, who desires me for himself – the dog!'

'No need to curse him for that,' grinned Conan. 'The old hyena has better taste than I thought.'

She ignored the bluff compliment. She was regaining her poise swiftly.

'My lover is a – a young Turanian soldier. To spite me, Totrasmek gave him a drug that drove him mad. Tonight he snatched up a sword and came at me to slay me in his madness, but I fled from him into the streets. The Negroes seized me and brought me to this – *what was that?*'

Conan had already moved. Soundlessly as a shadow he drew her behind the nearest hut, beneath the straggling palms. They stood in tense stillness, while the low mutterings both had heard grew louder until voices were distinguishable. A group of Negroes, some nine or ten, were coming along the road from the direction of the city. The girl clutched Conan's arm and he felt the terrified quivering of her supple body against his.

Now they could understand the gutturals of the black men.

'Our brothers are already assembled at the pit,' said one. 'We have had no luck. I hope they have enough for us.'

'Aram promised us a man,' muttered another, and Conan mentally promised Aram something.

'Aram keeps his word,' grunted yet another. 'Many a man we have taken from his tavern. But we pay him well. I myself have given him ten bales of silk I stole from my master. It was good silk, by Set!'

The blacks shuffled past, bare splay feet scuffing up the dust, and their voices dwindled down the road.

'Well for us those corpses are lying behind these huts,' muttered Conan. 'If they look in Aram's death room they'll find another. Let's begone.'

'Yes, let us hasten!' begged the girl, almost hysterical again. 'My lover is wandering somewhere in the streets alone. The Negroes may take him.'

'A devil of a custom this is!' growled Conan, as he led the way toward the city, paralleling the road but keeping behind the huts and straggling trees. 'Why don't the citizens clean out these black dogs?'

'They are valuable slaves,' murmured the girl. 'There are so many of them they might revolt if they were denied the flesh for which they lust. The people of Zamboula know they skulk the streets at night, and all are careful to remain within locked doors, except when something unforeseen happens, as it did to me. The blacks prey on anything they catch, but they seldom catch anybody but strangers. The people of Zamboula are not concerned with the strangers that pass through the city.

'Such men as Aram Baksh sell these strangers to the blacks. He would not dare attempt such a thing with a citizen.'

Conan spat in disgust, and a moment later led his companion out into the road which was becoming a street, with still, unlighted houses on each side. Slinking in the shadows was not congenial to his nature.

'Where did you want to go?' he asked. The girl did not seem to object to his arm about her waist.

'To my house, to rouse my servants,' she answered. 'To bid them search for my lover. I do not wish the city – the priests – anyone – to know of his madness. He – he is a young officer with a promising future. Perhaps we can drive this madness from him if we can find him.'

'If *we* find him?' rumbled Conan. 'What makes you think I want to spend the night scouring the streets for a lunatic?'

She cast a quick glance into his face, and properly interpreted the gleam in his blue eyes. Any woman could have known that he would follow her wherever she led – for a while, at least. But being a woman, she concealed her knowledge of that fact.

'Please,' she began with a hint of tears in her voice, 'I have no one else to ask for help – you have been kind—'

'All right!' he grunted. 'All right! What's the young reprobate's name?'

'Why – Alafdhal. I am Zabibi, a dancing-girl. I have danced often before the satrap, Jungir Khan, and his mistress Nafertari, and before all the lords and royal ladies of Zamboula. Totrasmek desired me and, because I repulsed him, he made me the innocent tool of his vengeance against Alafdhal. I asked a love potion of Totrasmek, not suspecting the depth of his guile and hate. He gave me a drug to mix with my lover's wine, and he swore that when Alafdhal drank it, he would love me even more madly than ever and grant my every wish. I mixed the drug secretly with my lover's wine. But having drunk, my lover went raving mad and things came about as I have told you. Curse Totrasmek, the hybrid snake – ahhh!'

She caught his arm convulsively and both stopped short. They had come into a district of shops and stalls, all deserted and unlighted, for the hour was late. They were passing an alley, and in its mouth a man was standing, motionless and silent. His head was lowered, but Conan caught the weird gleam of eery eyes regarding them unblinkingly. His skin crawled, not with fear of the sword in the man's hand, but because of the uncanny suggestion of his posture and silence. They suggested madness. Conan pushed the girl aside and drew his sword.

'Don't kill him!' she begged. 'In the name of Set, do not slay him! You are strong – overpower him!'

'We'll see,' he muttered, grasping his sword in his right hand and clenching his left into a malletlike fist.

He took a wary step toward the alley – and with a horrible moaning laugh the Turanian charged. As he came he swung his sword, rising on his toes as he put all the power of his body behind the blows. Sparks flashed blue as Conan parried the blade, and the next instant the madman was stretched senseless in the dust from a thundering buffet of Conan's left fist.

The girl ran forward.

'Oh, he is not – he is not—'

Conan bent swiftly, turned the man on his side, and ran quick fingers over him.

'He's not hurt much,' he grunted. 'Bleeding at the nose, but anybody's likely to do that, after a clout on the jaw. He'll come to after a bit, and maybe his mind will be right. In the meantime I'll tie his wrists with his sword belt – so. Now where do you want me to take him?'

'Wait!' She knelt beside the senseless figure, seized the bound hands, and scanned them avidly. Then, shaking her head as if in baffled disappointment, she rose. She came close to the giant Cimmerian and laid her slender hands on his arching breast. Her dark eyes, like wet black jewels in the starlight, gazed up into his.

'You are a man! Help me! Totrasmek must die! Slay him for me!'

'And put my neck into a Turanian noose?' he grunted.

'Nay!' The slender arms, strong as pliant steel, were around his corded neck. Her supple body throbbed against his. 'The Hyrkanians have no love for Totrasmek. The priests of Set fear him. He is a mongrel, who rules men by fear and superstition. I worship Set, and the Turanians bow to Erlik, but Totrasmek sacrifices to Hanuman the accursed! The Turanian lords fear his black arts and his power over the hybrid population, and they hate him. Even Jungir Khan and his mistress Nafertari fear and hate him. If he were slain in his temple at night, they would not seek his slayer very closely.'

'And what of his magic?' rumbled the Cimmerian.

'You are a fighting man,' she answered. 'To risk your life is part of your profession.'

'For a price,' he admitted.

'There will be a price!' she breathed, rising on tiptoes, to gaze into his eyes.

The nearness of her vibrant body drove a flame through his veins. The perfume of her breath mounted to his brain. But as his arms closed about her supple figure she avoided them with a lithe movement, saying: 'Wait! First serve me in this matter.'

'Name your price.' He spoke with some difficulty.

'Pick up my lover,' she directed, and the Cimmerian stooped and swung the tall form easily to his broad shoulder. At the moment he felt as if he could have toppled over Jungir Khan's palace with equal ease. The girl murmured an endearment to the unconscious man, and there was no hyprocrisy in her attitude. She obviously loved Alafdhal sincerely. Whatever business arrangement she made with Conan would have no bearing on her relationship with Alafdhal. Women are more practical about these things than men.

'Follow me!' She hurried along the street, while the Cimmerian strode easily after her, in no way discomforted by his limp burden. He kept a wary eye out for black shadows skulking under arches but saw nothing suspicious. Doubtless the men of Darfar were all gathered at the roasting pit. The girl turned down a narrow side street and presently knocked cautiously at an arched door.

Almost instantly a wicket opened in the upper panel, and a black face glanced out. She bent close to the open-

54

ing, whispering swiftly. Bolts creaked in their sockets, and the door opened. A giant black man stood framed against the soft glow of a copper lamp. A quick glance showed Conan the man was not from Darfar. His teeth were unfiled and his kinky hair was cropped close to his skull. He was from the Wadai.

At a word from Zabibi, Conan gave the limp body into the black's arms and saw the young officer laid on a velvet divan. He showed no signs of returning conciousness. The blow that had rendered him senseless might have felled an ox. Zabibi bent over him for an instant, her fingers nervously twining and twisting. Then she straightened and beckoned the Cimmerian.

The door closed softly, the locks clicked behind them, and the closing wicket shut off the glow of the lamps. In the starlight of the street Zabibi took Conan's hand. Her own hand trembled a little.

'You will not fail me?'

He shook his maned head, massive against the stars.

'Then follow me to Hanuman's shrine, and the gods have mercy on our souls.'

Along the silent streets they moved like phantoms of antiquity. They went in silence. Perhaps the girl was thinking of her lover lying senseless on the divan under the copper lamps or was shrinking with fear of what lay ahead of them in the demon-haunted shrine of Hanuman. The barbarian was thinking only of the woman moving so supplely beside him. The perfume of her scented hair was in his nostrils, the sensuous aura of her presence filled his brain and left room for no other thoughts.

Once they heard the clank of brass-shod feet, and drew into the shadows of a gloomy arch while a squad of Pelishti watchmen swung past. There were fifteen of them; they marched in close formation, pikes at the ready, and the rearmost men had their broad, brass shields slung on their backs, to protect them from a knife stroke from behind. The skulking menace of the black maneaters was a threat even to armed men.

As soon as the clang of their sandals had receded up the street, Conan and the girl emerged from their hiding place and hurried on. A few moments later, they saw the squat, flat-topped edifice they sought looming ahead of them.

The temple of Hanuman stood alone in the midst of a broad square, which lay silent and deserted beneath the stars. A marble wall surrounded the shrine, with a broad opening directly before the portico. This opening had no gate nor any sort of barrier.

'Why don't the blacks seek their prey here?' muttered Conan. 'There's nothing to keep them out of the temple.'

He could feel the trembling of Zabibi's body as she pressed close to him.

'They fear Totrasmek, as all in Zamboula fear him, even Jungir Khan and Nafertari. Come! Come quickly, before my courage flows from me like water!'

The girl's fear was evident, but she did not falter. Conan drew his sword and strode ahead of her as they advanced through the open gateway. He knew the hideous habits of the priests of the East and was aware that an invader of Hanuman's shrine might expect to encounter almost any sort of nightmare horror. He knew there was a good chance that neither he nor the girl would ever leave the shrine alive, but he had risked his life too many times before to devote much thought to that consideration.

They entered a court paved with marble which gleamed whitely in the starlight. A short flight of broad marble steps led up to the pillared portico. The great bronze doors stood wide open as they had stood for centuries. But no worshippers burnt incense within. In the day men and women might come timidly into the shrine and place offerings to the ape-god on the black altar. At night the people shunned the temple of Hanuman as hares shun the lair of the serpent.

Burning censers bathed the interior in a soft, weird glow that created an illusion of unreality. Near the rear wall, behind the black stone altar, sat the god with his gaze fixed for ever on the open door, through which for centuries his victims had come, dragged by chains of roses. A faint groove ran from the sill to the altar, and when Conan's foot felt it, he stepped away as quickly as if he had trodden upon a snake. That groove had been worn by the faltering feet of the multitude of those who had died screaming on that grim altar.

Bestial in the uncertain light, Hanuman leered with his carven mask. He sat, not as an ape would crouch, but cross-legged as a man would sit, but his aspect was no less simian for that reason. He was carved from black marble, but his eyes were rubies, which glowed red and lustful as the coals of hell's deepest pits. His great hands lay upon his lap, palms upward, taloned fingers spread and grasping. In the gross emphasis of his attributes, in the leer of his satyr-countenance, was reflected the abominable cynicism of the degenerate cult which deified him.

The girl moved around the image, making toward the back wall, and when her sleek flank brushed against a carven knee, she shrank aside and shuddered as if a reptile had touched her. There was a space of several feet between the broad back of the idol and the marble wall with its frieze of gold leaves. On either hand, flanking the idol, an ivory door under a gold arch was set in the wall.

'Those doors open into each end of a hairpin-shaped corridor,' she said hurriedly. 'Once I was in the interior of the shrine – once!' She shivered and twitched her slim shoulders at a memory both terrifying and obscene. 'The corridor is bent like a horseshoe, with each horn opening into this room. Totrasmek's chambers are enclosed within the curve of the corridor and open into it. But there is a secret door in this wall which opens directly into an inner chamber—'

She began to run her hands over the smooth surface, where no crack or crevice showed. Conan stood beside her, sword in hand, glancing warily about him. The silence, the emptiness of the shrine, with imagination picturing what might lie behind that wall, made him feel like a wild beast nosing a trap.

'Ah!' The girl had found a hidden spring at last; a square opening gaped blackly in the wall. Then: 'Set!' she screamed, and even as Conan leaped toward her, he saw that a great misshapen hand had fastened itself in her hair. She was snatched off her feet and jerked head-first through the opening. Conan, grabbing ineffectually at her, felt his fingers slip from a naked limb, and in an instant she had vanished and the wall showed black as before. Only from beyond it came the muffled sounds of a struggle, a scream, faintly heard, and a low laugh that made Conan's blood congeal in his veins.

3. *Black Hands Gripping*

With an oath the Cimmerian smote the wall a terrific blow with the pommel of his sword, and the marble cracked and chipped. But the hidden door did not give way, and reason told him that doubtless it had been bolted on the other side of the wall. Turning, he sprang across the chamber to one of the ivory doors.

He lifted his sword to shatter the panels, but on a venture tried the door first with his left hand. It swung open easily, and he glared into a long corridor that curved away into dimness under the weird light of censers similar to those in the shrine. A heavy gold bolt showed on the jamb of the door, and he touched it lightly with his finger tips. The faint warmness of the metal could have been detected only by a man whose faculties were akin to those of a wolf. That bolt had been touched – and therefore drawn – within the last few seconds. The affair was taking on more and more of the aspect of a baited trap. He might have known Totrasmek would know when anyone entered the temple.

To enter the corridor would undoubtedly be to walk into whatever trap the priest had set for him. But Conan did not hesitate. Somewhere in that dim-lit interior Zabibi was a captive, and, from what he knew of the characteristics of Hanuman's priests, he was sure that she needed help badly. Conan stalked into the corridor with a pantherish tread, poised to strike right or left.

On his left, ivory, arched doors opened into the corridor, and he tried each in turn. All were locked. He had gone perhaps seventy-five feet when the corridor bent sharply to the left, describing the curve the girl had mentioned. A door opened into this curve, and it gave under his hand.

He was looking into a broad, square chamber, somewhat more clearly lighted than the corridor. Its walls were of white marble, the floor of ivory, the ceiling of fretted silver. He saw divans of rich satin, gold-worked footstools of ivory, a disk-shaped table of some massive, metal-like substance. On one of the divans a man was reclining, looking toward the door. He laughed as he met the Cimmerian's startled glare.

This man was naked except for a loin cloth and high-

58

strapped sandals. He was brown-skinned, with close-cropped black hair and restless black eyes that set off a broad, arrogant face. In girth and breadth he was enormous, with huge limbs on which the great muscles swelled and rippled at each slightest movement. His hands were the largest Conan had ever seen. The assurance of gigantic physical strength colored his every action and inflection.

'Why not enter, barbarian?' he called mockingly, with an exaggerated gesture of invitation.

Conan's eyes began to smolder ominously, but he trod warily into the chamber, his sword ready.

'Who the devil are you?' he growled.

'I am Baal-pteor,' the man answered. 'Once, long ago and in another land, I had another name. But this is a good name, and why Totrasmek gave it to me, any temple wench can tell you.'

'So you're his dog!' grunted Conan. 'Well, curse your brown hide, Baal-pteor, where's the wench you jerked through the wall?'

'My master entertains her!' laughed Baal-pteor. 'Listen!'

From beyond a door opposite the one by which Conan had entered there sounded a woman's scream, faint and muffled in the distance.

'Blast your soul!' Conan took a stride toward the door, then wheeled with his skin tingling. Baal-pteor was laughing at him, and that laugh was edged with menace that made the hackles rise on Conan's neck and sent a red wave of murder-lust driving across his vision.

He started toward Baal-pteor, the knuckles on his swordhand showing white. With a swift motion the brown man threw something at him – a shining crystal sphere that glistened in the weird light.

Conan dodged instinctively, but, miraculously, the globe stopped short in midair, a few feet from his face. It did not fall to the floor. It hung suspended, as if by invisible filaments, some five feet above the floor. And as he glared in amazement, it began to rotate with growing speed. And as it revolved it grew, expanded, became nebulous. It filled the chamber. It enveloped him. It blotted out furniture, walls, the smiling countenance of Baal-pteor. He was lost in the midst of a blinding bluish blur of whirling speed.

59

Terrific winds screamed past Conan, tugging at him, striving to wrench him from his feet, to drag him into the vortex that spun madly before him.

With a choking cry Conan lurched backward, reeled, felt the solid wall against his back. At the contact the illusion ceased to be. The whirling, titanic sphere vanished like a bursting bubble. Conan reeled upright in the silver-ceilinged room, with a gray mist coiling about his feet, and saw Baal-pteor lolling on the divan, shaking with silent laughter.

'Son of a slut!' Conan lunged at him. But the mist swirled up from the floor, blotting out that giant brown form. Groping in a rolling cloud that blinded him, Conan felt a rending sensation of dislocation – and then room and mist and brown man were gone together. He was standing alone among the high reeds of a marshy fen, and a buffalo was lunging at him, head down. He leaped aside from the ripping scimitar-curved horns and drove his sword in behind the foreleg, through ribs and heart. And then it was not a buffalo dying there in the mud, but the brown-skinned Baal-pteor. With a curse Conan struck off his head; and the head soared from the ground and snapped beastlike tusks into his throat. For all his mighty strength he could not tear it loose – he was choking – strangling; then there was a rush and roar through space, the dislocating shock of an immeasurable impact, and he was back in the chamber with Baal-pteor, whose head was once more set firmly on his shoulders, and who laughed silently at him from the divan.

'Mesmerism!' muttered Conan, crouching and digging his toes hard against the marble.

His eyes blazed. This brown dog was playing with him, making sport of him! But this mummery, this child's play of mists and shadows of thought, it could not harm him. He had but to leap and strike and the brown acolyte would be a mangled corpse under his heel. This time he would not be fooled by shadows of illusion – but he was.

A blood-curdling snarl sounded behind him, and he wheeled and struck in a flash at the panther crouching to spring on him from the metal-colored table. Even as he struck, the apparition vanished and his blade clashed deafeningly on the adamantine surface. Instantly he

60

sensed something abnormal. The blade stuck to the table! He wrenched at it savagely. It did not give. This was no mesmeristic trick. The table was a giant magnet. He gripped the hilt with both hands, when a voice at his shoulder brought him about, to face the brown man, who had at last risen from the divan.

Slightly taller than Conan and much heavier, Baal-pteor loomed before him, a daunting image of muscular development. His mighty arms were unnaturally long, and his great hands opened and closed, twitching convulsively. Conan released the hilt of his imprisoned sword and fell silent, watching his enemy through slitted lids.

'Your head, Cimmerian!' taunted Baal-pteor. 'I shall take it with my bare hands, twisting it from your shoulders as the head of a fowl is twisted! Thus the sons of Kosala offer sacrifice to Yajur. Barbarian, you look upon a strangler of Yota-pong. I was chosen by the priests of Yajur in my infancy, and throughout childhood, boyhood, and youth I was trained in the art of slaying with the naked hands – for only thus are the sacrifices enacted. Yajur loves blood, and we waste not a drop from the victim's veins. When I was a child they gave me infants to throttle; when I was a boy I strangled young girls; as a youth, women, old men, and young boys. Not until I reached my full manhood was I given a strong man to slay on the altar of Yota-pong.

'For years I offered the sacrifices to Yajur. Hundreds of necks have snapped between these fingers—' he worked them before the Cimmerian's angry eyes. 'Why I fled from Yota-pong to become Totrasmek's servant is no concern of yours. In a moment you will be beyond curiosity. The priests of Kosala, the stranglers of Yajur, are strong beyond the belief of men. And I was stronger than any. With my hands, barbarian, I shall break your neck!'

And like the stroke of twin cobras, the great hands closed on Conan's throat. The Cimmerian made no attempt to dodge or fend them away, but his own hands darted to the Kosalan's bull-neck. Baal-pteor's black eyes widened as he felt the thick cords of muscles that protected the barbarian's throat. With a snarl he exerted his inhuman strength, and knots and lumps and ropes of thews rose along his massive arms. And then a choking gasp burst from him as Conan's fingers locked on his throat. For an instant they stood there like statues, their faces masks of effort, veins beginning to stand out purply on their temples. Conan's thin lips drew back from his teeth in a grinning snarl. Baal-pteor's eyes were distended in them grew an awful surprise and the glimmer of fear. Both men stood motionless as images, except for the expanding of their muscles on rigid arms and braced legs, but strength beyond common conception was warring there – strength that might have uprooted trees and crushed the skulls of bullocks.

The wind whistled suddenly from between Baal-pteor's parted teeth. His face was growing purple. Fear flooded his eyes. His thews seemed ready to burst from his arms and shoulders, yet the muscles of the Cimmerian's thick neck did not give; they felt like masses of woven iron cords under his desperate fingers. But his own flesh was giving way under the iron fingers of the Cimmerian which ground deeper and deeper into the yielding throat muscles, crushing them in upon jugular and windpipe.

The statuesque immobility of the group gave way to sudden, frenzied motion, as the Kosalan began to wrench and heave, seeking to throw himself backward. He let go of Conan's throat and grasped his wrists, trying to tear away those inexorable fingers.

With a sudden lunge Conan bore him backward until the small of his back crashed against the table. And still farther over its edge Conan bent him, back and back, until his spine was ready to snap.

Conan's low laugh was merciless as the ring of steel.

'You fool!' he all but whispered. 'I think you never saw a man from the West before. Did you deem yourself strong, because you were able to twist the heads off civilized folk, poor weaklings with muscles like rotten string? Hell! Break the neck of a wild Cimmerian bull before you call yourself strong. I did that, before I was a full-grown man – like this!'

And with a savage wrench he twisted Baal-pteor's head around until the ghastly face leered over the left shoulder, and the vertebrae snapped like a rotten branch.

Conan hurled the flopping corpse to the floor, turned to the sword again, and gripped the hilt with both hands, bracing his feet against the floor. Blood trickled down his broad breast from the wounds Baal-pteor's finger nails had torn in the skin of his neck. His black hair was damp, sweat ran down his face, and his chest heaved. For all his vocal scorn of Baal-pteor's strength, he had almost met his match in the inhuman Kosalan. But without pausing to catch his breath, he exerted all his strength in a mighty wrench that tore the sword from the magnet where it clung.

Another instant and he had pushed open the door from behind which the scream had sounded, and was looking down a long straight corridor, lined with ivory doors. The other end was masked by a rich velvet curtain, and from beyond that curtain came the devilish strains of such music as Conan had never heard, not even in nightmares. It made the short hairs bristle on the back of his neck. Mingled with it was the panting, hysterical sobbing of a woman. Grasping his sword firmly, he glided down the corridor.

4. Dance, Girl, Dance!

When Zabibi was jerked head-first through the aperture which opened in the wall behind the idol, her first, dizzy, disconnected thought was that her time had come. She instinctively shut her eyes and waited for the blow to fall. But instead she felt herself dumped unceremoniously onto the smooth marble floor, which bruised her knees and hip. Opening her eyes, she stared fearfully around her, just as a muffled impact sounded from beyond the wall. She saw a brown-skinned giant in a loin cloth standing over her, and, across the chamber into which she had come, a man sat on a divan, with his back to a rich black velvet curtain, a broad, fleshy man, with fat white hands and snaky eyes. And her flesh crawled, for this man was Totrasmek, the priest of Hanuman, who for years had spun his slimy webs of power throughout the city of Zamboula.

'The barbarian seeks to batter his way through the wall,' said Totrasmek sardonically, 'but the bolt will hold.'

The girl saw that a heavy golden bolt had been shot across the hidden door, which was plainly discernible from this side of the wall. The bolt and its sockets would have resisted the charge of an elephant.

'Go open one of the doors for him, Baal-pteor,' ordered Totrasmek. 'Slay him in the square chamber at the other end of the corridor.'

The Kosalan salaamed and departed by the way of a door in the side wall of the chamber. Zabibi rose, staring fearfully at the priest, whose eyes ran avidly over her splendid figure. To this she was indifferent. A dancer of Zamboula was accustomed to nakedness. But the cruelty in his eyes started her limbs to quivering.

'Again you come to me in my retreat, beautiful one,' he purred with cynical hypocrisy. 'It is an unexpected honor. You seemed to enjoy your former visit so little, that I dared not hope for you to repeat it. Yet I did all in my power to provide you with an interesting experience.'

For a Zamboulan dancer to blush would be an impossibility, but a smolder of anger mingled with the fear in Zabibi's dilated eyes.

'Fat pig! You know I did not come here for love of you.'

'No,' laughed Totrasmek, 'you came like a fool, creeping through the night with a stupid barbarian to cut my throat. Why should you seek my life?'

'You know why!' she cried, knowing the futility of trying to dissemble.

'You are thinking of your lover,' he laughed. 'The fact that you are here seeking my life shows that he quaffed the drug I gave you. Well, did you not ask for it? And did I not send what you asked for, out of the love I bear you?'

'I asked you for a drug that would make him slumber harmlessly for a few hours,' she said bitterly. 'And you – you sent your servant with a drug that drove him mad! I was a fool ever to trust you. I might have known your protestations of friendship were lies, to disguise your hate and spite.'

'Why did you wish your lover to sleep?' he retorted. 'So you could steal from him the only thing he would never give you – the ring with the jewel men call the Star of Khorala – the star stolen from the queen of Ophir, who would pay a roomful of gold for its return. He would not give it to you willingly, because he knew that it holds a magic which, when properly controlled, will enslave the hearts of any of the opposite sex. You wished to steal it from him, fearing that his magicians would discover the key to that magic and he would forget you in his conquests of the queens of the world. You would sell it back to the queen of Ophir, who understands its power and would use it to enslave me, as she did before it was stolen.'

'And why did *you* want it?' she demanded sulkily.

'I understand its powers. It would increase the power of my arts.'

'Well,' she snapped, 'you have it now!'

'*I* have the Star of Khorala? Nay, you err.'

'Why bother to lie?' she retorted bitterly. 'He had it on his finger when he drove me into the streets. He did not have it when I found him again. Your servant must have been watching the house, and have taken it from him, after I escaped him. To the devil with it! I want my lover back sane and whole. You have the ring; you have punished us both. Why do you not restore his mind to him? Can you?'

'I could,' he assured her, in evident enjoyment of her distress. He drew a phial from among his robes. 'This contains the juice of the golden lotus. If your lover drank it, he would be sane again. Yes, I will be merciful. You have both thwarted and flouted me, not once but many times; he has constantly opposed my wishes. But I will be merciful. Come and take the phial from my hand.'

She stared at Totrasmek, trembling with eagerness to seize it, but fearing it was but some cruel jest. She advanced timidly, with a hand extended, and he laughed heartlessly and drew back out of her reach. Even as her lips parted to curse him, some instinct snatched her eyes upward. From the gilded ceiling four jade-hued vessels were falling. She dodged, but they did not strike her. They crashed to the floor about her, forming the four corners of a square. And she screamed, and screamed again. For out of each ruin reared the hooded head of a cobra, and one struck at her bare leg. Her convulsive movement to evade it brought her within reach of the one on the other

65

side and again she had to shift like lightning to avoid the flash of its hideous head.

She was caught in a frightful trap. All four serpents were swaying and striking at foot, ankle, calf, knee, thigh, hip, whatever portion of her voluptuous body chanced to be nearest to them, and she could not spring over them or pass between them to safety. She could only whirl and spring aside and twist her body to avoid the strokes, and each time she moved to dodge one snake, the motion brought her within range of another, so that she had to keep shifting with the speed of light. She could move only a short space in any direction, and the fearful hooded crests were menacing her every second. Only a dancer of Zamboula could have lived in that grisly square.

She became, herself, a blurr of bewildering motion. The heads missed her by hair's breadths, but they missed, as she pitted her twinkling feet, flickering limbs, and perfect eye against the blinding speed of the scaly demons her enemy had conjured out of thin air.

Somewhere a thin, whining music struck up, mingling with the hissing of the serpents, like an evil night wind blowing through the empty sockets of a skull. Even in the flying speed of her urgent haste she realized that the darting of the serpents was no longer at random. They obeyed the grisly piping of the eery music. They struck with a horrible rhythm, and perforce her swaying, writhing, spinning body attuned itself to their rhythm. Her frantic motions melted into the measures of a dance compared to which the most obscene tarantella of Zamora would have seemed sane and restrained. Sick with shame and terror Zabibi heard the hateful mirth of her merciless tormenter.

'The Dance of the Cobras, my lovely one!' laughed Totrasmek. 'So maidens danced in the sacrifice to Hanuman centuries ago – but never with such beauty and suppleness. Dance, girl, dance! How long can you avoid the fangs of the Poison People? Minutes? Hours? You will weary at last. Your swift, sure feet will stumble, your legs falter, your hips slow in their rotations. Then the fangs will begin to sink deep into your ivory flesh—'

Behind him the curtain shook as if struck by a gust of wind, and Totrasmek screamed. His eyes dilated and his hands caught convulsively at the length of bright steel which jutted suddenly from his breast.

The music broke off short. The girl swayed dizzily in her dance, crying out in dreadful anticipation of the flickering fangs – and then only four wisps of harmless blue smoke curled up from the floor about her, as Totrasmek sprawled headlong from the divan.

Conan came from behind the curtain, wiping his broad blade. Looking through the hangings he had seen the girl dancing desperately between four swaying spirals of smoke, but he had guessed that their appearance was very different to her. He knew he had killed Totrasmek.

Zabibi sank down on the floor, panting, but even as Conan started toward her, she staggered up again, though her legs trembled with exhaustion.

'The phial!' she gasped. 'The phial!'

Totrasmek still grasped it in his stiffening hand. Ruthlessly she tore it from his locked fingers and then began frantically to ransack his garments.

'What the devil are you looking for?' Conan demanded.

'A ring – he stole it from Alafdhal. He must have, while my lover walked in madness through the streets. Set's devils!'

She had convinced herself that it was not on the person of Totrasmek. She began to cast about the chamber, tearing up divan covers and hangings and upsetting vessels.

She paused and raked a damp lock of hair out of her eyes.

'I forgot Baal-pteor!'

'He's in Hell with his neck broken,' Conan assured her.

She expressed vindictive gratification at the news, but an instant later swore expressively.

'We can't stay here. It's not many hours until dawn. Lesser priests are likely to visit the temple at any hour of the night, and if we're discovered here with his corpse, the people will tear us to pieces. The Turanians could not save us.'

She lifted the bolt on the secret door, and a few moments later they were in the streets and hurrying away from the silent square where brooded the age-old shrine of Hanuman.

In a winding street a short distance away, Conan halted

and checked his companion with a heavy hand on her naked shoulder.

'Don't forget there was a price—'

'I have not forgotten!' She twisted free. 'But we must go to – to Alafdhal first!'

A few minutes later the black slave let them through the wicket door. The young Turanian lay upon the divan, his arms and legs bound with heavy velvet ropes. His eyes were open, but they were like those of a mad dog, and foam was thick on his lips. Zabibi shuddered.

'Force his jaws open!' she commanded, and Conan's iron fingers accomplished the task.

Zabibi emptied the phial down the maniac's gullet. The effect was like magic. Instantly he became quiet. The glare faded from his eyes; he stared up at the girl in a puzzled way, but with recognition and intelligence. Then he fell into a normal slumber.

'When he awakes he will be quite sane,' she whispered, motioning to the silent slave.

With a deep bow he gave into her hands a small leathern bag and drew about her shoulders a silken cloak. Her manner had subtly changed when she beckoned Conan to follow her out of the chamber.

In an arch that opened on the street, she turned to him, drawing herself up with a new regality.

'I must now tell you the truth,' she said. 'I am not Zabibi. I am Nafertari. And *he* is not Alafdhal, a poor captain of the guardsmen. He is Jungir Khan, satrap of Zamboula.'

Conan made no comment; his scarred, dark countenance was immobile.

'I lied to you because I dared not divulge the truth to anyone,' she said. 'We were alone when Jungir Khan went mad. None knew of it but myself. Had it been known that the satrap of Zamboula was a madman, there would have been instant revolt and rioting, even as Totrasmek planned, who plotted our destruction.

'You see now how impossible is the reward for which you hoped. The satrap's mistress is not – cannot be for you. But you shall not go unrewarded. Here is a sack of gold.'

She gave him the bag she had received from the slave.

'Go now, and when the sun is up come to the palace.

I will have Jungir Khan make you captain of his guard. But you will take your orders from me, secretly. Your first duty will be to march a squad to the shrine of Hanuman, ostensibly to search for clues of the priest's slayer; in reality to search for the Star of Khorala. It must be hidden there somewhere. When you find it, bring it to me. You have my leave to go now.'

He nodded, still silent, and strode away. The girl, watching the swing of his broad shoulders, was piqued to note that there was nothing in his bearing to show that he was in any way chagrined or abashed.

When he had rounded a corner, he glanced back, and then changed his direction and quickened his pace. A few moments later he was in the quarter of the city containing the Horse Market. There he smote on a door until from the window above a bearded head was thrust to demand the reason for the disturbance.

'A horse,' demanded Conan. 'The swiftest steed you have.'

'I open no gates at this time of night,' grumbled the horse trader.

Conan rattled his coins.

'Dog's son knave! Don't you see I'm white, and alone? Come down, before I smash your door!'

Presently, on a bay stallion, Conan was riding toward the house of Aram Baksh.

He turned off the road into the alley that lay between the tavern compound and the date-palm garden, but he did not pause at the gate. He rode on to the northeast corner of the wall, then turned and rode along the north wall, to halt within a few paces of the northwest angle. No trees grew near the wall, but there were some low bushes. To one of these he tied his horse and was about to climb into the saddle again, when he heard a low muttering of voices beyond the corner of the wall.

Drawing his foot from the stirrup he stole to the angle and peered around it. Three men were moving down the road toward the palm groves, and from their slouching gait he knew they were Negroes. They halted at his low call, bunching themselves as he strode toward them, his sword in his hand. Their eyes gleamed whitely in the starlight. Their brutish lust shone in their ebony faces, but they knew their three cudgels could not prevail against his sword, just as he knew it.

'Where are you going?' he challenged.

'To bid our brothers put out the fire in the pit beyond the groves,' was the sullen, guttural reply. 'Aram Baksh promised us a man, but he lied. We found one of our brothers dead in the trap-chamber. We go hungry this night.'

'I think not,' smiled Conan. 'Aram Baksh will give you a man. Do you see that door?'

He pointed to a small, iron-bound portal set in the midst of the western wall.

'Wait there. Aram Baksh will give you a man.'

Backing warily away until he was out of reach of a sudden bludgeon blow, he turned and melted around the northwest angle of the wall. Reaching his horse he paused to ascertain that the blacks were not sneaking after him, and then he climbed into the saddle and stood upright on it, quieting the uneasy steed with a low word. He reached up, grasped the coping of the wall and drew himself up and over. There he studied the grounds for an instant. The tavern was built in the southwest corner of the enclosure, the remaining space of which was occupied by groves and gardens. He saw no one in the grounds. The tavern was dark and silent, and he knew all the doors and windows were barred and bolted.

Conan knew that Aram Baksh slept in a chamber that opened into a cypress-bordered path that led to the door in the western wall. Like a shadow he glided among the trees, and a few moments later he rapped lightly on the chamber door.

'What is it?' asked a rumbling, sleepy voice from within.

'Aram Baksh!' hissed Conan. 'The blacks are stealing over the wall!'

Almost instantly the door opened, framing the tavern-keeper, naked but for his shirt, with a dagger in his hand.

He craned his neck to stare into the Cimmerian's face.

'What tale is this – *you*!'

Conan's vengeful fingers strangled the yell in his throat. They went to the floor together and Conan wrenched the dagger from his enemy's hand. The blade glinted in the starlight, and blood spurted. Aram Baksh made hideous noises, gasping and gagging on a mouthful of blood. Conan dragged him to his feet and again the dagger slashed, and most of the curly beard fell to the floor.

Still gripping his captive's throat – for a man can scream incoherently even with his tongue slit – Conan dragged him out of the dark chamber and down the cypress-shadowed path, to the iron-bound door in the outer wall. With one hand he lifted the bolt and threw the door open, disclosing the three shadowy figures which waited like black vultures outside. Into their eager arms Conan thrust the innkeeper.

A horrible, blood-choked scream rose from the Zamboulan's throat, but there was no response from the silent tavern. The people there were used to screams outside the wall. Aram Baksh fought like a wild man, his distended eyes turned frantically on the Cimmerian's face. He found no mercy there. Conan was thinking of the scores of wretches who owed their bloody doom to this man's greed.

In glee the Negroes dragged him down the road, mocking his frenzied gibberings. How could they recognize Aram Baksh in this half-naked, bloodstained figure, with the grotesquely shorn beard and unintelligible babblings? The sounds of the struggle came back to Conan, standing beside the gate, even after the clump of figures had vanished among the palms.

Closing the door behind him, Conan returned to his horse, mounted, and turned westward, toward the open desert, swinging wide to skirt the sinister belt of palm groves. As he rode, he drew from his belt a ring in which gleamed a jewel that snared the starlight in a shimmering iridescence. He held it up to admire it, turning it this way and that. The compact bag of gold pieces clinked gently at his saddle bow, like a promise of the greater riches to come.

'I wonder what she'd say if she knew I recognized her as Nafertari and him as Jungir Khan the instant I saw them,' he mused. 'I knew the Star of Khorala, too. There'll be a fine scene if she ever guesses that I slipped it off his finger while I was tying him with his sword belt. But they'll never catch me, with the start I'm getting.'

He glanced back at the shadowy palm groves, among which a red glare was mounting. A chanting rose to the night, vibrating with savage exultation. And another sound mingled with it, a mad incoherent screaming, a frenzied gibbering in which no words could be distinguished. The noise followed Conan as he rode westward beneath the paling stars.

THE DEVIL IN IRON

Leaving Zamboula, Conan rides westward with the Star of Khorala into the meadowlands of Shem. Whether he reaches Ophir with it and claims his roomful of gold or whether he loses it to some thief or light lady along the road, there is no record. At any rate, the proceeds cannot have lasted him very long. He pays another short visit to his native Cimmeria, finding old friends dead and old ways duller than ever. When word comes that the kozaki have regained their old vigor and are making King Yezdigerd's life as unhappy as possible, Conan takes his horse and his sword back to the harrying of Turan.

Although the northlander arrives all but empty-handed, he has old friends both among the kozaki and among the Red Fellowship of Vilayet Sea. Presently, sizeable contingents from both groups of outlaws are operating under his command and finding the pickings better than ever.

1.

The fisherman loosened his knife in its scabbard. The gesture was instinctive, for what he feared was nothing a knife could slay, not even the saw-edged crescent blade of the Yuetshi that could disembowel a man with an upward stroke. Neither man nor beast threatened him in the solitude which brooded over the castellated isle of Xapur.

He had climbed the cliffs, passed through the jungle that bordered them, and now stood surrounded by evidences of a vanished state. Broken columns glimmered among the trees, the straggling lines of crumbling walls meandered off into the shadows, and under his feet were broad paves, cracked and bowed by roots growing beneath.

The fisherman was typical of his race, that strange people whose origin is lost in the gray dawn of the past, and who have dwelt in their rude fishing huts along the southern shore of the Sea of Vilayet since time immemorial. He was broadly built, with long, apish arms and a mighty chest, but with lean loins and thin, bandy legs. His face was broad, his forehead low and retreating, his hair thick and tangled. A belt for a knife and a rag for a loin cloth were all he wore in the way of clothing.

That he was where he was proved that he was less dully incurious than most of his people. Men seldom visited Xapur. It was uninhabited, all but forgotten, merely one among the myriad isles which dotted the great inland sea. Men called it Xapur, the Fortified, because of its ruins, remnants of some prehistoric kingdom, lost and forgotten before the conquering Hyborians had ridden southward. None knew who reared those stones, though dim legends lingered among the Yuetshi which half intelligibly suggested a connection of immeasurable antiquity between the fishers and the unknown island kingdom.

But it had been a thousand years since any Yuetshi had understood the import of these tales; they repeated them now as a meaningless formula, a gibberish framed to their lips by custom. No Yuetshi had come to Xapur for a century. The adjacent coast of the mainland was uninhabited, a reedy marsh given over to the grim beasts that haunted it. The fisher's village lay some distance to the south, on the mainland. A storm had blown his frail fishing craft far from his accustomed haunts and wrecked it in a night of flaring lightning and roaring waters on the towering cliffs of the isle. Now, in the dawn, the sky shone blue and clear; the rising sun made jewels of the dripping leaves. He had climbed the cliffs to which he had clung through the night because, in the midst of the storm, he had seen an appalling lance of lightning fork out of the black heavens, and the concussion of its stroke, which had shaken the whole island, had been accompanied by a cataclysmic crash that he doubted could have resulted from a riven tree.

A dull curiosity had caused him to investigate; and now

74

he had found what he sought, and an animal-like uneasiness possessed him, a sense of lurking peril.

Among the trees reared a broken domelike structure, built of gigantic blocks of the peculiar ironlike green stone found only on the islands of Vilayet. It seemed incredible that human hands could have shaped and placed them, and certainly it was beyond human power to have overthrown the structure they formed. But the thunderbolt had splintered the ton-heavy blocks like so much glass, reduced others to green dust, and ripped away the whole arch of the dome.

The fisherman climbed over the debris and peered in, and what he saw brought a grunt from him. Within the ruined dome, surrounded by stone dust and bits of broken masonry, lay a man on a golden block. He was clad in a sort of skirt and a shagreen girdle. His black hair, which fell in a square mane to his massive shoulders, was confined about his temples by a narrow gold band. On his bare, muscular breast lay a curious dagger with a jeweled pommel, a shagreen-bound hilt, and a broad, crescent blade. It was much like the knife the fisherman wore at his hip, but it lacked the serrated edge and was made with infinitely greater skill.

The fisherman lusted for the weapon. The man, of course, was dead; had been dead for many centuries. This dome was his tomb. The fisherman did not wonder by what art the ancients had preserved the body in such a vivid likeness of life, which kept the muscular limbs full and unshrunken, the dark flesh vital. The dull brain of the Yuetshi had room only for his desire for the knife with its delicate, waving lines along the dully gleaming blade.

Scrambling down into the dome, he lifted the weapon from the man's breast. As he did so, a strange and terrible thing came to pass. The muscular, dark hands knotted convulsively, the lids flared open, revealing great, dark, magnetic eyes, whose stare struck the startled fisherman like a physical blow. He recoiled, dropping the jeweled dagger in his peturbation. The man on the dais heaved up to a sitting position, and the fisherman gaped at the full extent of his size, thus revealed. His narrowed eyes held the Yuetshi, and in those slitted orbs he read neither friendliness nor gratitude; he saw only a fire as alien and hostile as that which burns in the eyes of a tiger.

Suddenly the man rose and towered above him, menace in his every aspect. There was no room in the fisherman's dull brain for fear, at least for such fear as might grip a man who has just seen the fundamental laws of nature defied. As the great hands fell to his shoulders, he drew his saw-edged knife and struck upward with the same motion. The blade splintered against the stranger's corded belly as against a steel column, and then the fisherman's thick neck broke like a rotten twig in the giant hands.

2.

Jehungir Agha, lord of Khawarizm and keeper of the coastal border, scanned once more the ornate parchment scroll with its peacock seal and laughed shortly and sardonically.

'Well?' bluntly demanded his counsellor Ghaznavi.

Jehungir shrugged his shoulders. He was a handsome man, with the merciless pride of birth and accomplishment.

'The king grows short of patience,' he said. 'In his own hand he complains bitterly of what he calls my failure to guard the frontier. By Tarim, if I cannot deal a blow to these robbers of the steppes, Khawarizm may own a new lord.'

Ghaznavi tugged his gray-shot beard in meditation. Yezdigerd, king of Turan, was the mightiest monarch in the world. In his palace in the great port city of Aghrapur was heaped the plunder of empires. His fleets of purple-sailed war galleys had made Vilayet an Hyrkanian lake. The dark-skinned people of Zamora paid him tribute, as did the eastern provinces of Koth. The Shemites bowed to his rule as far west as Shushan. His armies ravaged the borders of Stygia in the south and the snowy lands of the Hyperboreans in the north. His riders bore torch and sword westward into Brythunia and Ophir and Corinthia, even to the borders of Nemedia. His gilt-helmeted swordsmen had trampled hosts under their horses' hoofs, and walled cities went up in flames at his command. In the glutted slave markets of Aghrapur, Sultanapur, Khawarizm, Shahpur, and Khorusun, women were sold for three small silver coins – blonde Brythunians, tawny Stygians, dark-haired Zamorians, ebon Kushites, olive-skinned Shemites.

Yet, while his swift horsemen overthrew armies far from his frontiers, at his very borders an audacious foe plucked his beard with a red-dripping and smoke-stained hand.

On the broad steppes between the Sea of Vilayet and the borders of the easternmost Hyborian kingdoms, a new race had sprung up in the past half-century, formed originally of fleeing criminals, broken men, escaped slaves, and deserting soldiers. They were men of many crimes and countries, some born on the steppes, some fleeing from the kingdoms in the West. They were called *kozak*, which means wastrel.

Dwelling on the wild, open steppes, owning no law but their own peculiar code, they had become a people capable even of defying the Grand Monarch. Ceaselessly they raided the Turanian frontier, retiring in the steppes when defeated; with the pirates of Vilayet, men of much the same breed, they harried the coast, preying off the merchant ships which plied between the Hyrkanian ports.

'How am I to crush these wolves?' demanded Jehungir. 'If I follow them into the steppes, I run the risk either of being cut off and destroyed, or of having them elude me entirely and burn the city in my absence. Of late they have been more daring than ever.'

'That is because of the new chief who has risen among them,' answered Ghaznavi. 'You know whom I mean.'

'Aye!' replied Jehungir feelingly. 'It is that devil Conan; he is even wilder than the *kozaks*, yet he is crafty as a mountain lion.'

'It is more through wild animal instinct than through intelligence,' answered Ghaznavi. 'The other *kozaks* are at least descendants of civilized men. He is a barbarian. But to dispose of him would be to deal them a crippling blow.'

'But how?' demanded Jehungir. 'He has repeatedly cut his way out of spots that seemed certain death for him. And, instinct or cunning, he has avoided or escaped every trap set for him.'

'For every beast and for every man there is a trap he will not escape,' quoth Ghaznavi. 'When we have parleyed with

77

the *kozaks* for the ransom of captives, I have observed this man Conan. He has a keen relish for women and strong drink. Have your captive Octavia fetched here.'

Jehungir clapped his hands, and an impassive Kushite eunuch, an image of shining ebony in silken pantaloons, bowed before him and went to do his bidding. Presently he returned, leading by the wrist a tall, handsome girl, whose yellow hair, clear eyes, and fair skin identified her as a pure-blooded member of her race. Her scanty silk tunic, girded at the waist, displayed the marvelous contours of her magnificent figure. Her fine eyes flashed with resentment and her red lips were sulky, but submission had been taught her during her captivity. She stood with hanging head before her master until he motioned her to a seat on the divan beside him. Then he looked inquiringly at Ghaznavi.

'We must lure Conan away from the *kozaks*,' said the counsellor abruptly. 'Their war camp is at present pitched somewhere on the lower reaches of the Zaporoska River – which, as you well know, is a wilderness of reeds, a swampy jungle in which our last expedition was cut to pieces by those masterless devils.'

'I am not likely to forget that,' said Jehungir wryly.

'There is an uninhabited island near the mainland,' said Ghaznavi, 'known as Xapur, the Fortified, because of some ancient ruins upon it. There is a peculiarity about it which makes it perfect for our purpose. It has no shoreline but rises sheer out of the sea in cliffs a hundred and fifty feet tall. Not even an ape could negotiate them. The only place where a man can go up or down is a narrow path on the western side that has the appearance of a worn stair, carved into the solid rock of the cliffs.

'If we could trap Conan on that island, alone, we could hunt him down at our leisure, with bows, as men hunt a lion.'

'As well wish for the moon,' said Jehungir impatiently. 'Shall we send him a messenger, bidding him climb the cliffs and await our coming?'

'In effect, yes!' Seeing Jehungir's look of amazement, Ghaznavi continued: 'We will ask for a parley with the *kozaks* in regard to prisoners, at the edge of the steppes by Fort Ghori. As usual, we will go with a force and encamp outside the castle. They will come, with an equal force, and the parley will go forward with the usual distrust and suspicion. But this time we will take with us, as if by casual chance, your beautiful captive.' Octavia changed color and listened with intensified interest as the counsellor nodded toward her. 'She will use all her wiles to attract Conan's attention. That should not be difficult. To that wild reaver, she should appear a dazzling vision of loveliness. Her vitality and substantial figure should appeal to him more vividly than would one of the doll-like beauties of your seraglio.'

Octavia sprang up, her white fists clenched, her eyes blazing and her figure quivering with outraged anger.

'You would force me to play the trollop with this barbarian?' she exclaimed. 'I will not! I am no market-block slut to smirk and ogle at a steppes robber. I am the daughter of a Nemedian lord—'

'You were of the Nemedian nobility before my riders carried you off,' returned Jehungir cynically. 'Now you are merely a slave who will do as she is bid.'

'I will not!' she raged.

'On the contrary,' rejoined Jehungir with studied cruelty, 'you will. I like Ghaznavi's plan. Continue, prince among counsellors.'

'Conan will probably wish to buy her. You will refuse to sell her, of course, or to exchange her for Hyrkanian prisoners. He may then try to steal her, or take her by force – though I do not think even he would break the parley truce. Anyway, we must be prepared for whatever he might attempt.

'Then, shortly after the parley, before he has time to forget all about her, we will send a messenger to him, under a flag of truce, accusing him of stealing the girl and demanding her return. He may kill the messenger, but at least he will think that she has escaped.

'Then we will send a spy – a Yeutshi fisherman will do – to the *kozak* camp, who will tell Conan that Octavia is hiding on Xapur. If I know my man, he will go straight to that place.

'But we do not know that he will go alone,' Jehungir argued.

'Does a man take a band of warriors with him, when going to a rendezvous with a woman he desires?' retorted Ghaznavi. 'The chances are all that he *will* go alone. But we will take care of the other alternative. We will not await him on the island, where we might be trapped ourselves, but among the reeds of a marshy point, which juts out to within a thousand yards of Xapur. If he brings a large force, we'll beat a retreat and think up another plot. If he comes alone or with a small party, we will have him. Depend upon it, he will come, remembering your charming slave's smiles and meaning glances.'

'I will never descend to such shame!' Octavia was wild with fury and humiliation. 'I will die first!'

'You will not die, my rebellious beauty,' said Jehungir, 'but you will be subjected to a very painful and humiliating experience.'

He clapped his hands, and Octavia palled. This time it was not the Kushite who entered, but a Shemite, a heavily muscled man of medium height with a short, curled, blue-black beard.

'Here is work for you, Gilzan,' said Jehungir. 'Take this fool, and play with her awhile. Yet be careful not to spoil her beauty.'

With an inarticulate grunt the Shemite seized Octavia's wrist, and at the grasp of his iron fingers, all the defiance went out of her. With a piteous cry she tore away and threw herself on her knees before her implacable master, sobbing incoherently for mercy.

Jehungir dismissed the disappointed torturer with a gesture, and said to Ghaznavi: 'If your plan succeeds, I will fill your lap with gold.'

3.

In the darkness before dawn, an unaccustomed sound disturbed the solitude that slumbered over the reedy marshes and the misty waters of the coast. It was not a drowsy waterfowl nor a waking beast. It was a human who struggled through the thick reeds, which were taller than a man's head.

It was a woman, had there been anyone to see, tall, and

80

yellow-haired, her splendid limbs molded by her draggled tunic. Octavia had escaped in good earnest, every outraged fiber of her still tingling from her experience in a captivity that had become unendurable.

Jehungir's mastery of her had been bad enough; but with deliberate fiendishness Jehungir had given her to a nobleman whose name was a byword for degeneracy even in Khawarizm.

Octavia's resilient flesh crawled and quivered at her memories. Desperation had nerved her climb from Jelal Khan's castle on a rope made of strips from torn tapestries, and chance had led her to a picketed horse. She had ridden all night, and dawn found her with a foundered steed on the swampy shores of the sea. Quivering with the abhorrence of being dragged back to the revolting destiny planned for her by Jelal Khan, she plunged into the morass, seeking a hiding place from the pursuit she expected. When the reeds grew thinner around her and the water rose about her thighs, she saw the dim loom of an island ahead of her. A broad span of water lay between, but she did not hesitate. She waded out until the low waves were lapping about her waist; then she struck out strongly, swimming with a vigor that promised unusual endurance.

As she neared the island, she saw that it rose sheer from the water in castlelike cliffs. She reached them at last but found neither ledge to stand on below the water, nor to cling to above. She swam on, following the curve of the cliffs, the strain of her long flight beginning to weight her limbs. Her hands fluttered along the sheer stone, and suddenly they found a depression. With a sobbing gasp of relief, she pulled herself out of the water and clung there, a dripping white goddess in the dim starlight.

She had come upon what seemed to be steps carved in the cliff. Up them she went, flattening herself against the stone as she caught a faint clack of muffled oars. She strained her eyes and thought she made out a vague bulk moving toward the reedy point she had just quitted. But it was too far away for her to be sure in the darkness, and presently the faint sound ceased and she continued her climb. If it were her pursuers, she knew of no better course than to hide on the island. She knew that most of the islands off that marshy coast were uninhabited. This might

81

be a pirate's lair, but even pirates would be preferable to the beast she had escaped.

A vagrant thought crossed her mind as she climbed, in which she mentally compared her former master with the *kozak* chief with whom – by compulsion – she had shamelessly flirted in the pavilions of the camp by Fort Ghori, where the Hyrkanian lords had parleyed with the warriors of the steppes. His burning gaze had frightened and humiliated her, but his cleanly elemental fierceness set him above Jelal Khan, a monster such as only an overly opulent civilization can produce.

She scrambled up over the cliff edge and looked timidly at the dense shadows which confronted her. The trees grew close to the cliffs, presenting a solid mass of blackness. Something whirred above her head and she cowered, even though realizing it was only a bat.

She did not like the looks of those ebony shadows, but she set her teeth and went toward them, trying not to think of snakes. Her bare feet made no sound in the spongy loam under the trees.

Once among them, the darkness closed frighteningly about her. She had not taken a dozen steps when she was no longer able to look back and see the cliffs and the sea beyond. A few steps more and she became hopelessly confused and lost her sense of direction. Through the tangled branches not even a star peered. She groped and floundered on, blindly, and then came to a sudden halt.

Somewhere ahead there began the rhythmical booming of a drum. It was not such a sound as she would have expected to hear in the time and place. Then she forgot it as she was aware of a presence near her. She could not see, but she knew that something was standing beside her in the darkness.

With a stifled cry she shrank back, and as she did so, something that even in her panic she recognized as a human arm curved about her waist. She screamed and threw all her supple young strength into a wild lunge for freedom, but her captor caught her up like a child, crushing her frantic resistance with ease. The silence with which her frenzied pleas and protests were received added to her terror as she felt herself being carried through the darkness toward the distant drum, which still pulsed and muttered.

4.

As the first tinge of dawn reddened the sea, a small boat with a solitary occupant approached the cliffs. The man in the boat was a picturesque figure. A crimson scarf was knotted about his head; his wide silk breeches, of flaming hue, were upheld by a broad sash, which likewise supported a scimitar in a shagreen scabbard. His gilt-worked leather boots suggested the horseman rather than the seaman, but he handled his boat with skill. Through his widely open white silk shirt showed his broad, muscular breast, burned brown by the sun.

The muscles of his heavy, bronzed arms rippled as he pulled the oars with an almost feline ease of motion. A fierce vitality that was evident in each feature and motion set him apart from common men; yet his expression was neither savage nor somber, though the smoldering blue eyes hinted at ferocity easily wakened. This was Conan, who had wandered into the armed camps of the *kozaks* with no other possession than his wits and his sword, and who had carved his way to leadership among them.

He paddled to the carven stair as one familiar with his environs and moored the boat to a projection of the rock. Then he went up the worn steps without hesitation. He was keenly alert, not because he consciously suspected hidden danger, but because alertness was a part of him, whetted by the wild existence he followed.

What Ghaznavi had considered animal intuition or some sixth sense was merely the razor-edged faculties and savage wit of the barbarian. Conan had no instinct to tell him that men were watching him from a covert among the reeds of the mainland.

As he climbed the cliff, one of these men breathed deeply and stealthily lifted a bow. Jehungir caught his wrist and hissed an oath into his ear. 'Fool! Will you betray us? Don't you realize he is out of range? Let him get upon the island. He will go looking for the girl. We will stay here awhile. He *may* have sensed our presence or guessed our plot. He may have warriors hidden somewhere. We will wait. In an hour, if nothing suspicious occurs, we'll row up to the foot of the stair and wait him there. If he does not return in a reasonable time, some of us will go upon the island and hunt him down. But I do not wish to do that if it can be helped. Some of us are sure to die if we have to go into the bush after him. I had rather catch him with arrows from a safe distance.'

Meanwhile, the unsuspecting *kozak* had plunged into the forest. He went silently in his soft leather boots, his gaze sifting every shadow in eagerness to catch sight of the splendid, tawny-haired beauty of whom he had dreamed ever since he had seen her in the pavilion of Jehungir Agha by Fort Ghori. He would have desired her even if she had displayed repugnance toward him. But her cryptic smiles and glances had fired his blood, and with all the lawless violence which was his heritage he desired that white-skinned, golden-haired woman of civilization.

He had been on Xapur before. Less than a month ago, he had held a secret conclave here with a pirate crew. He knew that he was approaching a point where he could see the mysterious ruins which gave the island its name, and he wondered if he would find the girl hiding among them. Even with the thought, he stopped as though struck dead.

Ahead of him, among the trees, rose something that his reason told him was not possible. *It was a great dark green wall, with towers rearing beyond the battlements.*

Conan stood paralyzed in the disruption of the faculties which demoralizes anyone who is confronted by an impossible negation of sanity. He doubted neither his sight nor his reason, but something was monstrously out of joint. Less than a month ago, only broken ruins had showed among the trees. What human hands could rear such a mammoth pile as now met his eyes, in the few weeks which had elapsed? Besides, the buccaneers who roamed Vilayet ceaselessly would have learned of any work going on on such stupendous scale and would have informed the *kozaks*.

There was no explaining this thing, but it was so. He was on Xapur, and that fantastic heap of towering masonry was on Xapur, and all was madness and paradox; yet it was all true.

He wheeled to race back through the jungle, down the carven stair and across the blue waters to the distant camp at the mouth of the Zaporoska. In that moment of un-reasoning panic, even the thought of halting so near the inland sea was repugnant. He would leave it behind him, would quit the armed camps and the steppes and put a thousand miles between him and the blue, mysterious East where the most basic laws of nature could be set at naught, by what diabolism he could not guess.

For an instant, the future fate of kingdoms that hinged on this gay-clad barbarian hung in the balance. It was a small thing that tipped the scales – merely a shred of silk hanging on a bush that caught his uneasy glance. He leaned to it, his nostrils expanding, his nerves quivering to a subtle stimulant. On that bit of torn cloth, so faint that it was less with his physical faculties than by some obscure instinctive sense that he recognized it, lingered the tantalizing perfume that he connected with the sweet, firm flesh of the woman he had seen in Jehungir's pavilion. The fisherman had not lied, then; she *was* here! Then in the soil he saw a single track in the loam, the track of a bare foot, long and slender, but a man's, not a woman's, and sunk deeper than was natural. The conclusion was obvious; the man who made that track was carrying a burden, and what should it be but the girl the *kozak* was seeking?

He stood silently facing the dark towers that loomed through the trees, his eyes slits of blue balefire. Desire for the yellow-haired woman vied with a sullen, primordial rage at whoever had taken her. His human passion fought down his ultra-human fears, and dropping into the stalking crouch of a hunting panther, he glided toward the walls, taking advantage of the dense foliage to escape detection from the battlements.

As he approached, he saw that the walls were composed of the same green stone that had formed the ruins, and he was haunted by a vague sense of familiarity. It was as if he looked upon something he had never before seen but had dreamed of or pictured mentally. At last he recognized the sensation. The walls and towers followed the plan of the ruins. It was as if the crumbling lines had grown back into the structures they originally were.

No sound disturbed the morning quiet as Conan stole to the foot of the wall, which rose sheer from the luxuriant growth. On the southern reaches of the inland sea, the vegetation was almost tropical. He saw no one on the battlements, heard no sounds within. He saw a massive gate a short distance to his left and had no reason to suppose that it was not locked and guarded. But he believed that the woman he sought was somewhere beyond that wall, and the course he took was characteristically reckless.

Above him, vine-festooned branches reached out toward the battlements. He went up a great tree like a cat, and reaching a point above the parapet, he gripped a thick limb with both hands, swung back and forth at arm's length until he had gained momentum, and then let go and catapulted through the air, landing catlike on the battlements. Crouching there, he stared down into the streets of a city.

The circumference of the wall was not great, but the number of green stone buildings it contained was surprising. They were three or four stories in height, mainly flat-roofed, reflecting a fine architectural style. The streets converged like the spokes of a wheel into an octagon-shaped court in the centre of the town, which gave upon a lofty edifice, which, with its domes and towers, dominated the whole city. He saw no one moving in the streets or looking out of the windows, though the sun was already coming up. The silence that reigned there might have been that of a dead and deserted city. A narrow stone stair ascended the wall near him; down this he went.

Houses shouldered so closely to the wall that halfway down the stair, he found himself within arm's length of a window and halted to peer in. There were no bars, and the silk curtains were caught back with satin cords. He looked into a chamber whose walls were hidden by dark velvet tapestries. The floor was covered with thick rugs, and there were benches of polished ebony and an ivory dais heaped with furs.

He was about to continue his descent, when he heard the sound of someone approaching in the street below. Before the unknown person could round a corner and see him on the stair, he stepped quickly across the intervening space and dropped lightly into the room, drawing his scimitar. He stood for an instant statuelike; then, as nothing happened, he was moving across the rugs toward an arched doorway, when a hanging was drawn aside, revealing a cushioned alcove from which a slender, dark-haired girl regarded him with languid eyes.

Conan glared at her tensely, expecting her momentarily

to start screaming. But she merely smothered a yawn with a dainty hand, rose from the alcove, and leaned negligently against the hanging which she held with one hand.

She was undoubtedly a member of a white race, though her skin was very dark. Her square-cut hair was black as midnight, her only garment a wisp of silk about her supple hips.

Presently she spoke, but the tongue was unfamiliar to him, and he shook his head. She yawned again, stretched lithely and, without any show of fear or surprise, shifted to a language he did understand, a dialect of Yuetshi which sounded strangely archaic.

'Are you looking for someone?' she asked, as indifferently as if the invasion of her chamber by an armed stranger were the most common thing imaginable.

'Who are you?' he demanded.

'I am Yateli,' she answered languidly. 'I must have feasted late last night, I am so sleepy now. Who are you?'

'I am Conan, a *hetman* among the *kozaks*,' he answered, watching her narrowly. He believed her attitude to be a pose and expected her to try to escape from the chamber or rouse the house. But, though a velvet rope that might be a signal cord hung near her, she did not reach for it.

'Conan,' she repeated drowsily. 'You are not a Dagonian. I suppose you are a mercenary. Have you cut the heads off many Yuetshi?'

'I do not war on water rats!' he snorted.

'But they are very terrible,' she murmured. 'I remember when they were our slaves. But they revolted and burned and slew. Only the magic of Khosatral Khel has kept them from the walls—' she paused, a puzzled look struggling with the sleepiness of her expression. 'I forgot,' she muttered. 'They *did* climb the walls, last night. There was shouting and fire, and the people calling in vain on Khosatral.' She shook her head as if to clear it. 'But that cannot be,' she murmured, 'because I am alive, and I thought I was dead. Oh, to the devil with it!'

She came across the chamber, and taking Conan's hand, drew him to the dais. He yielded in bewilderment and uncertainty. The girl smiled at him like a sleepy child; her long silky lashes drooped over dusky, clouded eyes. She ran

87

her fingers through his thick black locks as if to assure herself of his reality.

'It was a dream,' she yawned. 'Perhaps it's all a dream. I feel like a dream now. I don't care. I can't remember something – I have forgotten – there is something I cannot understand, but I grow so sleepy when I try to think. Anyway, it doesn't matter.'

'What do you mean?' he asked uneasily. 'You said they climbed the walls last night? Who?'

'The Yuetshi. I thought so, anyway. A cloud of smoke hid everything, but a naked, bloodstained devil caught me by the throat and drove his knife into my breast. Oh, it hurt! But it was a dream, because see, there is no scar.' She idly inspected her smooth bosom, and then sank upon Conan's lap and passed her supple arms about his massive neck. 'I cannot remember,' she murmured, nestling her dark head against his mighty breast. 'Everything is dim and misty. It does not matter. You are no dream. You are strong. Let us live while we can. Love me!'

He cradled the girl's glossy head in the bend of his heavy arm and kissed her full red lips with unfeigned relish.

'You are strong,' she repeated, her voice waning. 'Love me – love—' The sleepy murmur faded away; the dusky eyes closed, the long lashes drooping over the sensuous cheeks; the supple body relaxed in Conan's arms.

He scowled down at her. She seemed to partake of the illusion that haunted this whole city, but the firm resilience of her limbs under his questing fingers convinced him that he had a living human girl in his arms, and not the shadow of a dream. No less disturbed, he hastily laid her on the furs upon the dais. Her sleep was too deep to be natural. He decided that she must be an addict of some drug, perhaps like the black lotus of Xuthal.

Then he found something else to make him wonder. Among the furs on the dais was a gorgeous spotted skin, whose predominant hue was golden. It was not a clever copy, but the skin of an actual beast. And that beast, Conan knew, had been extinct for at least a thousand years; it was the great golden leopard which figures so prominently in Hyborian legendry, and which the ancient artists delighted to portray in pigments and marble.

Shaking his head in bewilderment, Conan passed

through the archway into a winding corridor. Silence hung over the house, but outside he heard a sound which his keen ears recognized as something ascending the stair on the wall from which he had entered the building. An instant later he was startled to hear something land with a soft but weighty thud on the floor of the chamber he had just quitted. Turning quickly away, he hurried along the twisting hallway until something on the floor before him brought him to a halt.

It was a human figure, which lay half in the hall and half in an opening that obviously was normally concealed by a door, which was a duplicate of the panels of the wall. It was a man, dark and lean, clad only in a silk loincloth, with a shaven head and cruel features, and he lay as if death had struck him just as he was emerging from the panel. Conan bent above him, seeking the cause of his death, and discovered him to be merely sunk in the same deep sleep as the girl in the chamber.

But why should he select such a place for his slumbers? While meditating on the matter, Conan was galvanized by a sound behind him. Something was moving up the corridor in his direction. A quick glance down it showed that it ended in a great door, which might be locked. Conan jerked the supine body out of the panel entrance and stepped through, pulling the panel shut after him. A click told him it was locked in place. Standing in utter darkness, he heard a shuffling tread halt just outside the door, and a faint chill trickled along his spine. That was no human step, nor that of any beast he had ever encountered.

There was an instant of silence, then a faint creak of wood and metal. Putting out his hand he felt the door straining and bending inward, as if a great weight were being steadily borne against it from the outside. As he reached for his sword, this ceased and he heard a strange, slobbering mouthing that prickled the short hairs on his scalp. Scimitar in hand, he began backing away, and his heels felt steps, down which he nearly tumbled. He was in a narrow staircase leading downward.

He groped his way down in the blackness, feeling for, but not finding, some other opening in the walls. Just as he decided that he was no longer in the house, but deep in the earth under it, the steps ceased in a level tunnel.

5.

Along the black, silent tunnel Conan groped, momentarily dreading a fall into some unseen pit; but at last his feet struck steps again, and he went up them until he came to a door on which his fumbling fingers found a metal catch. He came out into a dim and lofty room of enormous proportions. Fantastic columns marched about the mottled walls, upholding a ceiling, which, at once translucent and dusky, seemed like a cloudy midnight sky, giving an illusion of impossible height. If any light filtered in from the outside, it was curiously altered.

In a brooding twilight, Conan moved across the bare green floor. The great room was circular, pierced on one side by the great, bronze valves of a giant door. Opposite this, on a dais against the wall, up to which led broad curving steps, there stood a throne of copper, and when Conan saw what was coiled on this throne, he retreated hastily, lifting his scimitar.

Then, as the thing did not move, he scanned it more closely and presently mounted the glass steps and stared down at it. It was a gigantic snake, apparently carved of some jadelike substance. Each scale stood out as distinctly as in real life, and the iridescent colors were vividly reproduced. The great wedge-shaped head was half submerged in the folds of its trunk; so neither the eyes nor jaws were visible. Recognition stirred in his mind. The snake was evidently meant to represent one of those grim monsters of the marsh, which in past ages had haunted the reedy edges of Vilayet's southern shores. But, like the golden leopard, they had been extinct for hundreds of years. Conan had seen rude images of them, in miniature, among the idol huts of the Yuetshi, and there was a description of them in the *Book of Skelos*, which drew on prehistoric sources.

Conan admired the scaly torso, thick as his thigh and obviously of great length, and he reached out and laid a curious hand on the thing. And as he did so, his heart nearly stopped. An icy chill congealed the blood in his veins and lifted the short hair on his scalp. Under his hand there was not the smooth, brittle surface of glass or metal or stone, but the yielding, fibrous mass of a *living* thing. He felt cold, sluggish life flowing under his fingers.

His hand jerked back in instinctive repulsion. Sword shaking in his grasp, horror and revulsion and fear almost choking him, he backed away and down the glass steps with painful care, glaring in awful fascination at the grisly thing that slumbered on the copper throne. It did not move.

He reached the bronze door and tried it, with his heart in his teeth, sweating with fear that he should find himself locked in with that slimy horror. But the valves yielded to his touch, and he glided through and closed them behind him.

He found himself in a wide hallway with lofty, tapestried walls, where the light was the same twilight gloom. It made distant objects indistinct, and that made him uneasy, rousing thoughts of serpents gliding unseen through the dimness. A door at the other end seemed miles away in the illusive light. Nearer at hand, the tapestry hung in such a way as to suggest an opening behind it, and lifting it cautiously he discovered a narrow stair leading up.

While he hesitated he heard, in the great room he had just left, the same shuffling tread he had heard outside the locked panel. Had he been followed through the tunnel? He went up the stair hastily, dropping the tapestry in place behind him.

Emerging presently into a twisting corridor, he took the first doorway he came to. He had a twofold purpose in his apparently aimless prowling: to escape from the building and its mysteries, and to find the Nemedian girl who, he felt, was imprisoned somewhere in this palace, temple, or whatever it was. He believed it was the great domed edifice in the center of the city, and it was likely that here dwelt the ruler of the town, to whom a captive woman would doubtless be brought.

He found himself in a chamber, not another corridor, and was about to retrace his steps, when he heard a voice which came from behind one of the walls. There was no door in that wall, but he leaned close and heard distinctly. And an icy chill crawled slowly along his spine. The tongue was Nemedian, but the voice was not human. There was a terrifying resonance about it, like a bell tolling at midnight.

'There was no life in the Abyss, save that which was in-

91

corporated in me,' it tolled. 'Nor was there light, nor motion, nor any sound. Only the urge behind and beyond life guided and impelled me on my upward journey, blind, insensate, inexorable. Through ages upon ages, and the changeless strata of darkness I climbed—'

Ensorcelled by that belling resonance, Conan crouched forgetful of all else, until its hypnotic power caused a strange replacement of faculties and perception, and sound created the illusion of sight. Conan was no longer aware of the voice, save as far-off rhythmical waves of sound. Transported beyond his age and his own individuality, he was seeing the transmutation of the being men called Khosatral Khel which crawled up from Night and the Abyss ages ago to clothe itself in the substance of the material universe.

But human flesh was too frail, too paltry to hold the terrific essence that was Khosatral Khel. So he stood up in the shape and aspect of a man, but his flesh was not flesh; nor the bone, bone; nor blood, blood. He became a blasphemy against all nature, for he caused to live and think and act a basic substance that before had never known the pulse and stir of animate being.

He stalked through the world like a god, for no earthly weapon could harm him, and to him a century was like an hour. In his wanderings he came upon a primitive people inhabiting the island of Dagonia, and it pleased him to give this race culture and civilization, and by his aid they built the city of Dagon and they abode there and worshipped him. Strange and grisly were his servants, called from the dark corners of the planet where grim survivals of forgotten ages yet lurked. His house in Dagon was connected with every other house by tunnels through which his shaven-headed priests bore victims for the sacrifice.

But after many ages, a fierce and brutish people appeared on the shores of the sea. They called themselves Yuetshi, and after a fierce battle were defeated and enslaved, and for nearly a generation they died on the altars of Khosatral.

His sorcery kept them in bonds. Then their priest, a strange, gaunt man of unknown race, plunged into the wilderness, and when he returned he bore a knife that was of no earthly substance. It was forged of a meteor, which flashed through the sky like a flaming arrow and fell in a far valley. The slaves rose. Their saw-edged crescents cut down the men of Dagon like sheep, and against that unearthly knife the magic of Khosatral was impotent. While carnage and slaughter bellowed through the red smoke that choked the streets, the grimmest act of that grim drama was played in the cryptic dome behind the great daised chamber with its copper throne and its walls mottled like the skin of serpents.

From that dome, the Yuetshi priest emerged alone. He had not slain his foe, because he wished to hold the threat of his loosing over the heads of his own rebellious subjects. He had left Khosatral lying upon the golden dais with the mystic knife across his breast for a spell to hold him senseless and inanimate until doomsday.

But the ages passed and the priest died, the towers of deserted Dagon crumbled, the tales became dim, and the Yuetshi were reduced by plagues and famines and war to scattered remnants, dwelling in squalor along the seashore.

Only the cryptic dome resisted the rot of time, until a chance thunderbolt and the curiosity of a fisherman lifted from the breast of the god the magic knife and broke the spell. Khosatral Khel rose and lived and waxed mighty once more. It pleased him to restore the city as it was in the days before its fall. By his necromancy he lifted the towers from the dust of forgotten millenia, and the folk which had been dust for ages moved in life again.

But folk who have tasted of death are only partly alive. In the dark corners of their souls and minds, death still lurks unconquered. By night the people of Dagon moved and loved, hated and feasted, and remembered the fall of Dagon and their own slaughter only as a dim dream; they moved in an enchanted mist of illusion, feeling the strangeness of their existence but not inquiring the reasons therefor. With the coming of day, they sank into deep sleep, to be roused again only by the coming of night, which is akin to death.

All this rolled in a terrible panorama before Conan's consciousness as he crouched beside the tapestried wall. His reason staggered. All certainty and sanity were swept away, leaving a shadowy universe through which stole hooded figures of grisly potentialities. Through the belling of the voice, which was like a tolling of triumph over the ordered laws of a sane planet, a human sound anchored Conan's mind from its flight through spheres of madness. It was the hysterical sobbing of a woman.

Involuntarily he sprang up.

6.

Jehungir Agha waited with growing impatience in his boat among the reeds. More than an hour passed, and Conan had not reappeared. Doubtless he was still searching the island for the girl he thought to be hidden there. But another surmise occurred to the Agha. Suppose the *hetman* had left his warriors near by, and that they should grow suspicious and come to investigate his long absence? Jehungir spoke to the oarsmen, and the long boat slid from among the reeds and glided toward the carven stairs.

Leaving half a dozen men in the boat, he took the rest, ten mighty archers of Khawarizm, in spired helmets and tiger-skin cloaks. Like hunters invading the retreat of the lion, they stole forward under the trees, arrows on strings. Silence reigned over the forest except when a great green thing that might have been a parrot swirled over their heads with a low thunder of broad wings and then sped off through the trees. With a sudden gesture, Jehungir halted his party, and they stared incredulously at the towers that showed through the verdure in the distance.

'Tarim!' muttered Jehungir. 'The pirates have rebuilt the ruins! Doubtless Conan is there. We must investigate this. A fortified town this close to the mainland! – Come!'

With renewed caution, they glided through the trees. The game had altered; from pursuers and hunters they had become spies.

And as they crept through the tangled growth, the man they sought was in peril more deadly than their filigreed arrows.

Conan realized with a crawling of his skin that beyond the wall the belling voice had ceased. He stood motionless as a statue, his gaze fixed on a curtained door through which he knew that a culminating horror would presently appear.

It was dim and misty in the chamber, and Conan's hair began to lift on his scalp as he looked. He saw a head and a pair of gigantic shoulders grow out of the twilight doom. There was no sound of footsteps, but the great dusky form grew more distinct until Conan recognized the figure of a man. He was clad in sandals, a skirt, and a broad shagreen girdle. His square-cut mane was confined by a circle of gold. Conan stared at the sweep of the monstrous shoulders, the breadth of swelling breast, the bands and ridges and clusters of muscles on torso and limbs. The face was without weakness and without mercy. The eyes were balls of dark fire. And Conan knew that this was Khosatral Khel, the ancient from the Abyss, the god of Dagonia.

No word was spoken. No word was necessary. Khosatral spread his great arms, and Conan, crouching beneath them, slashed at the giant's belly. Then he bounded back, eyes blazing with surprise. The keen edge had rung on the mighty body as on an anvil, rebounding without cutting. Then Khosatral came upon him in an irresistible surge.

There was a fleeting concussion, a fierce writhing and intertwining of limbs and bodies, and then Conan sprang clear, every thew quivering from the violence of his efforts; blood started where the grazing fingers had torn the skin. In that instant of contact, he had experienced the ultimate madness of blasphemed nature; no human flesh had bruised his, but *metal* animated and sentient; it was a body of living iron which opposed his.

Khosatral loomed above the warrior in the gloom. Once let those great fingers lock and they would not loosen until the human body hung limp in their grasp. In that twilit chamber it was as if a man fought with a dream-monster in a nightmare.

Flinging down his useless sword, Conan caught up a heavy bench and hurled it with all his power. It was such a missile as few men could even lift. On Khosatral's mighty breast it smashed into shreds and splinters. It did not even shake the giant on his braced legs. His face lost something of its human aspect, a nimbus of fire played about his awesome head, and like a moving tower he came on.

With a desperate wrench Conan ripped a whole section

95

of tapestry from the wall and whirling it, with a muscular effort greater than that required for throwing the bench, he flung it over the giant's head. For an instant Khosatral floundered, smothered and blinded by the clinging stuff that resisted his strength as wood or steel could not have done, and in that instant Conan caught up his scimitar and shot out into the corridor. Without checking his speed, he hurled himself through the door of the adjoining chamber, slammed the door, and shot the bolt.

Then as he wheeled, he stopped short, all the blood in him seeming to surge to his head. Crouching on a heap of silk cushions, golden hair streaming over her naked shoulders, eyes blank with terror, was the woman for whom he had dared so much. He almost forgot the horror at his heels until a splintering crash behind him brought him to his senses. He caught up the girl and sprang for the opposite door. She was too helpless with fright either to resist or to aid him. A faint whimper was the only sound of which she seemed capable.

Conan wasted no time trying the door. A shattering stroke of his scimitar hewed the lock asunder, and as he sprang through to the stair that loomed beyond it, he saw the head and shoulders of Khosatral crash through the other door. The colossus was splintering the massive panels as if they were of cardboard.

Conan raced up the stair, carrying the big girl over one shoulder as easily as if she had been a child. Where he was going he had no idea, but the stair ended at the door of a round, domed chamber. Khosatral was coming up the stair behind them, silently as a wind of death, and as swiftly.

The chamber's walls were of solid steel, and so was the door. Conan shut it and dropped in place the great bars with which it was furnished. The thought struck him that this was Khosatral's chamber, where he locked himself in to sleep securely from the monsters he had loosed from the Pits to do his bidding.

Hardly were the bolts in place when the great door shook and trembled to the giant's assault. Conan shrugged his shoulders. This was the end of the trail. There was no other door in the chamber, nor any window. Air, and the strange misty light, evidently came from interstices in the dome. He tested the nicked edge of his scimitar, quite cool now that he was at bay. He had done his volcanic best to escape; when the giant came crashing through that door, he would explode in another savage onslaught with his useless sword, not because he expected it to do any good, but because it was his nature to die fighting. For the moment there was no course of action to take, and his calmness was not forced or feigned.

The gaze he turned on his fair companion was as admiring and intense as if he had a hundred years to live. He had dumped her unceremoniously on the floor when he turned to close the door, and she had risen to her knees, mechanically arranging her streaming locks and her scanty garment. Conan's fierce eyes glowed with approval as they devoured her thick golden hair, her clear, wide eyes, her milky skin, sleek with exuberant health, the firm swell of her breasts, the contours of her splendid hips.

A low cry escaped her as the door shook and a bolt gave way with a groan.

Conan did not look around. He knew the door would hold a little while longer.

'They told me you had escaped,' he said. 'A Yuetshi fisher told me you were hiding here. What is your name?'

'Octavia,' she gasped mechanically. Then words came in a rush. She caught at him with desperate fingers. 'Oh Mitra! what nightmare is this? The people – the dark-skinned people – one of them caught me in the forest and brought me here. They carried me to – to that – that *thing*. He told me – he said – am I mad? Is this a dream?'

He glanced at the door which bulged inward as if from the impact of a battering-ram.

'No,' he said; 'it's no dream. That hinge is giving way. Strange that a devil has to break down a door like a common man; but after all, his strength itself is a diabolism.'

'Can you not kill him?' she panted. 'You are strong.'

Conan was too honest to lie to her. 'If a mortal man could kill him, he'd be dead now,' he answered. 'I nicked my blade on his belly.'

Her eyes dulled. 'Then you must die, and I must – oh, Mitra!' she screamed in sudden frenzy, and Conan caught her hands, fearing that she would harm herself. 'He told me what he was going to do to me!' she panted. 'Kill me! Kill me with your sword before he bursts the door!'

Conan looked at her, and shook his head.

'I'll do what I can,' he said. 'That won't be much, but it'll give you a chance to get past him down the stair. Then run for the cliffs. I have a boat tied at the foot of the steps. If you can get out of the palace, you may escape him yet. The people of this city are all asleep.'

She dropped her head in her hands. Conan took up his scimitar and moved over to stand before the echoing door. One watching him would not have realized that he was waiting for a death he regarded as inevitable. His eyes smoldered more vividly; his muscular hand knotted harder on his hilt; that was all.

The hinges had given under the giant's terrible assault, and the door rocked crazily, held only by the bolts. And these solid steel bars were buckling, bending, bulging out of their sockets. Conan watched in an almost impersonal fascination, envying the monster his inhuman strength.

Then, without warning, the bombardment ceased. In the stillness, Conan heard other noises on the landing outside – the beat of wings, and a muttering voice that was like the whining of wind through midnight branches. Then presently there was silence, but there was a new feel in the air. Only the whetted instincts of barbarism could have sensed it, but Conan knew, without seeing or hearing him leave, that the master of Dagon no longer stood outside the door.

He glared through a crack that had been started in the steel of the portal. The landing was empty. He drew the warped bolts and cautiously pulled aside the sagging door. Khosatral was not on the stair, but far below he heard the clang of a metal door. He did not know whether the giant was plotting new deviltries or had been summoned away by that muttering voice, but he wasted no time in conjectures.

He called to Octavia, and the new note in his voice brought her up to her feet and to his side almost without her conscious volition.

'What is it?' she gasped.

'Don't stop to talk!' He caught her wrist. 'Come on!' The chance for action had transformed him; his eyes blazed, his voice crackled. 'The knife!' he muttered, while almost dragging the girl down the stair in his fierce haste. 'The magic Yuetshi blade! He left it in the dome! I—' his voice died suddenly as a clear mental picture sprang up before him. That dome adjoined the great room where stood the copper throne – sweat started out on his body. The only way to that dome was through that room with its copper throne and the foul thing that slumbered in it.

But he did not hesitate. Swiftly they descended the stair, crossed the chamber, descended the next stair, and came into the great dim hall with its mysterious hangings. They had seen no sign of the colossus. Halting before the great bronze-valved door, Conan caught Octavia by her shoulders and shook her in his intensity.

'Listen!' he snapped. 'I'm going into the room and fasten the door. Stand here and listen; if Khosatral comes, call to me. If you hear me cry out for you to go, run as though the Devil were on your heels – which he probably will be. Make for that door at the other end of the hall, because I'll be past helping you. I'm going for the Yuetshi knife!'

Before she could voice the protest her lips were framing, he had slid through the valves and shut them behind him. He lowered the bolt cautiously, not noticing that it could be worked from the outside. In the dim twilight his gaze sought that grim copper throne; yes, the scaly brute was still there, filling the throne with its loathsome coils. He saw a door behind the throne and knew that it led into the dome. But to reach it he must mount the dais, a few feet from the throne itself.

A wind blowing across the green floor would have made more noise than Conan's slinking feet. Eyes glued on the sleeping reptile he reached the dais and mounted the glass steps. The snake had not moved. He was reaching for the door. . . .

The bolt on the bronze portal clanged and Conan stifled an awful oath as he saw Octavia come into the room. She stared about, uncertain in the deeper gloom, and he stood frozen, not daring to shout a warning. Then she saw his shadowy figure and ran toward the dais, crying: 'I want to go with you! I'm afraid to stay alone – *oh*!' She threw up her hands with a terrible scream as for the first time she saw the occupant of the throne. The wedge-shaped head had lifted from its coils and thrust out toward her on a yard of shining neck.

Then with a smooth, flowing motion, it began to ooze from the throne, coil by coil, its ugly head bobbing in the direction of the paralyzed girl.

Conan cleared the space between him and the throne with a desperate bound, his scimitar swinging with all his power. And with such blinding speed did the serpent move that it whipped about and met him in full midair, lapping his limbs and body with half a dozen coils. His half-checked stroke fell futilely as he crashed down on the dais, gashing the scaly trunk but not severing it.

Then he was writhing on the glass steps with fold after slimy fold knotting about him, twisting, crushing, killing him. His right arm was still free, but he could get no purchase to strike a killing blow, and he knew one blow must suffice. With a groaning convulsion of muscular expansion that bulged his veins almost to bursting on his temples and tied his muscles in quivering, tortured knots, he heaved up on his feet, lifting almost the full weight of that forty-foot devil.

An instant he reeled on wide-braced legs, feeling his ribs caving in on his vitals and his sight growing dark, while his scimitar gleamed above his head. Then it fell, shearing through the scales and flesh and vertebræ. And where there had been one huge, writhing cable, now there were horribly two, lashing and flopping in the death throes. Conan staggered away from their blind strokes. He was sick and dizzy, and blood oozed from his nose. Groping in a dark mist he clutched Octavia and shook her until she gasped for breath.

'Next time I tell you to stay somewhere,' he gasped, 'you stay!'

He was too dizzy even to know whether she replied. Taking her wrist like a truant schoolgirl, he led her around the hideous stumps that still looped and knotted on the floor. Somewhere, in the distance, he thought he heard men yelling, but his ears were still roaring so that he could not be sure.

The door gave to his efforts. If Khosatral had placed the snake there to guard the thing he feared, evidently he considered it ample precaution. Conan half expected some other monstrosity to leap at him with the opening of the door, but in the dimmer light he saw only the vague sweep of the arch above, a dully gleaming block of gold, and a half-moon glimmer on the stone.

With a gasp of gratification, he scooped it up and did not linger for further exploration. He turned and fled across the room and down the great hall toward the distant door that he felt led to the outer air. He was correct. A few minutes later he emerged into the silent streets, half carrying, half guiding his companion. There was no one to be seen, but beyond the western wall there sounded cries and moaning wails that made Octavia tremble. He led her to the southwestern wall and without difficulty found a stone stair that mounted the rampart. He had appropriated a thick tapestry rope in the great hall, and now, having reached the parapet, he looped the soft, strong cord about the girl's hips and lowered her to the earth. Then, making one end fast to a merlon, he slid down after her. There was but one way of escape from the island – the stair on the western cliffs. In that direction he hurried, swinging wide around the spot from which had come the cries and the sound of terrible blows.

Octavia sensed that grim peril lurked in those leafy fastnesses. Her breath came pantingly and she pressed close to her protector. But the forest was silent now, and they saw no shape of menace until they emerged from the trees and glimpsed a figure standing on the edge of the cliffs.

Jehungir Agha had escaped the doom that had overtaken his warriors when an iron giant sallied suddenly from the gate and battered and crushed them into bits of shredded flesh and splintered bone. When he saw the swords of his archers break on that manlike juggernaut, he had known it was no human foe they faced, and he had fled, hiding in the deep woods until the sounds of slaughter ceased. Then he crept back to the stair, but his boatmen were not waiting for him.

They had heard the screams, and presently, waiting nervously, had seen, on the cliff above them, a blood-smeared monster waving gigantic arms in awful triumph. They had waited for no more. When Jehungir came upon the cliffs, they were just vanishing among the reeds beyond

101

earshot. Khosatral was gone – had either returned to the city or was prowling the forest in search of the man who had escaped him outside the walls.

Jehungir was just preparing to descend the stairs and depart in Conan's boat, when he saw the *hetman* and the girl emerge from the trees. The experience which had congealed his blood and almost blasted his reason had not altered Jehungir's intentions towards the *kozak* chief. The sight of the man he had come to kill filled him with gratification. He was astonished to see the girl he had given to Jelal Khan, but he wasted no time on her. Lifting his bow he drew the shaft to its head and loosed. Conan crouched and the arrow splintered on a tree, and Conan laughed.

'Dog!' he taunted. 'You can't hit me! I was not born to die on Hyrkanian steel! Try again, pig of Turan!'

Jehungir did not try again. That was his last arrow. He drew his scimitar and advanced, confident in his spired helmet and close-meshed mail. Conan met him halfway in a blinding whirl of swords. The curved blades ground together, sprang apart, circled in glittering arcs that blurred the sight which tried to follow them. Octavia, watching, did not see the stroke, but she heard its chopping impact and saw Jehungir fall, blood spurting from his side where the Cimmerian's steel had sundered his mail and bitten to his spine.

But Octavia's scream was not caused by the death of her former master. With a crash of bending boughs, Khosatral Khel was upon them. The girl could not flee; a moaning cry escaped her as her knees gave way and pitched her grovelling to the sward.

Conan, stooping above the body of the Agha, made no move to escape. Shifting his reddened scimitar to his left hand, he drew the great half-blade of the Yuetshi. Khosatral Khel was towering above him, his arms lifted like mauls, but as the blade caught the sheen of the sun, the giant gave back suddenly.

But Conan's blood was up. He rushed in, slashing with the crescent blade. And it did not splinter. Under its edge, the dusky metal of Khosatral's body gave way like common flesh beneath a cleaver. From the deep gash flowed a strange ichor, and Khosatral cried out like the dirging of a great bell. His terrible arms flailed down, but Conan, quicker than the archers who had died beneath those awful flails, avoided their strokes and struck again and yet again. Khosatral reeled and tottered; his cries were awful to hear, as if metal were given a tongue of pain, as if iron shrieked and bellowed under torment.

Then, wheeling away, he staggered into the forest; he reeled in his gait, crashed through bushes, and caromed off trees. Yet though Conan followed him with the speed of hot passion, the walls and towers of Dagon loomed through the trees before the man came within dagger-reach of the giant.

Then Khosatral turned again, flailing the air with desperate blows, but Conan, fired to beserk fury, was not to be denied. As a panther strikes down a bull moose at bay, so he plunged under the bludgeoning arms and drove the crescent blade to the hilt under the spot where a human's heart would be.

Khosatral reeled and fell. In the shape of a man he reeled, but it was not the shape of a man that struck the loam. Where there had been the likeness of a human face, there was no face at all, and the metal limbs melted and changed. . . . Conan, who had not shrunk from Khosatral living, recoiled blenching from Khosatral dead, for he had witnessed an awful transmutation; in his dying throes Khosatral Khel had become again the *thing* that had crawled up from the Abyss millennia gone. Gagging with intolerable repugnance, Conan turned to flee the sight; and he was suddenly aware that the pinnacles of Dagon no longer glimmered through the trees. They had faded like smoke – the battlements, the crenellated towers, the great bronze gates, the velvets, the gold, the ivory, and the dark-haired women, and the men with their shaven skulls. With the passing of the inhuman intellect which had given them rebirth, they had faded back into the dust which they had been for ages uncounted. Only the stumps of broken columns rose above crumbling walls and broken paves and shattered dome. Conan again looked upon the ruins of Xapur as he remembered them.

The wild *hetman* stood like a statue for a space, dimly grasping something of the cosmic tragedy of the fitful ephemera called mankind and the hooded shapes of darkness which prey upon it. Then as he heard his voice called in accents of fear, he started, as one awakening from a dream, glanced again at the thing on the ground, shuddered and turned away toward the cliffs and the girl that waited there.

She was peering fearfully under the trees, and she greeted him with a half-stifled cry of relief. He had shaken off the dim monstrous visions which had momentarily haunted him, and was his exuberant self again.

'Where is *he*?' she shuddered.

'Gone back to Hell whence he crawled,' he replied cheerfully. 'Why didn't you climb the stair and make your escape in my boat?'

'I wouldn't desert—' she began, then changed her mind, and amnded rather sulkily, 'I have nowhere to go. The Hyrkanians would enslave me again, and the pirates would—'

'What of the *kozaks*?' he suggested.

'Are they better than the pirates?' she asked scornfully. Conan's admiration increased to see how well she had recovered her poise after having endured such frantic terror. Her arrogance amused him.

'You seemed to think so in the camp by Ghori,' he answered. 'You were free enough with your smiles then.'

Her red lip curled in disdain. 'Do you think I was enamored of you? Do you dream that I would have shamed myself before an ale-guzzling, meat-gorging barbarian unless I had to? My master – whose body lies there – forced me to do as I did.'

'Oh!' Conan seemed rather crestfallen. Then he laughed with undiminished zest. 'No matter. You belong to me now. Give me a kiss.'

'You dare ask—' she began angrily, when she felt herself snatched off her feet and crushed to the *hetman's* muscular breast. She fought him fiercely, with all the supple strength of her magnificent youth, but he only laughed exuberantly, drunk with the possession of this splendid creature writhing in his arms.

He crushed her struggles easily, drinking the nectar of her lips with all the unrestrained passion that was his, until the arms that strained against them melted and twined convulsively about his massive neck. Then he laughed down into the clear eyes, and said: 'Why should not a chief of the Free People be preferable to a city-bred dog of Turan?'

She shook back her tawny locks, still tingling in every nerve from the fire of his kisses. She did not loosen her arms from his neck. 'Do you deem yourself an Agha's equal?' she challenged.

He laughed and strode with her in his arms toward the stair. 'You shall judge,' he boasted. 'I'll burn Khawarizm for a torch to light your way to my tent.'

THE FLAME KNIFE

Conan may or may not have made good his boast to burn Jehungir's city of Khawarizm, but in any event he builds his combined kozak and pirate raiders into so formidable a threat that King Yezdigerd calls off his march of empire to crush them. The Turanian forces are ordered back from the frontiers and in one massive assault succeed in breaking up the kozak host. Some survivors ride east into the wilds of Hyrkania, others west to join the Zuagirs in the desert. With a sizeable band, Conan retreats southward through the passes of the Ilbars Mountains to take service as light cavalry in the army of one of Yezdigerd's strongest rivals, Kobad Shah, king of Iranistan.

1. *Knives in the Dark*

The scuff of swift and stealthy feet in the darkened doorway warned the giant Cimmerian. He wheeled to see a tall figure lunging at him from the black arch. It was dark in the alley, but Conan glimpsed a fierce, bearded face and the gleam of steel in a lifted hand, even as he avoided the blow with a twist of his body. The knife ripped his tunic and glanced along the shirt of light chain mail he wore beneath it. Before the assassin could recover his balance, the Cimmerian caught his arm and brought his massive fist down like a sledge hammer on the back of the fellow's neck. The man crumpled to earth without a sound.

Conan stood over him, listening with tense expectancy. Up the street, around the next corner, he caught the shuffle of sandaled feet, the muffled clink of steel. These sinister sounds told him the nighted streets of Anshan were a deathtrap. He hesitated, half-drew the scimitar at his side, then shrugged and hurried down the street. He swerved wide of the dark arches that gaped in the walls that lined it.

He turned into a wider street and a few moments later rapped softly on a door, above which burned a bronze lantern. The door opened almost instantly. Conan stepped inside, snapping:

'Lock the door!'

The massive Shemite who had admitted the Cimmerian shot home the heavy bolt and turned, tugging his curled blue-black beard as he inspected his commander.

'Your shirt is gashed, Conan!' he rumbled.

'A man tried to knife me,' answered Conan. 'Others followed.'

The Shemite's black eyes blazed as he laid a broad, hairy hand on the three-foot Ilbarsi knife that jutted from his hip. 'Let us sally forth and slay the dogs!' he urged.

Conan shook his head. He was a huge man, much taller than the Shemite, but for all his size he moved with the lightness of a cat. His thick chest, corded neck, and square shoulders spoke of primordial strength, speed, and endurance.

'Other things come first,' he said. 'They're enemies of Balash, who knew I quarreled with the king tonight.'

'You did!' cried the Shemite. 'This is dark news indeed. What said the king?'

Conan picked up a flagon of wine and gulped down half of it. 'Oh, Kobad Shan is mad with suspicion,' he said. 'Now it's our friend Balash. The chief's enemies have poisoned the king against him; but then, Balash is stubborn. He won't come in and surrender as Kobad demands, saying Kobad means to stick his head on a pike. So Kobad ordered me to take the *kozaki* into the Ilbars Mountains and bring back Balash – all of him if possible, but his head in any case.'

'And?'

'I refused.'

'You did?' said the Shemite in an awed whisper.

'Of course! What do you think I am? I told Kobad Shah how Balash and his tribe saved us when we got lost in the Ilbars in the middle of winter, on our ride south from the Vilayet Sea. Most hillmen would have wiped us

107

out. But the fool wouldn't listen. He began shouting about his divine right and the insolence of low-born barbarians and such stuff. One more word and I'd have stuffed his imperial turban down his throat.'

'You did not *strike* the king?' said the Shemite.

'Nay, though I felt like it. Crom! I can't understand the way you civilized men crawl on your bellies before any copper-riveted ass who happens to sit on a jeweled chair with a bauble on his head.'

'Because these asses can have us flayed or impaled at a nod. Now, we must flee from Iranistan to escape the king's wrath.'

Conan finished the wine and smacked his lips. 'I think not; he'll get over it. He knows his army is not what it was in his grandsire's time, and we're the only light horse he can count on. But that still leaves our friend Balash. I'm tempted to ride north to warn him.'

'Alone, Conan?'

'Why not? You can give it out that I'm sleeping off a debauch for a few days until—'

A light knock on the door made Conan cut off his sentence. He glanced at the Shemite, stepped to the door, and growled:

'Who's there?'

'It is I, Nanaia,' said a woman's voice.

Conan stared at his companion. 'Do you know any Nanaia, Tubal?'

'Not I. It must be some trick.'

'Let me in,' said the voice.

'We shall see,' muttered Conan, his eyes blazing a volcanic blue in the lamplight. He drew his scimitar and laid a hand on the bolt, while Tubal, knife drawn, took his place on the other side of the door.

Conan snapped the bolt and whipped open the door. A veiled figure stepped across the threshold, then gave a little shriek and shrank back at the sight of the gleaming blades poised on muscular arms.

Conan's blade darted out so that its tip touched the back of the visitor. 'Enter, my lady,' he rumbled in barbarously accented Iranistani.

The woman stepped forward. Conan slammed the door and shot home the bolt. 'Is anybody with you?'

'N-nay, I came alone . . .'

Conan's left arm shot out with the speed of a serpent's strike and ripped the veil from the woman's face. She was tall, lithe, young, and dark, with black hair and finely-chiseled features.

'Now, Nanaia, what is this all about?' he said.

'I am a girl from the king's seraglio—'

Tubal gave a long whistle. 'Now we are in for it.'

'Go on, Nanaia,' said Conan.

'Well, I have often seen you through the lattice behind the throne, when you were closeted with Kobad. It is the king's pleasure to let his women watch him at his royal business. We are supposed to be shut out of this gallery when weighty matters are discussed, but tonight Xathrita the eunuch was drunk and failed to lock the door between the gallery and the women's apartments. I stole back and heard your bitter speech with the king.

'When you had gone, Kobad was very angry. He called in Hakhamani the informer and bade him quietly murder you. Hakhamani was to make it look like an accident.'

'If I catch Hakhamani, I'll make him look like an accident,' gritted Conan. 'But why all this delicacy? Kobad is no more backward than most kings about shortening or lengthening the necks of people he likes not.'

'Because the king wants to keep the services of your *kozaki*, and if they knew he had slain you they would revolt or ride away.'

'And why did you bring me this news?'

She looked at him from large dark melting eyes. 'I perish in the harem from boredom. With hundreds of women, the king has no time for me. I have admired you through the screen ever since you took service here and hope you will take me with you. Anything is better than the suffocating monotony of this gilded prison, with its everlasting gossip and intrigue. I am the daughter of Kujala, chief of the Gwadiri. We are a tribe of fishermen and mariners, far to the south among the Islands of Pearl. I have steered my own ship through a typhoon, and such indolence drives me mad.'

'How did you get out of the palace?'

'A rope and an unguarded old window with the bars

109

broken away . . . But that is not important. Will you take me?'

'Send her back,' said Tubal in the *lingua franca* of the *kozaki*: a mixture of Zaporoskan, Hyrkanian, and other tongues. 'Or better yet, cut her throat and bury her in the garden. He might let us go unharmed, but he'd never let us get away with the wench. Let him find that you have run off with one of his concubines and he'll overturn every stone in Iranistan to find you.'

The girl evidently did not understand the words but quailed at the menace of the tone.

Conan grinned wolfishly. 'On the contrary. The thought of slinking out of the country with my tail between my legs makes my guts ache. But if I can take something like this along for a trophy – well, so long as we must leave anyway . . .' He turned to Nanaia. 'You understand that the pace will be fast, the going rough, and the company not so polite as you're used to?'

'I understand.'

'And furthermore,' he said with narrowed eyes, 'that I command absolutely?'

'Aye.'

'Good. Wake the dog-brothers, Tubal; we ride as soon as they can stow their gear and saddle up.'

Muttering his forebodings, the Shemite strode into an inner chamber and shook a man sleeping on a heap of carpets. 'Awaken, son of a long line of thieves. We ride northward.'

Hattusas, a slight, dark Zamorian, sat up yawning. 'Whither?'

'To Kushaf in the Ilbars Mountains, where we wintered, and where the rebel dog Balash will doubtless cut all our throats,' growled Tubal.

Hattusas grinned as he rose. 'You have no love for the Kushafi, but he is Conan's sworn friend.'

Tubal scowled as he stalked out into the courtyard and through the door that led to the adjacent barrack. Groans and curses came from the barrack as the men were shaken awake.

Two hours later, the shadowy figures that lurked about Conan's house shrank back into the shadows as the gate of the stable yard swung open and the three hundred Free

Companions clattered out in double file, leading pack mules and spare horses. They were men of all nations, the remnants of the band of *kozaki* whom Conan had led south from the steppes around the Vilayet Sea when King Yezdigerd of Turan had gathered a mighty army and broken the outlaw confederacy in an all-day battle. They had arrived in Anshan ragged and half-starved. Now they were gaudy in silken pantaloons and spired helmets of Iranistani pattern, and loaded down with weapons.

Meanwhile in the palace, the king of Iranistan brooded on his throne. Suspicion had eaten into his troubled soul until he saw enemies everywhere, within and without. For a time he had counted on the support of Conan, the leader of the squadron of mercenary light horse. The northern savage might lack the suave manners of the cultivated Iranistani court, but he did seem to have his own barbarian code of honor. Now, however, he had flatly refused to carry out Kobad Shah's order to seize the traitor Balash . . .

The king glanced at the curtain masking an alcove, absently reflecting that the wind must be rising, since the tapestry swayed a little. His eyes swept the gold-barred window and he went cold. The light curtains there hung motionless. Yet the hangings over the alcove had stirred . . .

Though short and fat, Kobad Shah did not lack personal courage. As he sprang, seized the tapestries, and tore them apart, a dagger in a dark hand licked from between them and smote him full in the breast. He cried out as he went down, dragging his assailant with him. The man snarled like a wild beast, his dilated eyes glaring madly. His dagger ribboned the king's robe, revealing the mail shirt that stopped his first thrust.

Outside, a deep shout echoed the king's shrill yells for help. Booted feet pounded in the corridor. The king had grasped his attacker by throat and knife wrist, but the man's stringy muscles were like knotted steel cords. As they rolled on the floor, the dagger, glancing from the links of the mail shirt, fleshed itself in arm, thigh, and hand. Then, as the bravo heaved the weakening ruler under him, grasped his throat, and lifted the knife again, something

111

flashed in the lamplight like a jet of blue lightning. The murderer collapsed, his head split to the teeth.

'Your majesty! Sire!' It was Gotarza, the towering captain of the royal guard, pale under his long black beard. As Kobad Shah sank down on a divan, Gotarza began ripping strips from the hangings to bind his wounds.

'Look!' gasped the king, pointing. His face was livid; his hand shook. 'The knife! By Asura, the knife!'

It lay glinting by the dead man's hand – a curious weapon with a wavy blade shaped like a flame. Gotarza stared and swore under his breath.

'The flame knife!' panted Kobad Shah. 'The same weapon that struck at the King of Vendhya and the King of Turan!'

'The mark of the Hidden Ones,' muttered Gotarza, uneasily eyeing the ominous symbol of the terrible cult.

The noise had roused the palace. Men were running down the corridors, shouting to know what had happened.

'Shut the door!' exclaimed the king. 'Admit no one but the major-domo of the palace!'

'But we must have a physician, your majesty,' protested the officer. 'These wounds will not slay of themselves, but the dagger might have been poisoned.'

'No, fetch no one! Whoever he is, he might be in the service of my foes. Asura! The Yezmites have marked me for doom!' The experience had shaken the king's courage. 'Who can fight the dagger in the dark, the serpent underfoot, the poison in the wine cup? There is that western barbarian, Conan – but no, not even he is to be trusted, now that he has defied my commands . . . Let the major-domo in, Gotarza.' When the officer admitted the stout official, the king asked: 'What news, Bardiya?'

'Oh, sire, what has happened? It is—'

'Never mind what has happened to me. I see by your eyes you have news. What know you?'

'The *kozaki* have ridden forth from the city with Conan, who told the guard at the North Gate they were on their way to take Balash as you commanded.'

'Good. Perhaps the fellow has repented his insolence. What else?'

'Hakhamani the informer caught Conan on his way home, but Conan slew one of his men and escaped.'

112

'That is just as well. Call off Hakhamani until we know what Conan intends by this foray. Anything more?'

'One of your women, Nanaia the daughter of Kujala, has fled the palace. We found the rope by which she escaped.'

Kobad Shah gave a roar. 'She must have gone with Conan! It is too much to have been pure chance! And he must be connected with the Hidden Ones too! Else why should they strike at me just after I have quarreled with him? He must have gone straight from my presence to send the Yezmite to slay me. Gotarza, turn out the royal guard. Ride after the *kozaki* and bring me Conan's head, or your own shall answer for it! Take at least five hundred men, for the barbarian is fierce and crafty and not to be trifled with.'

As Gotarza hurried from the chamber, the king groaned: 'Now, Bardiya, fetch a leech. My veins are afire. Gotarza was right; the dagger must have been envenomed.'

Three days after his hurried departure from Anshan, Conan sat cross-legged in the trail where it looped over the rock ridge to follow the slope down to the village of Kushaf.

'I would stand between you and death,' he said to the man who sat opposite him, 'as you did for me when your hill wolves would have massacred us.'

The man tugged his purple-stained beard reflectively. He was broad and powerful, with gray-flecked hair and a broad belt bristling with knife and dagger hilts. He was Balash, chief of the Kushafi tribesmen and overlord of Kushaf and its neighboring villages. But he spoke modestly:

'The gods favor you! Yet what man can pass the spot of his death?'

'A man can either fight or flee, and not sit on a rock like an apple in a tree, waiting to be picked. If you want to take a long chance of making your peace with the king, you can go to Anshan—'

'I have too many enemies at court. In Anshan, the king would listen to their lies and hang me up in an iron cage for the kites to eat. Nay, I will not go!'

113

'Then take your people and find another abode. There are places in these hills where not even the king could follow you.'

Balash glanced down the rocky slope to the cluster of mud-and-stone towers that rose above the encircling wall. His thin nostrils expanded, and into his eyes came a dark flame like that of an eagle surveying its eyrie.

'Nay, by Asura! My clan has held Kushaf since the days of Bahram. Let the king rule in Anshan; this is mine!'

'The king will likewise rule in Kushaf,' grunted Tubal, squatting behind Conan with Hattusas the Zamorian.

Balash glanced in the other direction where the trail disappeared to the east between jutting crags. On these crags, bits of white cloth were blown out by the wind, which the watchers knew were the garments of archers and javelin men who guarded the pass day and night.

'Let him come,' said Balash. 'We hold the passes.'

'He'll bring ten thousand men, in heavy armor, with catapults and other siege gear,' said Conan. 'He'll burn Kushaf and take your head back to Anshan.'

'That will happen which will happen,' said Balash.

Conan fought down a rising anger at the fatalism of these people. Every instinct of his strenuous nature was a negation of this inert philosophy. But, as they seemed to be deadlocked, he said nothing but sat staring at the western crags where the sun hung, a ball of fire in the sharp, windy blue.

Balash dismissed the matter with a wave of his hand and said: 'Conan, there is something I would show you. Down in yonder ruined hut outside the wall lies a dead man, whose like was never seen in Kushaf. Even in death, he is strange and evil. I think he is no natural man at all, but a demon. Come.'

He led the way down the slope to the hovel, explaining: 'My warriors came upon him lying at the base of a cliff, as if he had fallen or been thrown from the top. I made them bring him here, but he died on the way, babbling in a strange tongue. They deem him a demon with good cause.

'A long day's journey southward, among mountains so wild and barren not even a goat could dwell among them, lies the country we call Drujistan.'

'Drujistan!' echoed Conan. 'Land of demons, eh?'

114

'Aye! An evil region of black crags and wild gorges, shunned by wise men. It seems uninhabited, yet men dwell there – men or devils. Sometimes a man is slain or a child or woman stolen from a lonely trail, and we know it is their work. We have followed and glimpsed shadowy figures moving through the night, but always the trail ends against a blank cliff, through which only a demon could pass. Sometimes we hear drums echoing among the crags, or the roaring of the fiends. It is a sound to turn men's hearts to ice. The old legends say that among these mountains, thousands of years ago, the ghoul-king Ura built the magical city of Yanaidar, and that the deadly ghosts of Ura and his hideous subjects still haunt the ruins. Another legend tells how, a thousand years ago, a chief of the Ilbarsi hillmen settled in the ruins and began to repair them and make the city his stronghold; but in one night he and his followers vanished, nor were they ever seen again.'

They reached the ruined hut, and Balash pulled open the sagging door. A moment later, the five men were bending over a figure sprawled on the dirt floor.

It was a figure alien and incongruous: that of a stocky man with broad, square, flat features, colored like dark copper, and narrow, slanting eyes – an unmistakable son of Khitai. Blood clotted the coarse black hair on the back of his head, and the unnatural position of his body told of shattered bones.

'Has he not the look of an evil spirit?' asked Balash.

'He's no demon, whether he was a wizard in life or not,' answered Conan. 'He's a Khitan, from a country far to the east of Hyrkania, beyond mountains and deserts and jungles so vast you could lose a dozen Iranistans in them. I rode through that land when I soldiered for the king of Turan. But what this fellow is doing here I cannot say—'

Suddenly his blue eyes blazed and he tore the blood-stained tunic away from the squat throat. A stained woolen shirt came into view, and Tubal, looking over Conan's shoulder, grunted explosively. On the shirt, worked in thread so crimson it might at first glance have been mistaken for a splash of blood, appeared a curious emblem: a human fist grasping a hilt from which jutted a knife with a wavy blade.

115

'The flame knife!' whispered Balash, recoiling from that symbol of death and destruction.

All looked at Conan, who stared down at the sinister emblem, trying to recapture a vague train of associations it roused – dim memories of an ancient and evil cult, which used that symbol. Finally he said to Hattusas:

'When I was a thief in Zamora, I heard rumors of a cult called the Yezmites that used such a symbol. You're a Zamorian; what know you of this?'

Hattusas shrugged. 'There are many cults whose roots go back to the beginnings of time, to the days before the Cataclysm. Often rulers have thought they had stamped them out, and often they have come to life again. The Hidden Ones or Sons of Yezm are one of these, but more I cannot tell you. I meddle not in such matters.'

Conan spoke to Balash: 'Can your men guide me to where you found this man?'

'Aye. But it is an evil place, in the Gorge of Ghosts, on the borders of Drujistan, and—'

'Good. Everybody get some sleep. We ride at dawn.'

'To Anshan?' asked Balash.

'No. To Drujistan.'

'Then you think—?'

'I think nothing – yet.'

'Will the squadron ride with us?' asked Tubal. 'The horses are badly worn.'

'No, let the men and horses rest. You and Hattusas shall go with me, together with one of Balash's Kushafis for a guide. Codrus commands in my absence, and if there's any trouble as a result of my dogs laying hands on the Kushafi women, tell him he is to knock their heads in.'

2. The Black Country

Dusk mantled the serrated skyline when Conan's guide halted. Ahead, the rugged terrain was broken by a deep canyon. Beyond the canyon rose a forbidding array of black crags and frowning cliffs, a wild, haglike chaos of broken black rock.

'There begins Drujistan,' said the Kushafi. 'Beyond that

116

gorge, the Gorge of Ghosts, begins the country of horror and death. I go no farther.'

Conan nodded, his eyes picking out a trail that looped down rugged slopes into the canyon. It was a fading trace of the ancient road they had been following for many miles, but it looked as though it had often been used of late.

Conan glanced around. With him were Tubal, Hattusas, the guide – and Nanaia the girl. She had insisted on coming because, she said, she feared to be separated from Conan among all these wild foreigners, whose speech she could not understand. She had proved a good traveling companion, tough and uncomplaining, though of volatile and fiery disposition.

The Kushafi said: 'The trail is well-traveled, as you see. By it the demons of the black mountains come and go. But men who follow it do not return.'

Tubal peered. 'What need demons with a trail? They fly with wings like bats!'

'When they take the shape of men they walk like men,' said the Kushafi. He pointed to the jutting ledge over which the trail wound. 'At the foot of that slope we found the man you called a Khitan. Doubtless his brother demons quarreled with him and cast him down.'

'Doubtless he tripped and fell,' grunted Conan. 'Khitans of the desert are unused to climbing, their legs being bowed and weakened by a life in the saddle. Such a one would easily stumble on a narrow trail.'

'If he was a man, perhaps,' said the Kushafi. 'But – Asura!'

All but Conan jumped, and the Kushafi snatched at his bow, glaring wildly. Out over the crags, from the south, rolled an incredible sound – a strident, braying roar, which vibrated among the mountains.

'The voice of the demons!' cried the Kushafi, jerking the rein so that his horse squealed and reared. 'In the name of Asura, let us be gone! 'Tis madness to remain!'

'Go back to your village if you're afraid,' said Conan. 'I'm going on.' In truth, the hint of the supernatural made the Cimmerian's nape prickle too, but before his followers he did not wish to admit this.

117

'Without your men? It is madness! At least send back for your followers.'

Conan's eyes narrowed like those of a hunting wolf. 'Not this time. For scouting and spying, the fewer the better. I think I'll have a look at this land of demons; I could use a mountain stronghold.' To Nanaia he said: 'You had better go back, girl.'

She began to weep. 'Do not send me away, Conan! The wild mountaineers will ravish me.'

He glanced down her long, well-muscled figure. 'Anyone who tried it would have a task. Well, come on then, and do not say I didn't warn you.'

The guide wheeled his pony and kicked it into a run, calling back: 'Balash will weep for you! There will be woe in Kushaf! *Aie! Ahia!*'

His lamentations died away amidst the clatter of hoofs on stone as the Kushafi, flogging his pony, topped a ridge and vanished.

'Run, son of a noseless dam!' yelled Tubal. 'We'll brand your devils and drag them to Kushaf by their tails!' But he fell silent the instant the victim was out of hearing.

Conan spoke to Hattusas: 'Have you ever heard a sound like that?'

The lithe Zamorian nodded. 'Yes, in the mountains of the devil worshippers.'

Conan lifted his reins without comment. He, too, had heard the roar of the ten-foot bronze trumpets that blared over the bare black mountains of forbidden Pathenia, in the hands of shaven-headed priests of Erlik.

Tubal snorted like a rhinoceros. He had not heard those trumpets, and he thrust his horse in ahead of Hattusas so as to be next to Conan as they rode down the steep slopes in the purple dusk. He said roughly: 'Now that we have been lured into this country of devils by treacherous Kushafi dogs who will undoubtedly steal back and cut your throat while you sleep, what have you planned?'

It might have been an old hound growling at his master for patting another dog. Conan bent his head and spat to hide a grin. 'We'll camp in the canyon tonight. The horses are too tired for struggling through these gulches in the dark. Tomorrow we shall explore.

'I think the Hidden Ones have a camp in that country

118

across the gorge. The hills hereabouts are but thinly settled, Kushaf is the nearest village, and it's a hard day's ride away. Wandering clans stay out of these parts for fear of the Kushafis, and Balash's men are too superstitious to explore across the gorge. The Hidden Ones, over there, could come and go without being seen. I know not just what we shall do; our destiny is on the knees of the gods.'

As they came down into the canyon, they saw that the trail led across the rock-strewn floor and into the mouth of a deep, narrow gorge, which debouched into the canyon from the south. The south wall of the canyon was higher than the north and more sheer. It swept up in a sullen rampart of solid black rock, broken at intervals by narrow gorge mouths. Conan rode into the gulch into which the trail wound and followed it to the first bend. He found that this bend was but the first of a succession of kinks. The ravine, running between sheer walls of rock, writhed and twisted like the track of a serpent and was already filled with darkness.

'This is our road tomorrow,' said Conan. His men nodded silently as he led them back to the main canyon, where some light still lingered. The clang of their horses' hoofs on the flint seemed loud in the sullen silence.

A few score of paces west of the trail ravine, another, narrower gulch opened into the canyon. Its rocky floor showed no sign of any trail, and it narrowed so rapidly that Conan thought it ended in a blind alley.

Halfway between these ravine mouths, near the north wall, a tiny spring bubbled up in a natural basin of age-hollowed rock. Behind it, in a cavelike niche in the cliff, dry wiry grass grew sparsely. There they tethered the weary horses. They camped at the spring, eating dried meat and not risking a fire, which might be seen by hostile eyes.

Conan divided his party into two watches. Tubal he placed on guard west of the camp, near the mouth of the narrower ravine, while Hattusas had his station close to the mouth of the eastern ravine. Any hostile band coming up or down the canyon, or entering it from either ravine, would have to pass these vigilant sentries.

Darkness came swiftly in the canyon, seeming to flow in waves down the black slopes and ooze out of the mouths

119

of the ravines. Stars blinked out, cold, white, and impersonal. Above the invaders brooded the great dusky bulks of the broken mountain. Conan fell asleep wondering idly what grim spectacles they had witnessed since the beginning of time.

The razor-keen perceptions of the barbarian had never been dulled by Conan's years of contact with civilization. As Tubal approached him to lay a hand on his shoulder, Conan awoke and rose to a crouch, sword in hand, before the Shemite even had a chance to touch him.

'What is it?' muttered Conan.

Tubal squatted beside him, gigantic shoulders bulking dimly in the gloom. Back in the shadow of the cliffs, the unseen horses moved restlessly. Conan knew that peril was in the air even before Tubal spoke:

'Hattusas is slain and the girl is gone! Death is creeping upon us in the dark!'

'*What*?'

'Hattusas lies near the mouth of the ravine with his throat cut. I heard the sound of a rolling pebble from the mouth of the eastern ravine and stole thither without rousing you, and lo, there lay Hattusas in his blood. He must have died silently and suddenly. I saw no one and heard no further sound in the ravine. Then I hastened back to you and found Nanaia gone. The devils of the hills have slain one and snatched away the other without a sound. I sense that Death still skulks here. This is indeed the Gorge of Ghosts!'

Conan crouched silently on one knee, straining eyes and ears into the darkness. That the keen-sensed Zamorian should have died and Nanaia been spirited away without the sound of a struggle smacked of the diabolical.

'Who can fight devils, Conan? Let us mount and ride—'

'Listen!'

Somewhere a bare foot scuffed the rock floor. Conan rose, peering into the gloom. Men were moving out there in the darkness. Shadows detached themselves from the black background and slunk forward. Conan drew a dagger with his left hand. Tubal crouched beside him, gripping his Ilbarsi knife, silent and deadly as a wolf at bay.

The dim-seen line moved in slowly, widening as it came.

Conan and the Shemite fell back a few paces to have the rock wall at their backs and keep themselves from being surrounded.

The rush came suddenly, bare feet slapping softly over the rocky floor, steel glinting dully in the dim starlight. Conan could make out but few details of their assailants – only the bulks of them, and the shimmer of steel. He struck and parried by instinct and feel as much as by sight.

He killed the first man to come within sword reach. Tubal sounded a deep yell at the discovery that his foes were human after all and exploded in a burst of berserk ferocity. The sweep of his heavy, three-foot knife was devastating. Side by side, with the wall at their backs, the two companions were safe from attack on rear or flank.

Steel rang sharp on steel and blue sparks flew. There rose the ugly butcher-shop sound of blades cleaving flesh and bone. Men screamed or gasped death gurgles from severed throats. For a few moments a huddled knot writhed and milled near the rock wall. The work was too swift and blind and desperate to allow consecutive thought. But the advantage lay with the men at bay. They could see as well as their attackers; man for man they were stronger; and they knew that when they struck their steel would flesh itself only in hostile bodies. The others were handicapped by their numbers; for, the knowledge that they might kill a companion with a blind stroke must have tempered their frenzy.

Conan ducked a sword before he realized he had seen it swinging. His return stroke grated against mail; instead of hacking through it he slashed at an unprotected thigh and brought the man down. As he engaged the next man, the fallen one dragged himself forward and drove a knife at Conan's body, but Conan's own mail stopped it, and the dagger in Conan's left hand found the man's throat. Men spurted their blood on him as they died.

Then the rush ebbed. The attackers melted away like phantoms into the darkness, which was becoming less absolute. The eastern rim of the canyon was lined with a faint silvery fire that marked the moonrise.

Tubal gave tongue like a wolf and charged after the retreating figures, the foam of blood lust flecking his beard. He stumbled over a corpse and stabbed savagely downward before he realized it was a dead man. Then Conan grabbed his arm. He almost dragged the mighty Cimmerian off his feet as he plunged and snorted like a lassoed bull.

'Wait, fool!' snarled Conan. 'Do you want to run into a trap?'

Tubal subsided to a wolfish wariness. Together they glided after the vague figures, which disappeared into the mouth of the eastern ravine. There the pursuers halted, peering warily into the black depths. Somewhere far down it, a dislodged pebble rattled on the stone. Conan tensed like a suspicious panther.

'The dogs still flee,' muttered Tubal. 'Shall we follow?'

Conan shook his head. With Nanaia a captive, he could not afford to throw his life away by a mad rush into the well of blackness, where ambushes might make any step a march of death. They fell back to the camp and the frightened horses, which were frantic with the stench of fresh-spilt blood.

'When the moon rises high enough to flood the canyon with light,' said Tubal, 'they will shoot us with arrows from the ravine.'

'We must take the chance,' grunted Conan. 'Maybe they are poor shots.'

They squatted in the shadow of the cliffs in silence as the moonlight, weird and ghostly, grew in the canyon, and boulder, ledge, and wall took shape. No sound disturbed the brooding quiet. Then, by the waxing light, Conan investigated the four dead men left behind by the attackers. As he peered from face to bearded face, Tubal exclaimed:

'Devil-worshipers! Sabateans!'

'No wonder they could creep like cats,' muttered Conan. In Shem he had learned of the uncanny stealth of the people of that ancient and abominable cult, which worshipped the Golden Peacock in the nighted domes of accursed Sabatea. 'What are they doing here? Their homeland is in Shem. Let's see – Ha!'

Conan opened the man's robe. There on the linen jerkin that covered the Sabatean's thick chest appeared the emblem of a hand gripping a flame-shaped dagger. Tubal ripped the tunics from the other three corpses. Each displayed the fist and knife. He said:

122

'What sort of cult is this of the Hidden Ones, that draws men from Shem and Khitai, thousands of miles asunder?'

'That's what I mean to find out,' answered Conan. They squatted in the shadow of the cliffs in silence. Then Tubal rose and said:

'What now?'

Conan pointed to dark splotches on the bare rock floor, which the moonlight now made visible. 'We can follow that trail.'

Tubal wiped and sheathed his knife, while Conan wound around his waist a coil of thin, strong rope with a three-pointed iron hook at one end. He had found such a rope useful in his days as a thief. The moon had risen higher, drawing a silver thread along the middle of the ravine.

Through the moonlight, they approached the mouth of the ravine. No bowstring twanged; no javelin sighed through the night air; no furtive figures flitted among the shadows. The blood drops speckled the rocky floor; the Sabateans must have carried grim wounds away with them.

They pushed up the ravine, afoot, because Conan believed their foes were also afoot. Besides, the gulch was so narrow and rugged that a horseman would be at a disadvantage in a fight.

At each bend they expected an ambush, but the trail of blood drops led on, and no figures barred their way. The blood spots were not so thick now, but they were enough to mark the way.

Conan quickened his pace, hoping to overtake the Sabateans. Even though the latter had a long start, their wounds and their prisoner would slow them down. He thought Nanaia must still be alive, or they would have come upon her corpse.

The ravine pitched upward, narrowing, then widened, descended, bent, and came out into another canyon running east and west. This was a few hundred feet wide. The bloody trail ran straight across to the sheer south wall and ceased.

Tubal grunted. 'The Kushafi dogs spoke truth. The trail stops at a cliff that only a bird could fly over.'

Conan halted, puzzled. They had lost the trace of the ancient road in the Gorge of Ghosts, but this was undoubtedly the way the Sabateans had come. He raised his eyes up the wall, which rose straight for hundreds of feet. Above him, at a height of fifteen feet, jutted a narrow ledge, a mere outcropping a few feet wide and four or five paces long. It seemed to offer no solution, but halfway up to the ledge he saw a dull smear on the rock of the wall.

Uncoiling his rope, Conan whirled the weighted end and sent it soaring upward. The hook bit into the rim of the ledge and held. Conan went up it, clinging to the thin, smooth strand, as swiftly as most men would have climbed a ladder. As he passed the smear on the stone he confirmed his belief that it was dried blood, such as might have been made by a wounded man climbing or being hauled up to the ledge.

Tubal, below, fidgeted and tried to get a better view of the ledge, as if fearing it were peopled with unseen assassins. But the shelf lay bare when Conan pulled himself over the edge.

The first thing he saw was a heavy bronze ring set in the stone above the ledge, out of sight from below. The metal was polished by usage. More blood was smeared along the rim of the ledge. The drops led across the ledge to the sheer wall, which showed much weathering at that point. Conan saw something else: the blurred print of bloody fingers on the rock of the wall. He studied the cracks in the rock, then laid his hand over the bloody hand print and pushed. A section of the wall swung smoothly inward. He was staring into the door of a narrow tunnel, dimly lit by the moon somewhere at the far end.

Wary as a stalking leopard, he stepped into it. At once he heard a startled yelp from Tubal, to whose view it seemed that he had melted into solid rock. Conan emerged head and shoulders to exhort his follower to silence and then continued his investigation.

The tunnel was short; moonlight poured into it from the other end, where it opened into a cleft. The cleft ran straight for a hundred feet and made an abrupt bend, like a knife-cut through solid rock. The door through which he had entered was an irregular slab of rock hung on heavy, oiled bronze hinges. It fitted perfectly into its aperture, its irregular shape making the cracks appear to be merely natural seams in the cliff.

A rope ladder of heavy rawhide was coiled just inside the tunnel mouth. Conan returned to the ledge outside with this, made it fast to the bronze ring, and let it down. While Tubal swung up in a frenzy of impatience, Conan drew up his own rope and coiled it around his waist again.

Tubal swore strange Shemitic oaths as he grasped the mystery of the vanishing trail. He asked: 'But why was not the door bolted on the inside?'

'Probably men are coming and going constantly, and a man might be in a hurry to get through from the outside without having to shout to be let in. There was little chance of its being discovered; I should not have found it but for the blood marks.'

Tubal was for plunging instantly into the cleft, but Conan had become wary. He had seen no sign of a sentry but did not think a people so ingenious in hiding the entrance to their country would leave it unguarded.

He hauled up the ladder, coiled it back on its shelf, and closed the door, plunging that end of the tunnel into darkness. Commanding the unwilling Tubal to wait for him, he went down the tunnel and into the cleft.

From the bottom of the cleft, an irregular knife-edge of starlit sky was visible, hundreds of feet overhead. Enough moonlight found its way into the cleft to serve Conan's catlike eyes.

He had not reached the bend when a scuff of feet beyond it reached him. He had scarcely concealed himself behind a broken outcrop of rock, split away from the side wall, when the sentry came. He came in the leisurely manner of one who performs a perfunctory task, confident of his own security. He was a squat Khitan with a face like a copper mask. He swung along with the wide roll of a horseman, trailing a javelin.

He was passing Conan's hiding place when some instinct brought him about in a flash, teeth bared in a startled snarl, spear whipping up for a cast or a thrust. Even as he turned, Conan was upon him with the instant uncoiling of steel-spring muscles. As the javelin leaped to a level, the scimitar lashed down. The Khitan dropped like an ox, his round skull split like a ripe melon.

Conan froze to immobility, glaring along the passage. As he heard no sound to indicate the presence of any other

125

guard, he risked a low whistle which brought Tubal head-long into the cleft. The Shemite grunted at the sight of the dead man.

Conan stopped and pushed back the Khitan's upper lip, showing the canine teeth filed to points. 'Another son of Erlik, the Yellow God of Death. There is no telling how many more may be in this defile. We'll drag him behind these rocks.'

Beyond the bend, the long, deep defile ran empty to the next kink. As they advanced without opposition, Conan became sure that the Khitan was the only sentry in the cleft.

The moonlight in the narrow gash above them was paling into dawn when they came into the open at last. Here the defile broke into a chaos of shattered rock. The single gorge became half a dozen, threading between iso-lated crags and split-off rocks, as a river splits into sepa-rate streams at its delta. Crumbling pinnacles and turrets of black stone stood up like gaunt ghosts in the pale pre-dawn light.

Threading their way among these grim sentinels, the adventurers presently looked out upon a level, rock-strewn floor that stretched three hundred paces to the foot of a cliff. The trail they had followed, grooved by many feet in the weathered stone, crossed the level and twisted a tor-tuous way up the cliff on ramps cut in the rock. But what lay on top of the cliffs they could not guess. To right and left, the solid wall veered away, flanked by broken pin-nacles.

'What now, Conan?' In the gray light, the Shemite looked like a mountain goblin surprised out of his cave by dawn.

'I think we must be close to – listen!'

Over the cliffs rolled the blaring reverberation they had heard the night before, but now much nearer: the strident roar of the giant trumpet.

'Have we been seen?' wondered Tubal, fingering his knife.

Conan shrugged. 'Whether we have or not, we must see ourselves before we try to climb that cliff. Here!'

He indicated a weathered crag, which rose like a tower among its lesser fellows. The comrades went up it swiftly, keeping its bulk between them and the opposite cliffs. The summit was higher than the cliffs. Then they lay behind a spur of rock, staring through the rosy haze of the rising dawn.

'Pteor!' swore Tubal.

From their vantage point, the opposite cliffs assumed their real nature as one side of a gigantic mesalike block, which rose sheer from the surrounding level, four to five hundred feet high. Its vertical sides seemed unscalable, save where the trail had been cut into the stone. East, north, and west it was girdled by crumbling crags, separated from the plateau by the level canyon floor, which varied in width from three hundred paces to half a mile. On the south, the plateau abutted on a gigantic bare mountain, whose gaunt peaks dominated the surrounding pinnacles.

But the watchers gave but little attention to this topographical formation. Conan had expected, at the end of the bloody trail, to find some sort of rendezvous: a cluster of horsehide tents, a cavern, perhaps even a village of mud and stone nestling on a hillside. Instead, they were looking at a city, whose domes and towers glistened in the rosy dawn like a magical city of sorcerers stolen from some fabled land and set down in this wilderness.

'The city of the demons!' cried Tubal. 'It is enchantment and sorcery!' He snapped his fingers to ward off evil spells.

The plateau was oval, about a mile and a half long from north to south and somewhat less than a mile from east to west. The city stood near its southern end, etched against the dark mountain behind it. A large edifice, whose purple dome was shot with gold, gleamed in the dawn. It dominated the flat-topped stone houses and clustering trees.

The Cimmerian blood in Conan's veins responded to the somber aspect of the scene, the contrast of the gloomy black crags with the masses of green and the sheens of color in the city. The city awoke forebodings of evil. The gleam of its purple, gold-traced dome was somehow sinister. The black, crumbling crags formed a fitting setting for it. It was like a city of ancient, demonic mystery, rising with an evil glitter amidst ruin and decay.

'This must be the stronghold of the Hidden Ones,'

muttered Conan. 'Who'd have thought to find a city like this in an uninhabited country?'

'Not even we can fight a whole city,' grunted Tubal.

Conan fell silent while he studied the distant view. The city was not so large as it had looked at first glance. It was compact but unwalled; a parapet around the edge of the plateau furnished its defense. The two and three-storey houses stood among surprising groves and gardens – surprising because the plateau looked like solid rock without soil for growing things. He reached a decision and said:

'Tubal, go back to our camp in the Gorge of Ghosts. Take the horses and ride to Kushaf. Tell Balash I need all his swords, and bring the *kozaki* and the Kushafis through the cleft and halt them among these defiles until you get a signal from me, or know I'm dead.'

'Pteor devour Balash! What of you?'

'I go into the city.'

'You are mad!'

'Worry not, my friend. It is the only way I can get Nanaia out alive. Then we can make plans for attacking the city. If I live and am at liberty, I shall meet you here; otherwise, you and Balash follow your own judgment.'

'What do you want with this nest of fiends?'

Conan's eyes narrowed. 'I want a base for empire. We cannot stay in Iranistan nor yet return to Turan. In my hands, who knows what might not be made of this impregnable place? Now get along.'

'Balash loves me not. He'll spit in my beard, and then I'll kill him and his dogs will slay me.'

'He'll do no such thing.'

'He will not come.'

'He would come through Hell if I sent for him.'

'His men will not come; they fear devils.'

'They'll come when you tell them the devils are but men.'

Tubal tore his beard and voiced his real objection to leaving Conan. 'The swine in that city will flay you alive!'

'Nay, I'll match guile with guile. I shall be a fugitive from the wrath of the king, an outlaw seeking sanctuary.'

Tubal abandoned his argument. Grumbling in his beard, the thick-necked Shemite clambered down the crag and vanished into the defile. When he was out of sight, Conan also descended and walked toward the cliffs.

3. *The Hidden Ones*

Conan reached the foot of the cliffs and began mounting the steep road without having seen any human being. The trail wound interminably up a succession of ramps, with low, massive, cyclopean walls along the outer edges. This was no work of Ilbarsi hillmen; it looked ancient and as strong as the mountain itself.

For the last thirty feet, the ramps gave way to a flight of steep steps cut in the rock. Still no one challenged Conan. He passed through a line of low fortification along the edge of the mesa and came upon seven men squatting over a game.

At the crunch of Conan's boots on the gravel, the seven sprang to their feet, glaring wildly. They were Zuagirs – desert Shemites, lean, hawk-nosed warriors with fluttering kaffias over their heads and the hilts of daggers and scimitars protruding from their sashes. They snatched up the javelins they had laid beside them and poised them to throw.

Conan showed no surprise, halting and eyeing them tranquilly. The Zuagirs, as uncertain as cornered wildcats, merely glared.

'Conan!' exclaimed the tallest of the Zuagirs, his eyes ablaze with fear and suspicion. 'What do you here?'

Conan ran his eyes over them all and replied: 'I seek your master.'

This did not seem to reassure them. They muttered among themselves, moving their javelin arms back and forth as if to try for a cast. The tall Zuagir's voice rose:

'You chatter like crows! This thing is plain: We were gambling and did not see him come. We have failed in our duty. If it is known, there will be punishment. Let us slay him and throw him over the cliff.'

'Aye,' agreed Conan. 'Try it. And when your master asks: "Where is Conan, who brought me important news?" say "Lo, you did not consult with us about this man, so we slew him to teach you a lesson!"'

They winced at the irony. One growled: 'Spear him; none will know.'

'Nay! If we fail to bring him down with the first cast, he'll be among us like a wolf among sheep.'

'Seize him and cut his throat!' suggested the youngest of the band. The others scowled so murderously at him that he fell back in confusion.

'Aye, cut my throat,' taunted Conan, hitching the hilt of his scimitar around within easy reach. 'One of you might even live to tell of it!'

'Knives are silent,' muttered the youngster. He was rewarded by a javelin butt driven into his belly, which doubled him up gasping. Having vented some of their spleen on their tactless comrade, the Zuagirs grew calmer. The tall one asked Conan:

'You are expected?'

'Would I come otherwise? Does the lamb thrust his head unbidden into the lion's maw?'

'Lamb!' The Zuagir cackled. 'More like a gray wolf with blood on his fangs.'

'If there is fresh-spilt blood, it is but that of fools who disobeyed their master. Last night, in the Gorge of Ghosts—'

'By Hanuman! Was it you the Sabatean fools fought? They said they had slain a Vendhyan merchant and his servants in the gorge.'

So that was why the sentries were careless! For some reason the Sabateans had lied about the outcome of the battle, and the Watchers of the Road were not expecting pursuit.

'None of you was among them?' said Conan.

'Do we limp? Do we bleed? Do we weep from weariness and wounds? Nay, we have not fought Conan!'

'Then be wise and make not their mistake. Will you take me to him who awaits me, or will you cast dung in his beard by scorning his commands?'

'The gods forbid!' said the tall Zuagir. 'No order has been given us concerning you. But if this be a lie, our master shall see to your death, and if be not a lie, then we can have no blame. Give up your weapons and we will take you to him.'

Conan gave up his weapons. Ordinarily he would have

130

fought to the death before letting himself be disarmed, but now he was gambling for large stakes. The leader straightened up the young Zuagir with a kick in the rump, told him to watch the Stair as if his life depended on it; then barked orders at the others.

As they closed around the unarmed Cimmerian, Conan knew their hands itched to thrust a knife into his back. But he had sown the seeds of uncertainty in their primitive minds, so that they dared not strike.

They started along the wide road that led to the city. Conan asked casually: 'The Sabateans passed into the city just before dawn?'

'Aye,' was the terse reply.

'They couldn't march fast,' mused Conan. 'They had wounded men to carry, and the girl, their prisoner, to drag.'

One man began: 'Why, as to the girl—'

The tall leader barked him to silence and turned a baleful gaze on Conan. 'Do not answer him. If he mocks us, retort not. A serpent is less crafty. If we converse with him he'll have us beguiled ere we reach Yanaidar.'

Conan noted the name of the city, confirming the legend Balash had told him. 'Why mistrust me?' he demanded. 'Have I not come with open hands?'

'Aye!' The Zuagir laughed mirthlessly. 'Once I saw you come to the Hyrkanian masters of Khorusun with open hands, but when you closed those hands the streets ran red. Nay, Conan, I know you of old, from the days when you led your outlaws over the steppes of Turan. I cannot match my wits against yours, but I can keep my tongue between my teeth. You shall not snare and blind me with words. I'll not speak, and if any of my men answer you I will break his head.'

'I thought I knew you,' said Conan. 'You are Antar the son of Adi. You were a stout fighter.'

The Zuagir's scarred face lighted at the praise. Then he recollected himself, scowled, swore at one of his unoffending men, and marched stiffly ahead of the party.

Conan strolled with the air of a man walking amidst an escort of honor, and his bearing affected the warriors. By the time they reached the city they were carrying their javelins on their shoulders instead of poised for a thrust at Conan.

The secret of the plant life became apparent as they neared Yanaidar. Soil, laboriously brought from distant valleys, had been used to fill the many depressions pitting the surface of the plateau. An elaborate system of deep, narrow irrigation-ditches, originating in some natural water supply near the center of the city, threaded the gardens. Sheltered by a ring of peaks, the plateau would present a milder climate than was common in these mountains.

The road ran between large orchards and entered the city proper – lines of flat-roofed stone houses fronting each other across the wide, paved main street, each with an expanse of garden behind it. At the far end of the street began a half-mile of ravine-gashed plain separating the city from the mountain that frowned above and behind it. The plateau was like a great shelf jutting out from the massive slope.

Men working in the gardens or loitering along the street stared at the Zuagirs and their captive. Conan saw Iranistanis, Hyrkanians, Shemites, and even a few Vendhyans and black Kushites. But no Ilbarsis; evidently the mixed population had no connection with the native mountaineers.

The street widened into a *suk* closed on the south side by a broad wall, which enclosed the palatial building with the gorgeous dome.

There was no guard at the massive, bronze-barred, goldworked gates, only a gay-clad Negro who bowed deeply as he opened the portals. Conan and his escort came into a broad courtyard paved with colored tile, in the midst of which a fountain bubbled and pigeons fluttered. East and west, the court was bounded by inner walls, over which peeped the foliage of more gardens. Conan noticed a slim tower, which rose as high as the dome itself, its lacy tile work gleaming in the sunlight.

The Zuagirs marched across the court until they were halted on the pillared portico of the palace by a guard of thirty Hyrkanians, resplendent in plumed helmets of silvered steel, gilded corselets, rhinoceros-hide shields, and gold-chased scimitars. The hawk-faced captain of the guard conversed briefly with Antar the son of Adi. Conan divined from their manner that no love was lost between the two.

Then the captain, who was addressed as Zahak, gestured with his slim yellow hand, and Conan was surrounded by a dozen glittering Hyrkanians and marched up the broad marble steps and through the wide arch whose doors stood open. The Zuagirs, looking unhappy, followed.

They passed through wide, dimly-lit halls, from the vaulted and fretted ceilings of which hung smoking bronze censers, while on either hand velvet-curtained alcoves hinted at inner mysteries. Mystery and intangible menace lurked in those dim, gorgeous halls.

Presently they emerged into a broader hallway and approached a double-valved bronze door, flanked by even more gorgeously-clad guardsmen. These stood impassively as statues while the Hyrkanians strode by with their captive or guest and entered a semi-circular room. Here dragon-worked tapestries covered the walls, hiding all possible apertures except the one by which they had entered. Golden lamps hung from an arched ceiling fretted with gold and ebony.

Opposite the great doorway stood a marble dais. On the dais stood a great canopied chair, scrolled and carved like a throne, and on the velvet cushions which littered the seat sat a slender figure in a pearl-sewn robe. On the rose-colored turban glistened a great golden brooch in the shape of a hand gripping a wavy-bladed dagger. The face beneath the turban was oval, light-brown, with a small, pointed black beard. Conan guessed the man to be from farther east, Vendhya or Kosala. The dark eyes stared at a piece of carven crystal on a pedestal in front of the man, a piece the size of Conan's fist, roughly spherical but faceted like a great gem. It glittered with an intensity not accounted for by the lights of the throne room, as if a mystical fire burned in its depths.

On either side of the throne stood a giant Kushite. They were like images carved of black basalt, naked but for sandals and silken loincloths, with broad-tipped tulwars in their hands.

'Who is this?' languidly inquired the man on the throne in Hyrkanian.

'Conan the Cimmerian, my lord!' answered Zahak with a swagger.

The dark eyes quickened with interest, then sharpened with suspicion. 'How comes he into Yanaidar unannounced?'

'The Zuagir dogs who watch the Stair say he came to them, swearing that he had been sent for by the Magus of the Sons of Yezm.'

Conan stiffened at that title, his blue eyes fixed with fierce intensity on the oval face. But he did not speak. There was a time for silence as well as for bold speech. His next move depended upon the Magus' words. They might brand him as an impostor and doom him. But Conan depended on the belief that no ruler would order him slain without trying to learn why he was there, and the fact that few rulers wholly trust their own followers.

After a pause, the man on the throne spoke: 'This is the law of Yanaidar: No man may ascend the Stair unless he makes the Sign so the Watchers of the Stair can see. If he does not know the Sign, the Warder of the Gate must be summoned to converse with the stranger before he may mount the Stair. Conan was not announced. The Warder of the Gate was not summoned. Did Conan make the Sign, below the Stair?'

Antar sweated, shot a venomous glance at Conan, and spoke in a voice harsh with apprehension: 'The guard in the cleft did not give warning. Conan appeared upon the cliff before we saw him, though we were vigilant as eagles. He is a magician who makes himself invisible at will. We knew he spoke truth when he said you had sent for him, otherwise he could not have known the Secret Way—'

Perspiration beaded the Zuagir's narrow forehead. The man on the throne did not seem to hear his voice. Zahak struck Antar savagely in the mouth with his open hand. 'Dog, be silent until the Magus deigns to command your speech!'

Antar reeled, blood starting down his beard, and looked black murder at the Hyrkanian, but said nothing. The Magus moved his hand languidly, saying:

'Take the Zuagirs away. Keep them under guard until further orders. Even if a man is expected, the Watchers should not be surprised. Conan did not know the Sign, yet

134

he climbed the Stair unhindered. If they had been vigilant, not even Conan could have done this. He is no wizard. You may go. I will talk to Conan alone.'

Zahak bowed and led his glittering swordsmen away between the silent files of warriors lined on each side of the door, herding the shivering Zuagirs before them. These turned as they passed and fixed their burning eyes on Conan in a silent glare of hatred.

Zahak pulled the bronze doors shut behind them. The Magus spoke in Iranistani to Conan: 'Speak freely. These black men do not understand Iranistani.'

Conan, before replying, kicked a divan up before the dais and settled himself comfortably on it, with his feet propped up on a velvet footstool. The Magus showed no surprise that his visitor should seat himself unbidden. His first words showed that he had had much dealings with Westerners and had, for his own purposes, adopted some of their directness. He said: 'I did not send for you.'

'Of course not. But I had to tell those fools something or else slay them all.'

'What do you want here?'

'What does any man want who comes to a nest of outlaws?'

'He might come as a spy.'

Conan gave a rumbling laugh. 'For whom?'

'How did you know the Road?'

'I followed the vultures; they always lead me to my goal.'

'They should; you have fed them full often enough. What of the Khitan who watched the cleft?'

'Dead; he wouldn't listen to reason.'

'The vultures follow you, not you the vultures,' commented the Magus. 'Why sent you no word to me of your coming?'

'By whom? Last night in the Gorge of Ghosts a band of your fools fell upon my party, slew one, and carried another away. The fourth man was frightened and fled, so I came on alone when the moon rose.'

'They were Sabateans, whose duty it is to watch the Gorge of Ghosts. They did not know you sought me. They limped into the city at dawn, with one dying and most of the others wounded, and swore they had slain a

135

rich Vendhyan merchant and his servants in the Gorge of Ghosts. Evidently they feared to admit that they ran away leaving you alive. They shall smart for their lie, but you have not told me why you came here.'

'For refuge. The King of Iranistan and I have fallen out.'

The Magus shrugged. 'I know about that. Kobad Shah will not molest you for some time, if ever. He was wounded by one of our agents. However, the squadron he sent after you is still on your trail.'

Conan felt the prickling at his nape that magic aroused in him. 'Crom! You keep up to date on the news.'

The Magus gave a tiny nod towards the crystal. 'A toy, but not without its uses. However, we have kept our secret well. Therefore, since you knew of Yanaidar and the Road to Yanaidar, you must have been told of it by one of the Brotherhood. Did the Tiger send you?'

Conan recognized the trap. 'I know no Tiger,' he answered. 'I need not be told secrets; I learn them for myself. I came here because I had to have a hiding place. I'm out of favor at Anshan, and the Turanians would impale me if they caught me.'

The Magus said something in Stygian. Conan, knowing he would not change the language of their conversation without a reason, feigned ignorance.

The Magus spoke to one of the blacks, and that giant drew a silver hammer from his girdle and smote a golden gong hanging by the tapestries. The echoes had scarcely died away when the bronze doors opened long enough to admit a slim man in plain silken robes, who bowed before the dais – a Stygian from his shaven head. The Magus addressed him as 'Khaza' and questioned him in the tongue he had just tested on Conan. Khaza replied in the same language.

'Do you know this man?' said the Magus.

'Aye, my lord.'

'Have our spies included him in their reports?'

'Aye, my lord. The last dispatch from Anshan bore word of him. On the night that your servant tried to execute the king, this man talked with the king secretly an hour or so before the attack. After leaving the palace hurriedly he fled from the city with his three hundred horsemen and was last seen riding along the road to Kushaf. He was pursued by horsemen from Anshan, but whether these gave up the chase or still seek him I know not.'

'You have my leave to go.'

Khaza bowed and departed, and the Magus meditated for a space. Then he lifted his head and said: 'I believe you speak the truth. You fled from Anshan to Kushaf, where no friend of the king would be welcome. Your enmity toward the Turanians is well-known. We need such a man. But I cannot initiate you until the Tiger passes on you. He is not now in Yanaidar but will be here by tomorrow's dawn. Meanwhile I should like to know how you learned of our society and our city.'

Conan shrugged. 'I hear the secrets the wind sings as it blows through the branches of the dry tamarisks, and the tales the men of the caravans whispered about the dung-fires in the serais.'

'Then you know our purpose? Our ambition?'

'I know what you call yourselves.' Conan, groping his way, made his answer purposely ambiguous.

'Do you know what my title means?' asked the Magus.

'Magus of the Sons of Yezm – magician-in-chief of the Yezmites. In Turan they say the Yezmites were a pre-Catastrophic race who lived on the shores of the Vilayet Sea and practiced strange rites, with sorcery and cannibalism, before the coming of the Hyrkanians, who destroyed the last remnants of them.'

'So they say,' sneered the Magus. 'But their descendants still dwell in the hills of Shem.'

'So I suspected,' said Conan. 'I've heard tales of them, but until now I scorned them as legends.'

'Aye! The world deems them legends – but since the Beginning of Happenings the Fire of Yezm has not been wholly extinguished, though for centuries it smoldered to glowing embers. The Society of the Hidden Ones is the oldest cult of all. It lies behind the worship of Mitra, Ishtar, and Asura. It recognizes no difference in race or religion. In the ancient past its branches extended all over the world, from Grondar to Valusia. Men of many lands and races belong and have belonged to the society of the Hidden Ones. In the long, long ago the Yezmites were only one branch, though from their race the priests of the cult were chosen.

'After the Catastrophe, the cult reestablished itself. In Stygia, Acheron, Koth, and Zamora were bands of the cult, cloaked in mystery and only half-suspected by the races among which they dwelt. But, as the millennia passed, these groups became isolated and fell apart, each branch going its separate way and each dwindling in strength because of lack of unity.

'In olden days, the Hidden Ones swayed the destinies of empires. They did not lead armies in the field, but they fought by poison and fire and the flame-bladed dagger that bit in the dark. Their scarlet-cloaked emissaries of death went forth to do the bidding of the Magus of the Sons of Yezm, and kings died in Luxur, in Python, in Kuthchemes, in Dagon.

'And I am a descendant of that one who was Magus of Yezm in the days of Tuthamon, he whom all the world feared!' A fanatical gleam lit the dark eyes. 'Throughout my youth I dreamed of the former greatness of the cult, into which I was initiated as a child. Wealth that flowed from the mines of my estate made the dream a reality. Virata of Kosala became the Magus of the Sons of Yezm, the first to hold the title in five hundred years.

'The creed of the Hidden Ones is broad and deep as the sea, uniting men of opposing sects. Strand by strand I drew together and united the separate branches of the cult: the Zugites, the Jhilites, the Erlikites, the Yezudites. My emissaries traveled the world seeking members of the ancient society and finding them – in teeming cities, among barren mountains, in the silence of upland deserts. Slowly, surely, my band has grown, for I have not only united all the various branches of the cult but have also gained new recruits among the bold and desperate spirits of a score of races and sects. All are one before the Fire of Yezm; I have among my followers worshippers of Gullah, Set, and Mitra; of Derketo, Ishtar, and Yun.

'Ten years ago, I came with my followers to this city, then a crumbling mass of ruins, unknown to the hillmen because their superstitious legends made them shun this region. The buildings were crumbled stone, the canals filled with rubble, and the groves grown wild and tangled.

It took six years to rebuild it. Most of my fortune went into the labor, for bringing material hither in secret was tedious and dangerous work. We brought it out of Iranistan, over the old caravan route from the South and up an ancient ramp on the western side of the plateau which I have since destroyed. But at last I looked upon forgotten Yanaidar as it was in the days of old.

'Look!'

He rose and beckoned. The giant blacks closed in on each side of the Magus as he led the way into an alcove hidden behind a tapestry. They stood in a latticed balcony looking down into a garden enclosed by a fifteen-foot wall. This wall was almost completely masked by thick shrubbery. An exotic fragrance rose from masses of trees, shrubs and blossoms, and silvery fountains tinkled. Conan saw women moving among the trees, scantily clad in filmy silk and jewel-crusted velvet – slim, supple girls, mostly Vendhyan, Iranistani, and Shemite. Men, looking as if they were drugged, lay under the trees on silken cushions. Music wailed melodiously.

'This is the Paradise Garden, such as was used by the Magi of old times,' said Virata, closing the casement and turning back into the throne room. 'Those who serve me well are drugged with the juice of the purple lotus. Awakening in this garden with the fairest women of the world to serve them, they think they are in truth in the heaven promised for those who die serving the Magus.' The Kosalan smiled thinly. 'I show you this because I will not have you "taste Paradise" like these. You are not such a fool as to be duped so easily. It does no harm for you to know these secrets. If the Tiger does not approve of you, your knowledge will die with you; if he does, you have learned no more than you would in any event as one of the Sons of the Mountain.

'You can rise high in my empire. I shall become as mighty as my ancestor. Six years I prepared; then I began to strike. Within the last four years, my followers have gone forth with poisoned daggers as they went forth in the old days, knowing no law but my will, incorruptible, invincible, seeking death rather than life.'

'And your ultimate ambition?'

'Have you not guessed it?' The Kosalan almost whispered it, his eyes wide and blank with fanaticism.

'Who wouldn't?' grunted Conan. 'But I had rather hear it from you.'

'I shall rule the world! Sitting here in Yanaidar, I shall control its destinies! Kings on their thrones shall be but puppets dancing on my strings. Those who disobey my commands shall die. Soon none will dare disobey. Power will be mine. Power! Yajur! What is greater?'

Conan silently compared the Magus' boasts of absolute power with the rôle of the mysterious Tiger who must decide Conan's fate. Virata's authority was evidently not supreme after all.

'Where is the girl, Nanaia?' he demanded. 'Your Sabateans carried her away after they murdered my lieutenant Hattusas.'

Virata's expression of surprise was overdone. 'I know not to whom you refer. They brought back no captive.'

Conan was sure he was lying but realized it would be useless to press the question further now. He thought of various reasons why Virata should deny knowledge of the girl, all disquieting.

The Magus motioned to the black, who again smote the gong. Again Khaza entered, bowing.

'Khaza will show you to your chamber,' said Virata. 'There food and drink will be brought you. You are not a prisoner; no guard will be placed over you. But I must ask you not to leave your chamber unescorted. My men are suspicious of outsiders, and until you are initiated . . .' He let the sentence trail off into meaningful silence.

4. *Whispering Swords*

The impassive Stygian led Conan through the bronze doors, past the files of glittering guards, and along a narrow corridor, which branched off from the broad hallway. He conducted Conan into a chamber with a domed ceiling of ivory and sandalwood and one heavy, brass-bound, teakwood door. There were no windows; air and light came through apertures in the dome. The walls were hung with rich tapestries; the floor was hidden by cushion-strewn rugs.

Khaza bowed himself out without a word, shutting the door behind him. Conan seated himself on a velvet divan. This was the most bizarre situation he had found himself in during a life packed with wild and bloody adventures. He brooded over the fate of Nanaia and wondered at his next step.

Sandaled feet padded in the corridor. Khaza entered, followed by a huge Negro bearing viands in golden dishes and at golden jug of wine. Before Khaza closed the door, Conan had a glimpse of the spike of a helmet protruding from the tapestries before an alcove on the opposite side of the corridor. Virata had lied when he said no guard would be placed to watch him, which was no more than Conan expected.

'Wine of Kyros, my lord, and food,' said the Stygian. 'Presently a maiden beautiful as the dawn shall be sent to entertain you.'

'Good,' grunted Conan.

Khaza motioned the slave to set down the food. He himself tasted each dish and sipped liberally of the wine before bowing himself out. Conan, alert as a trapped wolf, noted that the Stygian tasted the wine last and stumbled a little as he left the chamber. When the door closed behind the men, Conan smelled of the wine. Mingled with the bouquet of the wine, so faint that only his keen barbarian nostrils could have detected it, was an aromatic odor he recognized. It was that of the purple lotus of the sullen swamps of southern Stygia, which induced a deep slumber for a short or a long time depending on the quantity. The taster had to hurry from the room before he was overcome. Conan wondered if Virata meant to convey him to the Paradise Garden after all.

Investigation convinced him that the food had not been tampered with, and he fell to with gusto.

He had scarcely finished the meal, and was staring at the tray hungrily as if in hope of finding something more to eat, when the door opened again. A slim, supple figure slipped in: a girl in golden breast-plates, a jewel-crusted girdle, and filmy silk trousers.

'Who are you?' growled Conan.

141

The girl shrank back, her brown skin paling. 'Oh, sire, do not hurt me! I have done nothing!' Her dark eyes were dilated with fear and excitement; her words tumbled over one another, and her fingers fluttered childishly.

'Who said anything about hurting you? I asked who you were.'

'I – am called Parusati.'

'How did you get here?'

'They stole me, my lord, the Hidden Ones, one night as I walked in my father's garden in Ayodhya. By secret, devious ways they brought me to this city of devils, to be a slave with the other girls they steal out of Vendhya and Iranistan and other lands.' She hurried on. 'I have d-dwelt here for a month. I have almost died of shame! I have been whipped! I have seen other girls die of torture. Oh, what shame for my father, that his daughter should be made a slave of devil worshipers!'

Conan said nothing, but the red glint in his blue eyes was eloquent. Though his own career had been red-spattered with slaying and rapine, towards women he possessed a rough, barbaric code of chivalry. Up till now he had toyed with the idea of actually joining Virata's cult – in hope of working up and making himself master of it, if need be by killing those above him. Now his intentions crystallized on the destruction of this den of snakes and the conversion of their lair to his own uses. Parusati continued:

'Today the Master of the Girls came to send a girl to you to learn if you had any hidden weapon. She was to search you while you lay in drugged stupor. Then, when you awoke, she was to beguile you to learn if you were a spy or a true man. He chose me for the task. I was terrified, and when I found you awake all my resolution melted. Do not slay me!'

Conan grunted. He would not have hurt a hair of her head, but he did not choose to tell her so just yet. Her terror could be useful. 'Parusati, do you know anything of a woman who was brought in earlier by a band of Sabateans?'

'Yes, my lord! They brought her here captive to make another pleasure girl like the rest of us. But she is strong, and after they reached the city and delivered her into the hands of the Hyrkanian guards, she broke free, snatched a dagger, and slew the brother of Zahak. Zahak demanded her life, and he is too powerful even for Virata to refuse in this matter.'

'So that's why the Magus lied about Nanaia,' muttered Conan.

'Aye, my lord. Nanaia lies in a dungeon below the palace, and tomorrow she is to be given to the Hyrkanian for torture and execution.'

Conan's dark face became sinister. 'Lead me tonight to Zahak's sleeping quarters,' he demanded, his narrowed eyes betraying his deadly intention.

'Nay, he sleeps among his warriors, all proven swordsmen of the steppes, too many even for so mighty a fighter as you. But I can lead you to Nanaia.'

'What of the guard in the corridor?'

'He will not see us, and he will not admit anyone else here until he has seen me depart.'

'Well, then?' Conan rose to his feet like a tiger setting out on its hunt.

Parusati hesitated. 'My lord – do I read your mind rightly, that you mean, not to join these devils, but to destroy them?'

Conan grinned wolfishly. 'You might say accidents have a way of happening to those I like not.'

'Then will you promise not to harm me, and if you can to free me?'

'If I can. Now let's not waste more time in chatter. Lead on.'

Parusati drew aside a tapestry on the wall opposite the door and pressed on the arabesqued design. A panel swung inward, revealing a narrow stair that slanted down into lightless depths.

'The masters think their slaves do not know their secrets,' she muttered. 'Come.'

She led the way into the stair, closing the panel after them. Conan found himself in darkness that was almost complete, save for a few gleams of light through holes in the panel. They descended until Conan guessed that they were well beneath the palace and then struck a narrow, level tunnel, which ran away from the foot of the stair.

'A Kshatriya who planned to flee Yanaidar showed me this secret way,' she said. 'I planned to escape with him. We hid food and weapons here. He was caught and tortured, but died without betraying me. Here is the sword he hid.' She fumbled in a niche and drew out a blade, which she gave to Conan.

A few moments later they reached an iron-bound door, and Parusati, gesturing for caution, drew Conan to it and showed him a tiny aperture to peer through. He looked down a wide corridor, flanked on one side by a blank wall in which showed a single ebon door, curiously ornate and heavily bolted, and on the other by a row of cells with barred doors. The other end of the corridor was not far distant and was closed by another heavy door. Archaic hanging bronze lamps cast a mellow glow.

Before one of the cell doors stood a resplendent Hyrkanian in glittering corselet and plumed helmet, scimitar in hand. Parusati's fingers tightened on Conan's arm.

'Nanaia is in that cell,' she whispered. 'Can you slay the Hyrkanian? He is a mighty swordsman.'

With a grim smile, Conan tried the balance of the blade she had given him – a long Vendhyan steel, light but well nigh unbreakable. Conan did not stop to explain that he was master alike of the straight blades of the West and the curved blades of the east, of the double-curved Ilbarsi knife and the leaf-shaped broadsword of Shem. He opened the secret door.

As he stepped into the corridor, Conan glimpsed the face of Nanaia staring through the bars behind the Hyrkanian. The hinges creaked, and the guard whirled catlike, lips drawn back in a snarl, and then instantly came to the attack.

Conan met him halfway, and the two women witnessed a play of swords that would have burned the blood of kings. The only sounds were the quick soft shuffle and thud of feet, the slither and rasp of steel, and the breathing of the fighters. The long, light blades flickered lethally in the illusive light, like living things, parts of the men who wielded them.

The hairline balance shifted. The Hyrkanian's lip curled in ferocious recognition of defeat and desperate resolve to take his enemy into death with him. A louder ring of blades, a flash of steel – and Conan's flickering blade seemed to caress his enemy's neck in passing. Then the Hyrkanian was stretched on the floor, his neck half severed. He had died without a cry.

Conan stood over him for an instant, the sword in his hand stained with a thread of crimson. His tunic had been torn open, and his muscular breast rose and fell easily. Only a film of sweat glistening there and on his brow betrayed the strain of his exertions. He tore a bunch of keys from the dead man's girdle, and the grate of steel in the lock seemed to awaken Nanaia from a trance.

'Conan! I had given up hope, but you came. What a fight! Would that I could have struck a blow in it!' The tall girl stepped forth lightly and picked up the Hyrkanian's sword. 'What now?'

'We shan't have a chance if we make a break before dark,' said Conan. 'Nanaia, how soon will another guard come to relieve the man I killed?'

'They change the guard every four hours. His watch had just begun.'

Conan turned to Parusati. 'What time of day is it? I have not seen the sun since early this morning.'

The Vendhyan girl said: 'It is well into the afternoon. Sundown should be within four hours.'

Conan perceived he had been in Yanaidar longer than he had realized. 'As soon as it's dark, we'll try to get away. We'll go back to my chamber now. Nanaia shall hide on the secret stair, while Parusati goes out the door and back to the girls' apartments.'

'But when the guard comes to relieve this one,' said Nanaia, 'he'll see I have escaped. You should leave me here till you're ready to go, Conan.'

'I dare not risk it; I might not be able to get you out then. When they find you gone, maybe the confusion will help us. We'll hide this body.'

He turned toward the curiously decorated door, but Parusati gasped: 'Not that way, my lord! Would you open the door to Hell?'

'What mean you? What lies beyond that door?'

'I know not. The bodies of executed men and women, and wretches who have been tortured but still live, are carried through this door. What becomes of them I do not know, but I have heard them scream more terribly than they did under torture. The girls say a man-eating demon has his lair beyond that door.'

'That may be,' said Nanaia. 'But some hours ago a slave came through here to hurl through that door something which was neither a man nor a woman, though what it was I could not see.'

'It was doubtless an infant,' said Parusati with a shudder.

'I'll tell you,' said Conan. 'We'll dress this body in your clothes and lay it in the cell, with the face turned away from the door. You're a big girl, and they will fit him. When the other guard comes, maybe he'll think it is you, asleep or dead, and start looking for the guard instead of you. The longer before they find you've escaped, the more time we shall have.'

Without hesitation, Nanaia slipped out of her jacket, whipped her shirt off over her head, and dropped her trousers while Conan pulled the clothes off the Hyrkanian. Parusati gave a gasp of shock.

'What's the matter, don't you know what a naked human being looks like?' snarled Conan. 'Help me with this.'

In a few minutes Nanaia was dressed in the Hyrkanian's garments, all but the helmet and corselet. She dabbed ineffectively at the blood that soaked the upper part of the longsleeved coat while Conan dragged the Hyrkanian, in Nanaia's clothes, into the cell. He turned the dead man's face down and toward the wall so that its wisp of beard and mustache should not show and pulled Nanaia's shirt up over the ghastly wound in the neck. Conan locked the cell-door behind him and handed the keys to Nanaia. He said:

'There's nothing we can do about the blood on the floor. I have no definite plan for escaping the city yet. If I can't get away I'll kill Virata – and the rest will be in Crom's hands. If you two get out and I don't, try to go back along the trail and meet the Kushafis as they come. I sent Tubal after them at dawn, so he should reach Kushaf after nightfall, and the Kushafis should get to the canyon below the plateau tomorrow morning.'

They returned to the secret door, which, when closed, looked like part of the blank stone wall. They traversed the tunnel and groped their way up the stair.

'Here you must hide until the time comes,' said Conan to

146

Nanaia. 'Keep the swords; they'll do me no good until then. If anything happens to me, open the panel-door and try to get away, with Parusati if she comes for you.'

'As you will, Conan.' Nanaia seated herself cross-legged on the topmost step.

When Conan and Parusati were back in the chamber, Conan said: 'Go now; if you stay too long, they may get suspicious. Contrive to return to me here as soon as it is well dark. I think I'm to stay here till this fellow Tiger returns. When you come back, tell the guard the Magus sent you. I'll attend to him when we are ready to go. And tell them you saw me drink this drugged wine, and that you searched me without finding any arms.'

'Aye, my lord! I will return after dark.' The girl was trembling with fear and excitement as she left.

Conan took up the winejug and smeared just enough wine on his mouth to make a detectable scent. Then he emptied the contents in a nook behind the tapestries and threw himself on his divan as if asleep.

In a few moments the door opened again and a girl entered. Conan did not open his eyes, but he knew it was a girl by the light rustle of her bare feet and the scent of her perfume, just as he knew by the same evidences that it was not Parusati returning. Evidently the Magus did not place too much trust in any one woman. Conan did not believe she had been sent there to slay him – poison in the wine would have been enough – so he did not risk peering through slitted lids.

That the girl was afraid was evident by the quick tremor of her breathing. Her nostrils all but touched his lips as she sniffed to detect the drugged wine on his breath. Her soft hands stole over him, searching for hidden weapons. Then with a sigh of relief she glided away.

Conan relaxed. It would be hours before he could make any move, so he might as well snatch sleep when he could. His life and those of the girls depended on his being able to find or make a way out of the city that night. In the meantime, he slept as soundly as if he lay in the house of a friend.

5. *The Mask Falls*

Conan awoke the instant a hand touched the door to his room, and came to his feet, fully alert, as Khaza entered with a bow. The Stygian said:

'The Magus of the Sons of Yezm desires your presence, my lord. The Tiger has returned.'

So the Tiger had returned sooner than the Magus had expected! Conan felt a premonitory tenseness as he followed the Stygian out of the chamber. Khaza did not lead him back to the chamber where the Magus had first received him. He was conducted through a winding corridor to a gilded door before which stood a Hyrkanian swordsman. This man opened the door, and Khaza hurried Conan across the threshold. The door closed behind them. Conan halted.

He stood in a broad room without windows but with several doors. Across the chamber, the Magus lounged on a divan with his black slaves behind him. Clustered about him were a dozen armed men of various races: Zuagirs, Hyrkanians, Iranistanis, Shemites, and even a villainous-looking Kothian, the first Hyborian that Conan had seen in Yanaidar.

But the Cimmerian spared these men only the briefest glance. His attention was fixed on the man who dominated the scene. This man stood between him and the Magus' divan, with the wide-legged stance of a horseman. He was as tall as Conan, though not so massive. His shoulders were broad; his supple figure hard as steel and springy as whalebone. A short black beard failed to hide the aggressive jut of his lean jaw, and grey eyes cold and piercing gleamed under his tall Zaporoskan fur cap. Tight breeches emphasized his leanness. One hand caressed the hilt of his jeweled saber; the other stroked his thin mustache.

Conan knew the game was up. For this was Olgerd Vladislav, a Zaporoskan adventurer, who knew Conan too well to be deceived. He would hardly have forgotten how Conan had forced him out of the leadership of a band of Zuagirs and given him a broken arm as a farewell gift, less than three years previously.

'This man desires to join us,' said Virata.

The man they called the Tiger smiled thinly. 'It would

148

be safer to bed with a leopard. I know Conan of old. He'll worm his way into your band, turn the men against you, and run you through when you least expect it.'

The eyes fixed on the Cimmerian grew murderous. No more than the Tiger's word was needed to convince his men.

Conan laughed. He had done what he could with guile and subtlety, and now the game was up. He could drop the mask from the untamed soul of the berserk barbarian and plunge into the bright madness of battle without doubts or regrets.

The Magus made a gesture of repudiation. 'I defer to your judgment in these matters, Tiger. Do what you will; he is unarmed.'

At the assurance of the helplessness of their prey, wolfish cruelty sharpened the faces of the warriors. Edged steel slid into view. Olgerd said:

'Your end will be interesting. Let us see if you are still as stoical as when you hung on the cross in Khauran. Bind him, men—'

As he spoke, the Zaporoskan reached for his saber in a leisurely manner, as if he had forgotten just how dangerous the black-haired barbarian could be, what savage quickness lurked in Conan's massive thews. Before Olgerd could draw his sword, Conan sprang and struck as a panther slashes. The impact of his clenched fist was like that of a sledgehammer. Olgerd went down, blood spurting from his jaw.

Before Conan could snatch the Zaporoskan's sword, the Kothian was upon him. Only he had realized Conan's deadly quickness and ferocity, and even he had not been swift enough to save Olgerd. But he kept Conan from securing the saber, for he had to whirl and grapple as the three-foot Ilbarsi knife rose above him. Conan caught the knife wrist as it fell, checking the stroke in mid-air, the iron sinews springing out of his own wrist in the effort. His right hand ripped a dagger from the Kothian's girdle and sank it to the hilt under his ribs almost with the same motion. The Kothian groaned and sank down dying, and Conan wrenched away the long knife as he crumpled.

All this had happened in a stunning explosion of speed, embracing a mere tick of time. Olgerd was down and the Kothian dying before the others could get into action. When they did, they were met by the yard-long knife in the hand of the most terrible knife fighter of the Hyborian Age.

Even as Conan whirled to meet the rush, the long blade licked out and a Zuagir went down, choking out his life through a severed jugular. A Hyrkanian shrieked, disemboweled. A Stygian overreached with a ferocious dagger lunge and reeled away, clutching the crimson-gushing stump of a wrist.

Conan did not put his back to the wall this time. He sprang into the thick of his foes, wielding his dripping knife murderously. They swirled and milled about him. He was the center of a whirlwind of blades that flickered and lunged and slashed, and yet somehow missed their mark again and again as he shifted his position constantly and so swiftly that he baffled the eye which sought to follow him. Their numbers hindered them; they cut thin air and gashed one another, confused by his speed and demoralized by the wolfish ferocity of his onslaught.

At such deadly close quarters, the long knife was more effective than the scimitars and tulwars. Conan had mastered its every use, whether the downward swing that splits a skull or the upward rip that spills out a man's entrails.

It was butcher's work, but Conan made no false motion. He waded through that mêlée of straining bodies and lashing blades like a typhoon, leaving a red wake behind him.

The mêlée lasted only a moment. Then the survivors gave back, stunned and appalled by the havoc wrought among them. Conan wheeled and located the Magus against the farther wall between the stolid Kushites. Then, even as his leg-muscles tensed for a leap, a shout brought him around.

A group of Hyrkanian guardsmen appeared at the door opening into the corridor, drawing thick, double-curved bows to the chin, while those in the room scurried out of the way. Conan's hesitation lasted no longer than an eyeblink, while the archers' right arms, bulging with taut muscles, drew back their bowsprings. In that flash of consciousness he weighed his chances of reaching the Magus and killing him before he himself died. He knew he would be struck in mid-leap by a half-dozen shafts, driven by the powerful compound bows of the Hyrkanian deserts, which slay at five hundred paces. Their force would tear through his light mail shirt, and their impact alone would be enough to knock him down.

As the commander of the squad of archers opened his mouth to cry 'Loose!', Conan threw himself flat on the floor. He struck just as the archers' fingers released their bowstrings. The arrows whipped through the air inches above his back, criss-crossing in their flight with a simultaneous whistling screech.

As the archers reached back for the arrows in their quivers, Conan drove his fists, still holding the knife and the dagger, downward with such force that his body flew into the air and landed on its feet again. Before the Hyrkanians could nock their second flight of arrows, Conan was among them. His tigerish rush and darting blades left a trail of writhing figures behind him. Then he was through the milling mob and racing down the corridor. He dodged through rooms and slammed doors behind him, while the uproar in the palace grew. Then he found himself racing down a narrow corridor, which ended in a cul-de-sac with a barred window.

A Himelian hillman sprang from an alcove, raising a pike. Conan came at him like a mountain storm. Daunted by the sight of the blood-stained stranger, the Himelian thrust blindly with his weapon, missed, drew it back for another stab, and screamed as Conan, maddened with battle lust, struck with murderous fury. The hillman's head jumped from his shoulders on a spurt of crimson and thudded to the floor.

Conan lunged at the window, hacked once at the bars with his knife, then gripped them with both hands and braced his legs. A heaving surge of iron strength, a savage wrench, and the bars came away in his hands with a splintering crash. He plunged through into a latticed balcony overlooking a garden. Behind him, men were storming down the corridor. An arrow swished past him. He dove at the lattice headfirst, the knife extended before him, smashed through the flimsy material without checking his flight, and landed catlike on his feet in the garden below.

The garden was empty but for half a dozen scantily-clad women, who screamed and ran. Conan raced toward the opposite wall, quartering among the low trees to avoid the arrows that rained after him. A backward glance showed the broken lattice crowded with furious faces and arms brandishing weapons. Another shout warned him of peril ahead.

A man was running along the wall, swinging a tulwar.

The fellow, a dark, fleshily-built Vendhyan, had accurately judged the point where the fugitive would reach the wall, but he himself reached that point a few seconds too late. The wall was not higher than a man's head. Conan caught the coping with one hand and swung himself up almost without checking his speed. An instant later, on his feet on the parapet, he ducked the sweep of the tulwar and drove his knife through the Vendhyan's huge belly.

The man bellowed like an ox in pain, threw his arms about his slayer in a death grip, and they went over the parapet together. Conan had only time to glimpse the sheer-walled ravine which gaped below them. They struck on its narrow lip, rolled off, and fell fifteen feet to crash to the rocky floor. As they rushed downward, Conan turned in mid-air so that the Vendhyan was under him when they hit, and the fat, limp body cushioned his fall. Even so, it jolted the breath out of him.

6. *The Haunter of the Gulches*

Conan staggered to his feet empty-handed. As he glared about, a row of turbaned and helmeted heads bobbed up along the wall. Bows appeared and arrows were nocked.

A glance showed Conan that there was no cover within leaping distance. Because of the steep angle at which the archers were shooting down at him, there was little chance that he could escape by falling flat a second time.

As the first bowstring twanged and the arrow screeched past him to splinter on the rocks, Conan threw himself down beside the body of the Vendhyan he had killed. He thrust an arm under the body and rolled the dripping, still-warm carcass over on top of himself. As he did so, a storm of arrows struck the corpse. Conan, underneath, could feel the impacts as if a gang were pounding the body with sledge-hammers. But such was the girth of the Vendhyan that the shafts failed to pierce through to Conan.

'Crom!' Conan exploded as an arrow nicked his calf.

The tattoo of impacts stopped as the Yezmites saw that they were merely feathering the corpse. Conan gathered up the thick hairy wrists of the body. He rolled to one side, so that the corpse fell squashily on to the rock beside him; sprang to his feet, and heaved the corpse up on his back. Now, as he faced away from the wall, the corpse still made a shield. His muscles quivered under the strain, for the Vendhyan weighed more than he did.

He walked away from the wall down the ravine. The Yezmites yelled as they saw their prey escaping and sent another blast of arrows after him, which struck the corpse again.

Conan slipped around the first buttress of rock and dropped the corpse. The face and the front of the body were pierced by more than a dozen arrows.

'If I had a bow, I'd show those dogs a thing or two about shooting!' Conan muttered wrathfully. He peeked around the buttress.

The wall was crowded with heads, but no more arrows came. Instead, Conan recognized Olgerd Vladislav's fur hat in the middle of the row. Olgerd shouted:

'Do you think you've escaped? Ha ha! Go on; you'll wish you had stayed in Yanaidar with my slayers. Farewell, dead man!'

With a brusque nod to his followers, Olgerd disappeared. The other heads vanished from the wall too. Conan stood alone save for the corpse at his feet.

He frowned as he peered suspiciously about him. He knew that the southern end of the plateau was cut up into a network of ravines. Obviously he was in one that ran out of that network just south of the palace. It was a straight gulch, like a giant knife-cut, ten paces wide, which issued from a maze of gullies straight toward the city, ceasing abruptly at a sheer cliff of solid stone below the garden wall from which he had fallen. This cliff was fifteen feet high and too smooth to be wholly the work of nature.

The side walls at that end of the gulch were sheer, too, showing signs of having been smoothed by tools. Across the rim of the wall at the end and for fifteen feet out on each side ran a strip of iron with short, knife-edged blades slanting down. He had missed them in his fall, but anyone trying

153

to climb over the wall would be cut to ribbons by them. The bottom of the gulch sloped down away from the city so that beyond the ends of the strips on the side walls, these walls were more than twenty feet high. Conan was in a prison, partly natural, partly manmade.

Looking down the ravine, he saw that it widened and broke into a tangle of smaller gulches, separated by ridges of solid stone, beyond and above which he saw the gaunt bulk of the mountain looming. The other end of the ravine was not blocked, but he knew his pursuers would not safeguard one end of his prison so carefully while leaving an avenue of escape open at the other.

Still, it was not his nature to resign himself to whatever fate they had planned for him. They evidently thought they had him safely trapped, but others had thought that before.

He pulled the knife out of the Vendhyan's carcass, wiped off the blood, and went down the ravine.

A hundred yards from the city wall, he came to the mouths of the smaller ravines, chose one at random, and at once found himself in a nightmarish labyrinth. Channels hollowed in the rock meandered bafflingly though a crumbling waste of stone. For the most part they ran north and south, but they merged, split, and looped chaotically. He was forever coming to the ends of blind alleys; if he climbed the walls to surmount them, it was only to descend into another equally confusing branch of the network.

As he slid down one ridge, his heel crunched something that broke with a dry crack. He had stepped upon the dried rib bone of a headless skeleton. A few yards away lay the skull, crushed and splintered. He began to stumble upon similar grisly relics with appalling frequency. Each skeleton showed broken, disjointed bones and a smashed skull. The elements could not have done that.

Conan went on warily, narrowly eyeing every spur of rock and shadowed recess. In one spot there was a faint smell of garbage, and he saw bits of melon rind and turnip lying about. In one of the few sandy spots, he saw a partly-effaced track. It was not the spoor of a leopard, bear, or tiger, such as he would have expected in this country. It looked more like the print of a bare, mis-shapen human foot.

Once he came upon a rough out-jut of rock, to which clung strands of coarse gray hair that might have rubbed

154

off against the stone. Here and there, mixed with the taint of garbage, was an unpleasant, rank odor that he could not define. It hung heavily in cavelike recesses where a beast, or man, or demon might curl up to sleep.

Baffled in his efforts to steer a straight course through the stony maze, Conan scrambled up a weathered ridge, which looked to be higher than most. Crouching on its sharp crest, he stared out over the waste. His view was limited except to the north, but the glimpses he had of sheer cliffs rising above the spurs and ridges to east, west, and south made him believe that they formed parts of a continuous wall, which enclosed the tangle of gullies. To the north, this wall was split by the ravine that ran to the outer palace garden.

Presently the nature of the labyrinth became evident. At one time or another, a section of that part of the plateau which lay between the site of the present city and the mountain had sunk, leaving a great bowl-shaped depression, and the surface of the depression had been cut up into gullies by erosion over an immense period of time.

There was no use wandering about the gulches. Conan's problem was to get to the cliffs that hemmed in the corrugated bowl and skirt them to find if there was any way to surmount them, or any break in them through which water falling on the bowl drained off. To the south he thought he could trace the route of a ravine more continuous than the others, and which ran more or less directly to the base of the mountain whose sheer wall hung over the bowl. He also saw that, to reach this ravine, he would save time by returning to the gulch below the city wall and following another of the ravines that led into it, instead of scrambling over a score of knife-edged ridges between him and the gully he wished to reach.

Therefore he climbed down the ridge and retraced his steps. The sun was swinging low as he reentered the mouth of the outer ravine and started toward the gulch that, he believed, would lead him to his goal. He glanced idly toward the cliff at the other end of the wider ravine – and stopped dead.

The body of the Vendhyan was gone, though his tulwar still lay on the rocks at the foot of the wall. Several arrows lay about as if they had fallen out of the body when it was

155

moved. A tiny gleam from the rocky floor caught Conan's eye. He ran to the place and found that it was made by a couple of silver coins.

Conan scooped up the coins and stared at them. Then he glared about with narrowed eyes. The natural explanation would be that the Yezmites had come out somehow to recover the body. But if they had, they would probably have picked up the undamaged arrows and would hardly have left money lying about.

On the other hand, if not the folk of Yanaidar, then who? Conan thought of the broken skeletons and remembered Parusati's remark about the 'door to Hell.' There was every reason to suspect that something inimical to human beings haunted this maze. What if the ornate door in the dungeon led out to this ravine?

A careful search disclosed the door whose existence Conan suspected. The thin cracks that betrayed its presence would have escaped the casual glance. On the side of the ravine, the door looked like the material of the cliff and fitted perfectly. Conan thrust powerfully at it, but it did not yield. He remembered its heavy, metal-bound construction and stout bolts. It would take a battering-ram to shake that door. The strength of the door, together with the projecting blades overhead, implied that the Yezmites were taking no chances that the haunter of the gulches might get into their city. On the other hand, there was comfort in the thought that it must be a creature of flesh and blood, not a demon against whom bolts and spikes would be of no avail.

Conan looked down the gully toward the mysterious labyrinth, wondering what skulking horror its mazes hid. The sun had not yet set but was hidden from the bottoms of the gulches. Although vision was still clear, the ravine was full of shadows.

Then Conan became aware of another sound: a muffled drumming, a slow boom – boom – boom, as if the drummer were striking alternate beats for marching men. There was something odd about the quality of the sound. Conan knew the clacking hollow log-drums of the Kushites, the whirring copper kettledrums of the Hyrkanians, and the thundering infantry drums of the Hyborians, but this did not sound like any of these. He glanced back at Yanaidar, but the sound did not seem to come from the city. It seemed to come from everywhere and nowhere – from beneath his feet as much as anything.

Then the sound ceased.

A mystical blue twilight hovered over the gulches as Conan reentered the labyrinth. Threading among winding channels, he came out into a slightly wider gully, which Conan believed was the one he had seen from the ridge, which ran to the south wall of the bowl. But he had not gone fifty yards when it split on a sharp spur into two narrower gorges. This division had not been visible from the ridge, and Conan did not know which branch to follow.

As he hesitated, peering along his alternative paths, he suddenly stiffened. Down the right-hand ravine, a still narrower gulch opened into it, forming a well of blue shadows. And in that well something moved. Conan tensed rigidly as he stared at the monstrous, manlike thing that stood in the twilight before him.

It was like a ghoulish incarnation of a terrible legend, clad in flesh and bone; a giant ape, as tall on its gnarled legs as a gorilla. It was like the monstrous man-apes that hunted the mountains around the Vilayet Sea, which Conan had seen and fought before. But it was even larger, its hair was longer and shaggier, as of an arctic beast, and paler, an ashen grey that was almost white.

Its feet and hands were more manlike than those of a gorilla, the great toes and thumbs being more like those of man than of the anthropoid. It was no tree-dweller but a beast bred on great plains and gaunt mountains. The face was apish in general appearance, though the nose-bridge was more pronounced, the jaw less bestial. But its manlike features merely increased the dreadfulness of its aspect, and the intelligence which gleamed from its small red eyes was wholly malignant.

Conan knew it for what it was: the monster named in myth and legend of the north – the snow ape, the desert man of forbidden Pathenia. He had heard rumors of its existence in wild tales drifting down from the lost, bleak plateau country of Loulan. Tribesmen had sworn to the stories of a manlike beast, which had dwelt there since time immemorial, adapted to the famine and bitter chill of the northern uplands.

All this flashed through Conan's mind as the two stood facing each other in menacing tenseness. Then the rocky walls of the ravine echoed to the ape's high, penetrating scream as it charged, low-hanging arms swinging wide, yellow fangs bared and dripping.

Conan waited, poised on the balls of his feet, craft and long knife pitted against the strength of the mighty ape.

The monster's victims had been given to it broken and shattered from torture, or dead. The semi-human spark in its brain, which set it apart from the true beasts, had found a horrible exultation in the death agonies of its prey. This man was only another weak creature to be torn and dismembered, and his skull broken to get at the brain, even though he stood up with a gleaming thing in his hand.

Conan, as he faced that onrushing death, knew his only chance was to keep out of the grip of those huge arms, which could crush him in an instant. The monster was swifter than its clumsy appearance indicated. It hurled itself through the air for the last few feet in a giant grotesque spring. Not until it was looming over him, the great arms closing upon him, did Conan move, and then his action would have shamed a striking leopard.

The talonlike nails only shredded his ragged tunic as he sprang clear, slashing, and a hideous scream ripped echoing through the ridges. The ape's right hand was half severed at the wrist. The thick mat of pale hair prevented Conan's slash from altogether severing the member. With blood spouting from the wound, the brute wheeled and rushed again. This time its lunge was too lightning-quick for any human thews to avoid.

Conan evaded the disembowelling sweep of the great misshapen left hand with its thick black nails, but the massive shoulder struck him and knocked him staggering. He was carried to the wall with the lunging brute, but even as he was swept back he drove his knife to the hilt in the great belly and ripped up in desperation in what he thought was his dying stroke.

They crashed together into the wall. The ape's great arm hooked terrifyingly about Conan's straining frame. The scream of the beast deafened him as the foaming jaws gaped above his head. Then they snapped in empty air as a great shudder shook the mighty body. A frightful convulsion hurled the Cimmerian clear, and he staggered up to see the ape thrashing in its death throes at the foot of the wall. His desperate upward rip had disembowelled it, and the tearing blade had plowed up through muscle and bone to find the anthropoid's fierce heart.

Conan's corded muscles were quivering as if from a long strain. His iron-hard frame had resisted the terrible strength of the ape long enough to let him come alive out of that awful grapple, which would have torn a weaker man to pieces. But the terrific exertion had shaken even him. His tunic had been ripped nearly off his body and some links of the mail-shirt underneath were broken. Those horny-taloned fingers had left bloody marks across his back. He stood panting as if from a long run, smeared with blood, his own and the ape's.

Conan shuddered, then stood in thought as the red sun impaled itself on a far peak. The pattern was becoming clear now. Broken captives were thrown out to the ape through the door in the city wall. The ape, like those that lived around the Sea of Vilayet, ate flesh as well as fodder. But the irregular supply of captives would not satisfy the enormous appetite of so large and active a beast. Therefore the Yezmites must feed it a regular ration; hence the remains of melons and turnips.

Conan swallowed, aware of thirst. He had rid the ravines of their haunter, but he could still perish of hunger and thirst if he did not find a way out of the depression. There was no doubt a spring or pool somewhere in the waste, where the ape had drunk, but it might take a month to find it.

Dusk masked the gullies and hung over the ridges as Conan moved off down the right-hand ravine. Forty paces further, the left branch rejoined its brother. As he advanced, the walls were more thickly pitted with cavelike lairs, in which the rank scent of the ape hung strongly. It occurred to him that there might be more than one of the creatures, but that was unlikely, because the scream of the first as it charged would have attracted any others.

Then the mountains loomed above him. The ravine he was following shallowed until Conan found himself climbing up a bank of talus until he stood at its apex and could look out over the depression to the city of Yanaidar. He leaned against a smooth vertical cliff on which a fly would hardly be able to find a foothold.

'Crom and Mitra!' he grumbled.

He jounced down the side of the fan of débris and struggled along the base of the cliff to the edge of the bowl. Here the plateau dropped sheerly away below. It was either straight up or straight down; there was no other choice.

He could not be sure of the distance in the gathering darkness, but he judged the bottom to be several times as far as the length of his rope. To make sure he uncoiled the line from around his waist and dangled the grapnel on its end the full length of the rope. The hook swung freely.

Next, Conan retraced his steps across the base of the cliff and kept on going to the other side of the plateau. Here the walls were not quite so steep. By dangling his rope he ascertained that there was a ledge about thirty feet down, and from where it ran off and ended on the side of the mountain among broken rocks there seemed to be a chance of getting down by arduous climbing and sliding. It would not be a safe route – a misstep would send the climber bouncing down the rocky slope for hundreds of paces – but he thought a strong girl like Nanaia could make it.

He still, however, had to try to get back into Yanaidar. Nanaia was still hidden in the secret stairway in Virata's palace – if she had not been discovered. There was a chance that, by lurking outside the door to Hell, he could get in when the Yezmite in charge of feeding the ape opened the door to put out food. There was a chance that the men from Kushaf, roused by Tubal, were on their way to Yanaidar.

In any case, Conan could only try. He shrugged a little and turned toward the city.

7. *Death in the Palace*

Conan groped his way back through the gulches until he came into the outer ravine and saw the wall and the cliff at the other end. The lights of Yanaidar glowed in the sky above the wall, and he could catch the weird melody of whining citherns. A woman's voice was lifted in plaintive song. He smiled grimly in the dark, skeleton-littered gorges around him.

There was no food on the rocks before the door. He had no way of knowing how often the brute had been fed or whether it would be fed at all that night.

He must gamble, as he often had. The thought of what might be happening to Nanaia maddened him with impatience, but he flattened himself against the rock on the side against which the door opened and waited still as a statue.

An hour later, even his patience was wearing thin when there came a rattle of chains, and the door opened a crack.

Someone was peering out to be sure the grisly guardian of the gorges was not near before opening the door further. More bolts clanged, and a man stepped out with a great copper bowl full of vegetables. As he set it down, he sounded a weird call. And as he bent, Conan struck with his knife. The man dropped, his head rolling off down the ravine.

Conan peered through the open door and saw that the lamplit corridor was empty; the barred cells stood vacant. He dragged the headless body down the ravine and hid it among broken rocks.

Then he returned and entered the corridor, shut the door, and shot the bolts. Knife in hand, he started toward the secret door that opened into the tunnel that led to the hidden stair. If hiding in the secret passage did not prove feasible, he might barricade himself and Nanaia in this corridor and hold it until the Kushafis came – if they came.

Conan had not reached the secret door when the creak of a hinge behind him made him whirl. The plain door at the opposite end was opening. Conan sprinted for it as an armed man stepped through.

It was a Hyrkanian like the one Conan had slain earlier. As he sighted Conan rushing upon him, his breath hissed between his teeth and he reached for his scimitar.

With a leap Conan was upon him and drove him back against the closing door with the point of his knife pricking the Hyrkanian's chest. 'Silence!' he hissed.

The guard froze, pallor tinging his yellowish skin. Gingerly he drew his hand away from his sword hilt and spread both arms in token of surrender.

'Are there any other guards?' asked Conan.

'Nay, by Tarim! I am the only one.'

'Where's the Iranistani girl, Nanaia?' Conan thought he knew where she was but hoped to learn by indirection whether her escape had been discovered and whether she had been recaptured.

'The gods know!' said the guard. 'I was with the party of guards who brought the Zuagir dogs to the dungeon and found our comrade in the cell with his neck half sliced through and the wench gone. Such shouting and rushing to and fro in the palace! But I was told off to guard the Zuagirs, so I cannot tell more.'

'Zuagirs?' said Conan.

'Aye, those who wrongly let you up the Stair. For that they will die tomorrow.'

'Where are they now?'

'In the other bank of cells, through yonder door. I have just now come from them.'

'Then turn around and march back through that door. No tricks!'

The man opened the door and stepped through as if he were treading on naked razors. They came into another corridor lined with cells. At Conan's appearance, there was a hiss of breath from two of these cells. Bearded faces crowded the grilles and lean hands gripped the bars. The seven prisoners glared silently at him with venomous hate in their eyes. Conan dragged his prisoner in front of these cells and said:

'You were faithful minions; why are you locked up?'

Antar the son of Adi spat at him. 'Because of you, outland dog! You surprised us on the Stair, and the Magus sentenced us to die even before he learned you were a spy. He said we were either knaves or fools to be caught off guard, so at dawn we die under the knives of Zahak's slayers, may Hanuman curse him and you!'

'Yet you will attain Paradise,' Conan reminded them, 'because you have faithfully served the Magus of the Sons of Yezm.'

'May the dogs gnaw the bones of the Magus of Yezm!' replied one with whole-hearted venom, and another said: 'Would that you and the Magus were chained together in Hell!' 'We spit on his Paradise! It is all lies and tricks with drugs!'

162

Conan reflected that Virata had fallen short of getting the allegiance his ancestors boasted, whose followers gladly slew themselves at command.

He had taken a bunch of keys from the guard and now weighed them thoughtfully in his hand. The eyes of the Zuagirs fixed upon them with the aspect of men in Hell who look upon an open door.

'Antar the son of Adi,' he said, 'your hands are stained with the blood of many men, but when I knew you before, you did not violate your sworn oaths. The Magus has abandoned you and cast you from his service. You are no longer his men, you Zuagirs. You owe him nothing.'

Antar's eyes were those of a wolf. 'Could I but send him to Arallu ahead of me, I should die happy!'

All stared tensely at Conan, who said: 'Will you swear, each man by the honor of his clan, to follow and serve me until vengeance is accomplished, or death releases you from the vow?' He put the keys behind him so as not to seem to flaunt them too flagrantly before helpless men. 'Virata will give you nothing but the death of a dog. I offer you revenge and, at worst, a chance to die with honor.'

Antar's eyes blazed and his sinewy hands quivered as they gripped the bars. 'Trust us!' he said.

'Aye, we swear!' clamored the men behind him. 'Harken, Conan, we swear, each by the honor of his clan!'

He was turning the key in the lock before they finished swearing. Wild, cruel, turbulent, and treacherous these desert men might be by civilized standards, but they had their code of honor, and it was close enough to that of Conan's kin in far-distant Cimmeria so that he understood it.

Tumbling out of the cell they laid hold of the Hyrkanian, shouting: 'Slay him! He is one of Zahak's dogs!'

Conan tore the man from their grasp and dealt the most persistent a buffet that stretched him on the floor, though it did not seem to arouse any particular resentment.

'Have done!' he growled. 'This is *my* man, to do with as I like.' He thrust the cowering Hyrkanian before him down the corridor and back into the other dungeon corridor, followed by the Zuagirs. Having sworn allegiance, they followed blindly without questions. In the other corridor,

163

Conan ordered the Hyrkanian to strip. The man did, shivering in fear of torture.

'Change clothes with him,' was Conan's next command to Antar. As the fierce Zuagir began to obey, Conan said to another man: 'Step through that door at the end of the corridor—'

'But the devil-ape!' cried the man addressed. 'He'll tear me to pieces!'

'He's dead. I slew him with this. Outside the door, behind a rock, you'll find a dead man. Take his dagger, and also fetch the sword you'll see lying near there.'

The desert Shemite gave Conan an awed glance and departed. Conan handed his dagger to another Zuagir and the Hyrkanian's wavy-edged dagger to still another. Others at his direction bound and gagged the guard and thrust him through the secret door, which Conan opened, into the tunnel. Antar stood up in the spired helmet, long-sleeved coat, and silken trousers of the Hyrkanian. His features were oriental enough to fool anyone who was expecting to see a Hyrkanian in that garb. Conan meanwhile pulled Antar's kaffia over his own head, letting it hang well down in front to hide his features.

'Two still unarmed,' said Conan, running his eyes over them. 'Follow me.'

He reentered the tunnel, stepped over the body of the bound guardsman, and strode along the tunnel, past the peepholes and into the darker stretch beyond. At the foot of the stair he halted.

'Nanaia!' he called softly. There was no response.

Scowling in the dark, Conan groped his way up the stair. There was no sign of Nanaia, although at the top of the stair, just inside the masked panel, he found the two swords he had left there earlier. Now each of the eight men had a weapon of some sort.

A glance through a peephole in the masked panel showed the chamber where Conan had slept to be empty. Conan opened the panel, a crack at first, then all the way.

'They must have found the girl,' he whispered to Antar. 'Where would they take her if not back to the cells?'

'The Magus has girls who have committed faults chastised in his throne room, where he gave you audience this morning.'

164

'Then lead – what's that?'

Conan whirled at the sound of the slow drumming that he had heard earlier, in the ravines. Again it seemed to come out of the earth. The Zuagirs looked at one another, paling under their swarthy skins.

'None knows,' said Antar with a visible shudder. 'The sound started months ago and since then has become stronger and comes more and more often. The first time, the Magus turned the city upside down looking for the source. When he found none he desisted and ordered that no man should pay heed to the drumming or even speak of it. Gossip says he has been busy of nights in his oratory, striving with spells and divinations to learn the source of the sound, but the gossip does not say he has found anything.'

The sound had ceased while Antar was speaking. Conan said: 'Well, lead me to this chamber of chastisement. The rest of you close up and walk as if you owned the place, but quietly. We may fool some of the palace dogs.'

'Through the Paradise Garden would be the best way,' said Antar. 'A strong guard of Stygians would be posted before the main door to the throne room at night.'

The corridor outside the chamber was empty. The Zuagirs took the lead. With nightfall, the atmosphere of silence and mystery had thickened over the palace of the Magus. Lights burned dimly; shadows hung thickly, and no breeze stole in to ruffle the dully shimmering tapestries.

The Zuagirs knew the way well. A ragged-looking gang, with furtive feet and blazing eyes, they stole swiftly along the dim, richly-decorated hallways like a band of midnight thieves. They kept to passages little frequented at that time of night. The party had encountered no one when they came suddenly to a door, gilded and barred, before which stood two giant black Kushites with naked tulwars.

The Kushites silently lifted their tulwars at the sight of the unauthorized invaders; they were mutes. Eager to begin their vengeance, the Zuagirs swarmed over the two blacks, the men with swords engaging them while the others grappled and dragged them down and stabbed them to death in a straining, sweating, swearing knot of convulsing effort. It was butchery, but necessary.

'Keep watch here,' Conan commanded one of the

Zuagirs. He threw open the door and strode out into the garden, now empty in the starlight, its blossoms glimmering whitely, its dense trees and shrubbery masses of dusky mystery. The Zuagirs, now armed with the swords of the blacks, swaggered after him.

Conan headed for the balcony, which he knew overhung the garden, cleverly masked by the branches of trees. Three Zuagirs bent their backs for him to stand upon. In an instant he had found the window from which he and Virata had looked. The next instant he was through it, making no more noise than a cat.

Sounds came from beyond the curtain that masked the balcony alcove: a woman sobbing in terror and the voice of Virata.

Peering through the hanging, Conan saw the Magus lolling on the throne under the pearl-sewn canopy. The guards no longer stood like ebon images on either side of him. They were squatting before the dais in the middle of the floor, whetting daggers and heating irons in a glowing brazier. Nanaia was stretched out between them, naked, spread-eagled on the floor with her wrists and ankles lashed to pegs driven into holes in the floor. No one else was in the room, and the bronze doors were closed and bolted.

'Tell me how you escaped from the cell,' commanded Virata.

'No! Never!' She bit her lip in her struggle to keep her self-control.

'Was it Conan?'

'Did you ask for me?' said Conan as he stepped from the alcove, a grim smile on his dark, scarred face.

Virata sprang up with a cry. The Kushites straightened, snarling and reaching for weapons.

Conan sprang forward and drove his knife through the throat of one before he could get his sword clear. The other lunged toward the girl, lifting his scimitar to slay the victim before he died. Conan caught the descending blow on his knife and, with a lightning riposte, drove the knife to the hilt in the man's midriff. The Kushite's momentum carried him forward against Conan, who crouched, placed his free hand on the black's belly, and straightened, raising the Kushite over his head. The Kushite squirmed and groaned.

166

Conan threw him to one side, to fall with a heavy thump and expire.

Conan turned again to the Magus, who, instead of trying to flee, was advancing upon him with a fixed, wide-eyed stare. His eyes developed a peculiar luminous quality, which caught and held Conan's gaze like a magnet.

Conan, straining forward to reach the wizard with his knife, felt as if he were suddenly laden with chains, or as if he were wading through the slimy swamps of Stygia where the black lotus grows. His muscles stood out like lumps of iron. Sweat beaded his skin as he strained at the invisible bonds.

Virata stalked slowly toward the Cimmerian, hands outspread before him, making little rhythmic gestures with his fingers and never taking his weird gaze from Conan's eyes. The hands neared Conan's throat. Conan had a flash of foreboding that, with the help of his arcane arts, this frail-looking man could snap even the Cimmerian's bull-neck like a rotten stick.

Nearer came the spreading hands. Conan strained harder than ever, but the resistance seemed to increase with every inch the Magus advanced toward him.

And then Nanaia screamed a long, high, piercing shriek, as of a soul being flayed in Hell.

The Magus half-turned, and in that instant his eyes left Conan's. It was as if a ton had been lifted instantly from Conan's back. Virata snapped his gaze back to Conan, but the Cimmerian knew better than to meet his eyes again. Peering through narrowed lids at the Magus' chest, Conan made a disembowelling thrust with his knife. The attack met only air as the Kosalan avoided it with a backward bound of superhuman litheness, then turned and ran toward the door, crying:

'Help! Guard! To me!'

Men were yelling and hammering against the door on the far side. Conan waited until the Magus' fingers were clawing at the bolts. Then he threw the knife so that the point struck Virata in the middle of his back and drove through his body, pinning him to the door like an insect to a board.

8. *Wolves at Bay*

Conan strode to the door and wrenched out his knife, letting the body of the Magus slip to the floor. Beyond the door the clamor grew, and out in the garden the Zuagirs were bawling to know if he was safe and loudly demanding permission to join him. He shouted to them to wait and hurriedly freed the girl, snatching up a piece of silk from a divan to wrap around her. She clasped his neck with a hysterical sob, crying:

'Oh, Conan, I knew you would come! They told me you were dead, but I knew they could not slay you—'

'Save that till later,' he said gruffly. Carrying the Kushites' swords, he strode back to the balcony and handed Nanaia down through the window to the Zuagirs, then swung down beside her.

'And now, lord?' said the Zuagirs, eager for more desperate work.

'Back the way we came, through the secret passage and out the door to Hell.'

They started at a run across the garden, Conan leading Nanaia by the hand. They had not gone a dozen paces when ahead of them a clang of steel vied with the din in the palace behind them. Lusty curses mingled with the clangor, a door slammed like a clap of thunder, and a figure came headlong through the shrubbery. It was the Zuagir they had left on guard at the gilded door. He was swearing and wringing blood from a slashed forearm.

'Hyrkanian dogs at the door!' he yelled. 'Someone saw us kill the Kushites and ran for Zahak. I sworded one in the belly and slammed the door, but they'll soon have it down!'

'Is there a way out of this garden that does not lead through the palace, Antar?' asked Conan.

'This way!' The Zuagir ran to the north wall, all but hidden in masses of foliage. Across the garden they could hear the gilded door splintering under the onslaught of the nomads of the steppes. Antar slashed and tore at the fronds until he disclosed a cunningly-masked door set in the wall. Conan slipped the hilt of his knife into the chain of the antiquated lock and twisted the heavy weapon by the blade. His muscles knotted: the Zuagirs watched him, breathing heavily, while the clamor behind them grew. With a final heave Conan snapped the chain. They burst through into another, smaller garden, lit with hanging lanterns, just as the gilded door gave way and a stream of armed figures flooded into the Paradise Garden.

In the midst of the garden into which the fugitives had come stood the tall, slim tower Conan had noticed when he first entered the palace. A latticed balcony extended out a few feet from its second storey. Above the balcony, the tower rose square and slim to a height of over a hundred yards, then widened out into a walled observation platform.

'Is there another way out of here?' asked Conan.

'That door leads into the palace at a place not far from the stair down to the dungeon,' said Antar, pointing.

'Make for it, then!' said Conan, slamming the door behind him and wedging it with a dagger. 'That might hold it for a few seconds at least.'

They raced across the garden to the door indicated, but it proved to be closed and bolted from the inside. Conan threw himself against it but failed to shake it.

Vengeful yells reached a crescendo behind them as the dagger-wedged door splintered inward. The aperture was crowded with wild faces and waving arms as Zahak's men jammed there in their frantic eagerness.

'The tower!' roared Conan. 'If we can get in there . . .'

'The Magus often made magics in the upper chamber,' panted a Zuagir running after Conan. 'He let none other than the Tiger in that chamber, but men say arms are stored there. Guards sleep below—'

'Come on!' bellowed Conan, racing in the lead and dragging Nanaia so that she seemed to fly through the air. The door in the wall gave way altogether, spilling a knot of Hyrkanians into the garden, falling over one another in their haste. From the noise that came from every other direction, it would be only a matter of minutes before men swarmed into the Garden of the Tower from all its apertures.

As Conan neared the tower, the door in the base opened as five bewildered guards came out. They yelped in astonishment as they saw a knot of men rushing upon them with teeth bared and eyes blazing in the light of the hanging lanterns. Even as they reached for their blades, Conan was upon them. Two fell to his whirling blade as the Zuagirs swarmed over the remaining three, slashing and stabbing until the glittering figures lay still in puddles of crimson.

But now the Hyrkanians from the Paradise Garden were racing towards the tower too, their armor flashing and their accouterments jingling. The Zuagirs stormed into the tower. Conan slammed the bronze door and shot home a bolt that would have stopped the charge of an elephant, just as the Hyrkanians piled up against the door on the outside.

Conan and his people rushed up the stairs, eyes and teeth gleaming, all but one who collapsed halfway up from loss of blood. Conan carried him the rest of the way, laid him on the floor, and told Nanaia to bandage the ghastly gash made by the sword of one of the guards they had just killed. Then he took stock of their surroundings. They were in an upper chamber of the tower, with small windows and a door opening out on to the latticed balcony. The light from the lanterns in the garden, coming in little twinkles through the lattice and the windows, shone faintly on racks of arms lining the walls: helms, cuirasses, bucklers, spears, swords, axes, maces, bows and sheaves of arrows. There were enough arms here to equip a troop, and no doubt there were more in the higher chambers. Virata had made the tower his arsenal and keep as well as his magical oratory.

The Zuagirs chanted gleefully as they snatched bows and quivers from the walls and went out on the balcony. Though several had minor wounds, they began shooting through the holes in the lattice into the yelling mob of soldiery swarming below.

A storm of arrows came back, clattering against the lattice-work and a few coming through. The men outside shot at random, as they could not see the Zuagirs in the shadow. The mob had surged to the tower from all directions. Zahak was not in sight, but a hundred or so of his Hyrkanians were, and a welter of men of a dozen other races. They swarmed about the garden yelling like fiends.

The lanterns, swinging wildly under the impact of bodies stumbling against the slender trees, lit a mass of twisted faces with white eyeballs rolling madly upward. Blades flickered lightninglike all over the garden. Bowstrings twanged blindly. Bushes and shrubs were shredded underfoot as the mob milled and eddied. *Thump*! They had obtained a beam and were using it as a ram against the door.

'Get those men with the ram!' barked Conan, bending the stiffest bow he had been able to find in the racks.

The overhang of the balcony kept the besieged from seeing those at the front end of the ram, but as they picked off those in the rear, those in front had to drop the timber because of its weight. Looking around, Conan was astonished to see Nanaia, her sheet of silk wrapped around her waist to make a skirt, shooting with the Zuagirs.

'I thought I told you—' he began, but she only said:

'Curse it, have you nothing I can use as a bracer? The bowstring is cutting my arm to ribbons.'

Conan turned away with a baffled sigh and resumed shooting his own bow. He understood the celerity with which he and his men had been trapped when he heard Olgerd Vladislav's voice lifted like the slash of a saber above the clamor. The Zaporoskan must have learned of Virata's death within minutes and taken instant command.

'They bring ladders,' said Antar.

Conan peered into the dark. By the light of the bobbing lanterns he saw three ladders coming towards the tower, each carried by several men. He stepped into the armory and presently came out on the balcony again with a spear.

A pair of men were holding the base of one ladder against the ground while two more raised it by walking toward the tower holding the ladder's uprights over their heads. The ends of the ladder crunched against the lattice.

'Push it over! Throw it down!' cried the Zuagirs, and one started to thrust his sword through the lattice.

'Back!' snarled Conan. 'Let me take care of this.'

He waited until several men had swarmed up the ladder. The top man was a burly fellow with an ax. As he swung the ax to hack away the flimsy wooden lattice-work, Conan thrust his spear through one of the holes, placed the point against a rung, and pushed. The ladder swayed back. The men on it screamed, dropping their weapons to clutch at the rungs. Down crashed the ladder and its load into the front ranks of the besiegers.

'Come! Here's another!' cried a Zuagir, and Conan hurried to another side of the balcony to push over a second ladder. The third was only half raised when arrows brought down two of the men raising it, so that it fell back.

'Keep shooting,' growled Conan, laying down his spear and bending the great bow.

The continuous rain of arrows, to which they could make no effective reply, wore down the spirits of the throng below. They broke and scattered for cover, and the Zuagirs whooped with frantic glee and sent long, arching flights of missiles after them.

In a few moments, the garden was empty except for the dead and dying, though Conan could see the movement of men along the surrounding walls and roofs.

Conan reentered the armoury and climbed the stair. He passed through several more rooms lined with arms, then came to the magical laboratory of the Magus. He spared only a brief glance at the dusty manuscripts, the strange instruments and diagrams, and climbed the remaining flight to the observation platform.

From here he could take stock of their position. The palace, he now saw, was surrounded by gardens except in front, where there was a wide courtyard. All was enclosed by an outer wall. Lower, inner walls separated the gardens somewhat like the spokes of a wheel, with the high outer wall taking the place of the rim.

The garden in which they were at bay lay on the northwest side of the palace, next to the courtyard, which was separated from it by a wall. Another wall lay between it and the next garden to the west. Both this garden and the Garden of the Tower lay outside the Paradise Garden, which was half-enclosed by the walls of the palace itself.

Over the outer wall that surrounded the whole of the palace grounds, Conan looked down on the roofs of the city. The nearest house was not over thirty paces from the wall. Lights blazed everywhere, in the palace, the gardens, and the adjacent houses.

The noise, the shouts and groans and curses and the clatter of arms, died down to a murmur. Then Olgerd Vladislav's voice was raised from behind the courtyard wall: 'Are you ready to yield, Conan?'

Conan laughed at him. 'Come and get us!'

'I shall – at dawn,' the Zaporoskan assured him. 'You're as good as dead now.'

'So you said when you left me in the ravine of the devil-ape, but I'm alive and the ape is dead!'

Conan had spoken in Hyrkanian. A shout of anger and unbelief arose from all quarters. Conan continued: 'Do the Yezmites know that the Magus is dead, Olgerd?'

'They know that Olgerd Vladislav is the real ruler of Yanaidar, as he has always been! I know not how you slew the ape, nor how you got those Zuagiri dogs out of their cells, but I'll have your skins hanging on this wall before the sun is an hour high!'

Presently a banging and hammering sounded on the other side of the courtyard, out of sight. Olgerd yelled: 'Do you hear that, you Cimmerian swine? My men are building a helepolis – a siege tower on wheels, which will stop your shafts and shelter fifty men behind it. At dawn we'll push it up to the tower and swarm in. That will be your finish, dog!'

'Send your men on in. Tower or no tower, we'll pick them off just as fast.'

The Zaporoskan replied with a shout of derisive laughter, and thereafter there was no more parleying. Conan considered a sudden break for freedom but abandoned the idea. Men clustered thickly behind every wall around the garden, and such an attempt would be suicide. The fortress had become a prison.

Conan admitted to himself that if the Kushafis did not appear on time, he and his party were finished despite all his strength and speed and ferocity and the help of the Zuagirs.

The hammering went on unseen. Even if the Kushafis came at sunrise, they might be too late. The Yezmites would have to break down a section of the garden wall to get the machine into the garden, but that would not take long.

The Zuagirs did not share their leader's somber forebodings. They had already wrought a glorious slaughter; they had a strong position, a leader they worshipped, and an unlimited supply of missiles. What more could a warrior desire?

The Zuagir with the sword cut died just as dawn was paling the lanterns in the garden below. Conan stared at his pitiful band. The Zuagirs prowled the balcony, peering through the lattice, while Nanaia slept the sleep of exhaustion on the floor, wrapped in the silken sheet.

The hammering ceased. Presently, in the stillness, Conan

173

heard the creak of massive wheels. He could not yet see the juggernaut the Yezmites had built, but he could make out the black forms of men huddled on the roofs of the houses beyond the outer wall. He looked further, over the roofs and clustering trees, toward the northern edge of the plateau. He saw no sign of life, in the growing light, among the fortifications that lined the rim of the cliffs. Evidently the guards, undeterred by the fate of Antar and the original sentries, had deserted their posts to join the fighting at the palace. But, as he watched, Conan saw a group of a dozen men trudging along the road that led to the Stair. Olgerd would not long leave that point unguarded.

Conan turned back toward his six Zuagirs, whose bearded faces looked silently at him out of bloodshot eyes.

'The Kushafis have not come,' he said. 'Presently Olgerd will send his slayers against us under cover of a great shield on wheels. They will climb up ladders behind this shield and burst in here. We shall slay some of them; then we shall die.'

'As Hanuman has decreed,' they answered. 'We shall slay many ere we die.' They grinned like hungry wolves in the dawn and thumbed their weapons.

Conan looked out and saw the storming machine rumbling across the courtyard. It was a massive affair of beams and bronze and iron, on oxcart wheels. At least fifty men could huddle behind it, safe from arrows. It rolled toward the wall and halted. Sledge-hammers began to crash against the wall.

The noise awakened Nanaia. She sat up, rubbed her eyes, stared about, and ran to Conan with a cry.

'Hush up. We'll beat them yet,' he said gruffly, although he thought otherwise. There was nothing he could do for her now but stand before her in the last charge and perhaps spare one last merciful sword stroke for her.

'The wall crumbles,' muttered a lynx-eyed Zuagir, peering through the lattice. 'Dust rises under the hammers. Soon we shall see the workmen who swing the sledges.'

Stones toppled out of the weakened wall; then a whole section crashed down. Men ran into the gap, picked up stones, and carried them away. Conan bent the strong Hyrkanian bow he had been using and sent a long arching shot

174

at the gap. It skewered a Yezmite, who fell shrieking and thrashing. Others dragged the wounded man out of the way and continued clearing the passage. Behind them loomed the siege tower, whose crew shouted impatiently to those toiling in the gap to hurry and clear the way. Conan sent shaft after shaft at the crowd. Some bounced from the stones, but now and then one found a human target. When the men flinched at their task, Olgerd's whiplash voice drove them back to it.

As the sun rose, casting long shadows across the courts, the last remains of the wall in front of the tower were shoveled out of the way. Then, with a mighty creaking and groaning, the tower advanced. The Zuagirs shot at it, but their arrows merely stuck in the hides that covered its front. The tower was of the same height as the storey on which they stood, with ladders going up its rear side. When it reached the tower in the garden, the Yezmites would swarm up, rush across the small platform on top, and burst through the flimsy lattice on to the balcony on which Conan and his men crouched.

'You have fought well,' he told them. 'Let us end well by taking as many Yezmite dogs with us as we can. Instead of waiting for them to swarm in here, let us burst the lattice ourselves, charge out on to the platform, and hurl the Yezmites off it. Then we can slay those that climb the ladders as they come up.'

'Their archers will riddle us from the ground,' said Antar.

Conan shrugged, his lip curling in a somber smile. 'We can have some fun in the meantime. Send the men to fetch pikes from the armory; for this kind of push, a solid line of spears is useful. And there are some big shields there; let those on the flanks carry these to protect the rest of us.'

A moment later Conan lined up the six surviving Zuagirs with pikes, while he stood in front of them with a massive battle-ax, ready to chop away the lattice and lead the charge on to the platform.

Nearer rolled the tower, the men huddled behind it shouting their triumph.

Then, when the siege tower was hardly a spear's length from the balcony, it stopped. The long trumpets blared, a great hubbub arose, and presently the men behind the tower began running back through the gap in the wall.

9. *The Fate of Yanaidar*

'Crom, Mitra, and Asura!' roared Conan, throwing down his ax. 'The dogs can't be running before they are even hurt!'

He strode back and forth on the balcony, trying to see what was happening, but the bulk of the deserted siege tower blocked his view. Then he dashed into the armory chamber and up the winding stair to the observation platform.

Toward the north, he looked out over the roofs of Yanaidar along the road that stretched out in the white dawn. Half a dozen men were running along the road. Behind them, other figures were swarming through the fortifications at the rim of the plateau. A fierce, deep yelling came to the ears listening in the suddenly silent city. And in the silence Conan again heard the mysterious drumming that had disturbed him on previous occasions. Now, however, he did not care if all the fiends of Hell were drumming under Yanaidar.

'Balash!' he cried.

Again, the negligence of the guards of the Stair had helped him. The Kushafis had climbed the unguarded Stair in time to slaughter the sentries coming to mount guard there. The numbers swarming up on to the plateau were greater than the village of Kushaf could furnish, and he could recognize, even at this distance, the red silken breeches of his own *kozaki*.

In Yanaidar, frozen amazement gave way to hasty action. Men yelled on the roofs and ran about in the street. From housetop to housetop the news of the invasion spread. Conan was not surprised, a few moments later, to hear Olgerd's whiplash voice shouting orders.

Soon, men poured into the square from the gardens and court and from the houses around the square. Conan glimpsed Olgerd, far down the street amidst a glittering company of armored Hyrkanians, at the head of which gleamed Zahak's plumed helmet. After them thronged hundreds of Yezmite warriors, in good order for tribesmen. Evidently Olgerd had taught them the rudiments of civilized warfare.

They swung along as if they meant to march out on to

176

the plain and meet the oncoming horde in battle, but at the
end of the street they scattered, taking cover in the gardens
and the houses on each side of the street.

The Kushafis were still too far away to see what was
going on in the city. By the time they reached a point where
they could look down the street, it seemed empty. But
Conan, from his vantage point, could see the gardens at the
northern end of the town clustered with menacing figures,
the roofs loaded with men with double-curved bows strung
for action. The Kushafis were marching into a trap, while
he stood there helpless. Conan gave a strangled groan.

A Zuagir panted up the stair and stood beside Conan,
knotting a rude bandage about a wounded wrist. He spoke
through his teeth, with which he was tugging at the rag.
'Are those your friends? The fools run headlong into the
fangs of death.'

'I know,' growled Conan.

'I know what will happen. When I was a palace guardsman, I heard the Tiger tell his officers his plan for defense.
See you that orchard at the end of the street, on the east
side? Fifty swordsmen hide there. Across the road is a
garden we call the Garden of the Stygian. There too, fifty
warriors lurk in ambush. The house next to it is full of
warriors, and so are the first three houses on the other side
of the street.'

'Why tell me? I can see the dogs crouching in the orchard and on the roofs.'

'Aye! Then men in the orchard and the garden will wait
until the Ilbarsis have passed beyond them and are between
the houses. Then the archers on the roofs will pour arrows
down upon them, while the swordsmen close in from all
sides. Not a man will escape.'

'Could I but warn them!' muttered Conan. 'Come on,
we're going down.'

He leaped down the stairs and called in Antar and the
other Zuagirs. 'We're going out to fight.'

'Seven against seven hundred?' said Antar. 'I am no
craven, but—'

In a few words Conan told him what he had seen from
the top of the tower. 'If, when Olgerd springs his trap, we
can take the Yezmites in the rear in turn, we might just be

able to turn the tide. We have nothing to lose, for if Olgerd destroys my friends he'll come back and finish us.'

'But how shall we be known from Olgerd's dogs?' persisted the Zuagir. 'Your reavers will hew us down with the rest and ask questions afterwards.'

'In here,' said Conan. In the armory, he handed out silvered coats of scale mail and bronze helmets of an antique pattern, with tall, horsehair crests, unlike any he had seen in Yanaidar. 'Put these on. Keep together and shout "Conan!" as your war-cry, and we shall do all right.' He donned one of the helms himself.

The Zuagirs grumbled at the weight of the armor and complained that they were half blinded by the helmets, whose cheek plates covered most of their faces.

'Put them on!' roared Conan. 'This is a stand-up fight, no desert jackal's slash-and-run raid. Now, wait here until I fetch you.'

He climbed back to the top of the tower. The Free Companions and the Kushafis were marching along the road in compact companies. Then they halted. Balash was too crafty an old wolf to rush headlong into a city he knew nothing about. A few men detached themselves from the mass and ran toward the town to scout. They disappeared behind the houses, then reappeared again, running back towards the main forces. After them came a hundred or so Yezmites, running in ragged formation.

The invaders spread out into a battle line. The sun glinted on sheets of arrows arching between the two groups. A few Yezmites fell, while the rest closed with the Kushafis and the *kozaki*. There was an instant of dusty confusion through which sparkled the whirl of blades. Then the Yezmites broke and fled back towards the houses. Just as Conan feared, the invaders poured after them, howling like blood-mad demons. Conan knew the hundred had been sent out to draw his men into the trap. Olgerd would never have sent such an inferior force to charge the invaders otherwise.

They converged from both sides into the road. There, though Balash was unable to check their headlong rush, he did at least manage to beat and curse them into a more compact formation as they surged into the end of the street.

Before they reached it, not fifty paces behind the last Yezmites, Conan was racing down the stairs.

'Come on!' he shouted. 'Nanaia, bolt the door behind us and stay here!'

Down the stair to the first storey they pelted, out the door, past the deserted siege tower, and through the gap in the wall. Nobody barred their way. Olgerd must have taken from the palace every man who could bear arms.

Antar led them into the palace and out again through the front entrance. As they emerged, the signal for the Yezmite attack was given by a deafening roar of a dozen long bronze trumpets in the hands of Olgerd's Hyrkanians. By the time they reached the street, the trap had closed. Conan could see the backs of a mass of Yezmites struggling with the invaders, filling the street from side to side, while archers poured arrows into the mass from the roofs of the houses on either side.

With a silent rush Conan led his little group straight into the rear of the Yezmites. The latter knew nothing until the pikes of the Zuagirs thrust them through the back. As the first victims fell, the desert Shemites wrenched out their spears and thrust again and again, while in the middle of the line Conan whirled his ax, splitting skulls and lopping off arms at the shoulder. As the pikes broke or became jammed in the bodies of the Yezmites, the Zuagirs dropped them and took to their swords.

Such was the mad fury of Conan's onslaught that he and his little squad had felled thrice their own number before the Yezmites realized they were taken in the rear. As they looked around, the unfamiliar harness and the shambles of mangled bodies made them give back with cries of dismay. To their imaginations the seven madly slashing and chopping attackers seemed like an army.

'Conan! Conan!' howled the Zuagirs.

At the cry, the trapped force roused itself. There were only two men between Conan and his own force. One was thrust through by the *kozak* facing him. Conan brought his ax down on the other's helmet so hard that it not only split helm and head but also broke the ax handle.

In an instant of lull, when Conan and the Zuagirs faced the *kozaki* and nobody was sure of the others' identity, Conan pushed his helmet back so that his face showed.

'To me!' he bellowed above the clatter. 'Smite them, dog-brothers!'

'It is Conan!' cried the nearest Free Companions, and the cry was taken up through the host.

'Ten thousand pieces of gold for the Cimmerian's head!' came the sharp voice of Olgerd Vladislav.

The clatter of weapons redoubled. So did the chorus of cries, curses, threats, shrieks, and groans. The battle began to break up into hundreds of single combats and fights among small groups. They swirled up and down the street, trampling the dead and wounded; they surged into the houses, smashed furniture, thundered up and down stairs, and erupted on to the roofs, where the Kushafis and *kozaki* made short work of the archers posted there.

After that, there was no semblance of order or plan, no chance to obey commands and no time to give them. It was all blind, gasping, sweating butchery, hand-to-hand, with straining feet splashing through pools of blood. Mingled inextricably, the heaving mass of fighters surged and eddied up and down Yanaidar's main street and overflowed into the alleys and gardens. There was little difference in the numbers of the rival hordes. The outcome hung in the balance, and no man knew how the general battle was going; each was too busy killing and trying not to be killed to see what was going on around him.

Conan did not waste breath trying to command order out of chaos. Craft and strategy had gone by the board; the fight would be decided by sheer muscle and ferocity. Hemmed in by howling madmen, there was nothing for him to do but split as many heads and spill as many guts as he could and let the gods of chance decide the issue.

Then, as a fog thins when the wind strikes it, the battle began to thin, knotted masses splitting and melting into groups and individuals. Conan knew that one side or the other was giving way as men turned their backs on the slaughter. It was the Yezmites who wavered, the madness inspired by the drugs their leaders had given them beginning to die out.

Then Conan saw Olgerd Vladislav. The Zaporoskan's helmet and cuirass were dented and blood-splashed, his garments shredded, his corded muscles quivering and knotting to the lightning play of his saber. His gray eyes blazed and his lips wore a reckless smile. Three dead Kushafis lay at his feet and his saber kept half a dozen blades in play at

180

once. Right and left of him corseleted Hyrkanians and slit-eyed Khitans in lacquered leather smote and wrestled breast to breast with wild Kushafi tribesmen.

Conan also saw Tubal for the first time, plowing through the wrack of battle like a black-bearded buffalo as he glutted his wild-beast fury in stupendous blows. And he saw Balash reeling out of the battle covered with blood. Conan began beating his way through to Olgerd.

Olgerd laughed with a wild gleam in his eyes as he saw the Cimmerian coming toward him. Blood streamed down Conan's mail and coursed in tiny rivulets down his massive, sun-browned arms. His knife was red to the hilt.

'Come and die, Conan!' shouted Olgerd. Conan came in as a *kozak* would come, in a blazing whirl of action. Olgerd sprang to meet him, and they fought as the *kozaki* fight, both attacking simultaneously, stroke raining on stroke too swiftly for the eye to follow.

In a circle about them, the panting, blood-stained warriors ceased their own work of slaughter to stare at the two leaders settling the destiny of Yanaidar.

'*Aie!*' cried a hundred throats as Conan stumbled, losing contact with the Zaporoskan blade.

Olgerd cried out ringingly and whirled up his sword. Before he could strike, or even realize the Cimmerian had tricked him, the long knife, driven by Conan's iron muscles, punched through his breastplate and through the heart beneath. He was dead before he struck the ground, tearing the blade out of the wound as he fell.

As Conan straightened to look around, there came a new outcry, somehow different from what he would have expected to hear as his men set upon the broken Yezmites. He looked up and saw a new force of armed men clattering down the street in a solid, disciplined formation crushing and brushing aside the knots of fighters in their way. As they came close, Conan made out the gilded mail and nodding plumes of the Iranistanian royal guard. At their head raged the mighty Gotarza, striking with his great scimitar at Yezmite and *kozak* alike.

In a twinkling the whole aspect of the battle had changed. Some Yezmites fled. Conan shouted: 'To me, *kozaki!*' and his band began to cluster around him, mixed with the Kushafis and some of the Yezmites. The latter, finding

Conan the only active leader against the new common foe, fell in with the men with whom they had just been locked in a death grapple, while along the front between the two masses, swords flashed and more men fell.

Conan found himself facing Gotarza, who swept the field with blows that would have felled small oaks. Conan's notched blade sang and flashed too fast for the eye to follow, but the Iranistani was not behind him. Blood from a cut on the forehead ran down the side of Gotarza's face; blood from another flesh wound in Conan's shoulder crimsoned the front of his mail. But still the blades whirled and clashed, neither finding an opening in the other's guard.

Then the roar of the battle rose in pitch to screams of pure terror. On all sides, men began to leave the fight to run for the road to the Stair. The panic push drove Conan into a *corps-à-corps* with Gotarza. Breast to breast they strained and wrestled. Conan, opening his mouth to shout, found it full of Gotarza's long black beard. He spat it out and roared:

'What in Hell is going on, you palace-bred lap dog?'

'The real owners of Yanaidar have come back,' shouted Gotarza. 'Look, swine!'

Conan risked a glance. From all sides, hordes of slinking gray shadows with unblinking, soulless eyes and misshapen, doglike jaws swarmed, to fasten upon any man they met, wherever a clawed but manlike hand could find a hold, and begin to tear him apart and devour him on the spot. Men struck at them with the strength of maniacal terror, but their corpselike skins seemed almost impervious to weapons. Where one fell, three others leaped to take its place.

'The ghouls of Yanaidar!' gasped Gotarza. 'We must flee. Smite me not in the back till we win clear, and I'll hold my hand from you. We can settle our own score later.'

The rush of fugitives bowled the two off their feet. Conan felt human feet on his back. With a tremendous effort he forced himself back on his knees and then to his feet, striking out with fists and elbows to clear enough space to breathe.

The rout flowed out northward along the road to the Stair, Yezmites, *kozaki*, Kushafis, and Iranistanian guards all mixed together but forgetting their three-cornered battle in the face of this subhuman menace. Women and children mingled with the warriors. Along the flanks of the rout swarmed the ghouls, like great gray lice, flowing over any person who became momentarily separated from the rest. Conan, thrust out to the edges of the crowd by the buffeting of the fugitives, came upon Gotarza staggering under the attack of four ghouls. He had lost his sword but gripped two by the throat, one with each hand, while a third clung to his legs and a fourth circled around, trying to reach his throat with its jaws.

A swipe of Conan's knife cut one ghoul in half; a second took off the head of another. Gotarza hurled the others from him, and then they swarmed over Conan, ripping and snapping with claws and fangs. For an instant they almost pulled him down. He was dimly aware that Gotarza had pulled one off him, thrown it to the ground, and was stamping on it with a sticklike snapping of ribs. Conan broke his knife on another and crushed the skull of a third with the hilt.

Then he was running on again with the rest. They poured through the gate in the cyclopean wall, down the Stair, down the ramps, and out across the floor of the canyon. The ghouls pursued them as far as the gate, pulling down man after man. As the last fugitives jammed through the gate, the ghouls fell back, scurrying along the road and into the orchards to fall snarling upon the bodies over which little knots of their own kind already snapped and fought.

In the canyon, men collapsed from weariness, lying down upon the rock heedless of the proximity of their late foes or sitting with their backs against boulders and crags. Most were wounded. All were blood-spattered, disheveled, and bloodshot of eye, in ragged garments and hacked and dented armor. Many had lost their weapons. Of the hundreds of warriors who had gathered for the battle in Yanaidar in the dawn, less than half emerged from the city. For a time the only sounds were those of heavy breathing, the groans of the wounded, the ripping of garments as men made them into crude bandages, and the occasional clink of weapons on the rock as they moved about.

Though he had been fighting, running, and climbing most of the time since the previous afternoon, Conan was one of the first on his feet. He yawned and stretched, winced at the

183

sting of his wounds, and stalked about, caring for his own men and gathering them into a compact mass. Of his squad of Zuagirs, he could find only three including Antar. Tubal he found, but not Codrus.

On the other side of the canyon, Balash, sitting with his leg swathed in bandages, ordered his Kushafis in a weak voice. Gotarza collected his guardsmen. The Yezmites, who had suffered the heaviest losses, wandered about like lost sheep, staring fearfully at the other gathering groups.

'I slew Zahak with my own hands,' explained Antar, 'so they have no high officer to rally them.'

Conan strode over to where Balash lay. 'How are you doing, old wolf?'

'Well enough, though I cannot walk unaided. So the old legends are true after all! Every so often, the ghouls issue from chambers under Yanaidar to devour any men so rash as to have taken up residence there.' He shuddered. 'I do not think anybody will soon try to rebuild the city again.'

'Conan!' called Gotarza. 'We have things to discuss.'

'I'm ready,' growled Conan. To Tubal he said: 'Gather the men into formation, with those least wounded and best armed on the outside.' Then he strode between his group and Gotarza's. The latter came forward too, saying:

'I still have orders to fetch you and Balash back to Anshan, dead or alive.'

'Try it,' said Conan.

Balash called from his sitting-place: 'I am wounded, but if you try to bear me off by force, my people will harry you through the hills till not one lives.'

'A brave threat, but after another battle you would not have enough men,' said Gotarza. 'You know the other tribes would take advantage of your weakness to plunder your village and carry off your women. The king rules the Ilbars because the Ilbarsi tribes have never united and never will.'

Balash remained silent for a moment, then said: 'Tell me, Gotarza, how did you find whither we had gone?'

'We came to Kushaf last night, and the prickle of a skinning knife persuaded a boy of the village to tell us you had gone into Drujistan and guide us on your trail. In the light before dawn, we came up to that place where you climb a cliff by a rope ladder, and the fools in their haste

184

did not draw it up after them. We bound the men you had left to guard your horses and came up after you.

'But now to business. I have nought against either of you, but I have sworn an oath by Asura to obey the commands of Kobad Shah, and I will obey them while I can drew breath. On the other hand, it seems a shame to begin a further slaughter when our men are so weary and so many brave warriors have fallen.'

'What had you in mind?' growled Conan.

'I thought you and I might settle the question by single combat. If I fall, you may go your ways, as there will be none to stop you. If you fall, Balash shall return to Anshan with me. You may be able to prove your innocence at that,' Gotarza added to the Kushafi chief. 'The king shall know of your part in ending the cult of the Hidden Ones.'

'Not from what I know of Kobad's mad suspiciousness,' said Balash. 'But I'll agree, as no city-bred Iranistani dog could worst Conan in such a duel.'

'Agreed,' said Conan shortly, and turned back to his men. 'Who has the biggest sword?'

He hefted several and chose a long, straight one of Hyborian pattern. Then he faced Gotarza. 'Are you ready?'

'Ready,' said Gotarza, and came on with a rush.

The two blades flashed and clanged in a whirl of steel, so fast that the onlookers could not see clearly what was happening. The warriors leaped, circled, advanced, retreated, and ducked decapitating slashes, while the blades continued their din, never stopping for a second. Slash – parry – thrust – cut – lunge – parry they went. Never in Yanaidar's thousands of years had those crags looked down upon so magnificent a display of swordsmanship.

'Hold!' cried a voice. Then, as the fight continued: 'I said *hold*!'

Conan and Gotarza backed away from each other warily and turned to see who was shouting.

'Bardiya!' cried Gotarza at the stout major-domo, who stood in the notch of the gully that led to the cliff of the rope ladder. 'What do you here?'

'Cease your battle,' said the Iranistani. 'I have killed three horses catching up with you. Kobad Shah has died of the poison on the flame knife, and his son Arshak reigns. He has withdrawn all charges against Conan and Balash and urges Balash to resume his loyal protection of the northern frontier and Conan to return to his service. Iranistan will need such warriors, as Yezdigerd of Turan, having dispersed the bands of *kozaki*, is again sending his armies forth to ravage and subdue his neighbors.'

'If that's so,' said Conan, 'there will be rich pickings on the Turanian steppe again, and I'm tired of the intrigues of your perfumed court.' He turned to his men. 'Those who want to return to Anshan may go; the rest ride north with me tomorrow.'

'But what of us?' wailed a plumed Hyrkanian guard from Yanaidar. 'The Iranistanis will slay us out of hand. Our city is taken by ghouls, our families are slaughtered, our leaders are slain. What will become of us?'

'Those who like may come with me,' said Conan indifferently. 'The others might ask Balash if he'll accept them. Many of the women of his tribe will be looking for new husbands – Crom!'

Conan's roving eye had lighted on a group of women in which he recognized Parusati. The sight reminded him of something he had forgotten.

'What is it, Conan?' said Tubal.

'I forgot the wench, Nanaia. She's still in the tower. Now how in Hell am I to get back to rescue her from the ghouls?'

'You needn't,' said a voice. One of the surviving Zuagirs who had followed Conan pulled off a bronze helmet, revealing Nanaia's features as her black hair tumbled down her back.

Conan started, then laughed thunderously. 'I thought I told you to stay – oh, well, it's just as well you didn't.' He kissed her loudly and spanked her sharply. 'One's for fighting beside us; the other's for disobedience. Now come along. Rouse yourselves, dog-brothers; will you sit on your fat behinds on these bare rocks until you starve?'

Leading the tall dark girl, he strode into the cleft that led to the road to Kushaf.

A Selection of Science Fiction from Sphere

A Selection of Occult Titles from Sphere

Sphere now have an exciting new list of tantalising books which cover the many theories about man's origins, about the part that alien beings have played and the hidden mysteries they have left behind them and about the unknown powers of mankind. Can he cross the time barrier? Is yesterday real today? Can we predict the future? These are some of the questions posed and answered in these books.

The Stainless Steel Rat

HARRY HARRISON   30p

The first in a series to be published by Sphere, 'The Stainless
Steel Rat' is the story of a cosmic criminal written by one
of the best writers on the science fiction scene. Slippery
Jim diGriz is the smoothest, sneakiest con-man in the known
Universe and when the law finally catches up with him,
there is only one thing to do – make him a cop.

Look out for more stories about The Stainless Steel Rat
in the future . . .

To be published in May 1974 – THE STAINLESS
STEEL RAT'S REVENGE.

Some Science Fiction Anthologies
from Sphere

The year's best Science Fiction Series edited by
Harry Harrison and Brian Aldiss:

THE YEAR'S BEST SCIENCE FICTION No. 2   25p
THE YEAR'S BEST SCIENCE FICTION No. 4   30p
THE YEAR'S BEST SCIENCE FICTION No. 5   35p
THE YEAR'S BEST SCIENCE FICTION No. 6   35p

TWO ANTHOLOGIES edited by Isaac Asimov:
THE HUGO WINNERS Vol. 1. 1963–67   40p
THE HUGO WINNERS Vol. 2 1968–70   40p

SCIENCE AGAINST MAN
  edited by Anthony Cheetham   30p

S.F. HALL OF FAME Vol. 1
  edited by Robert Silverberg   40p

S.F. HALL OF FAME Vol. 2
  edited by Robert Silverberg   40p

THE SECOND 'IF' READER edited by Frederik Pohl 35p

Two Great Novels by Burt Hirschfeld from Sphere

FIRE ISLAND   45p

This is a number one bestseller from the greatest storyteller
since Harold Robbins. New York's beautiful beach resort is
a sun-soaked playground for the bored and rich, where
the wealthy, the housewives, the hippies all come to find
freedom. This is the story of six friends who share a summer
house every year. It is a story of friendship, of love and of
passion, money, murder, joy and despair.

CINDY ON FIRE   50p

This great novel is the story of a girl who is alone in a
decadent world where she brushes with the jet-setters and
the drop-outs. She rejects her middle-class background and
struggles to find herself. She has to become a prostitute to
support her lover who's a drug addict. She hungers after
more and more lovers and eventually becomes involved
with revolutionaries in Chicago. It is a story of youth, sex,
despair and a kind of freedom.

SPHERE BOOKS

All Sphere Books are available at your bookshop or
newsagent, or can be ordered from the following address:

Sphere Books, Cash Sales Department,
P.O. Box 11, Falmouth, Cornwall.

Please send cheque or postal order (no currency), and allow
7p per copy to cover the cost of postage and packing
in U.K. or overseas.